Night People

by

A. Molise

Night People

Contact Information: info@thewildrosepress.com

Cover Art by *Kim Mendoza*

The Wild Rose Press, Inc.
PO Box 708
Adams Basin, NY 14410-0708
Visit us at www.thewildrosepress.com

Publishing History
First Edition, 2022
Trade Paperback ISBN 978-1-5092-4223-8
Digital ISBN 978-1-5092-4224-5

Published in the United States of America

I fell into her dark eyes, inhaled her warm, peppermint breath. My lips parted with wanting; my eyes closed with hoping. Considering her past, I feared her kiss would be rough and lustful. Her lips brushed mine and set me shivering. I sensed our kiss meant much to her and scared her, too. How I relished her tenderness and the hope of love. Her bold second kiss whispered of lust and sweet satisfaction. Her third kiss promised belonging, a freedom from limits, kinship. I'd never experienced such careful and deliberate kisses. Her fingers played against my neck as if she would hold me by my most vulnerable part. Everything melted away, the café, the city, my life. Nothing in the world existed but the two of us, wholly connected. The world with all its weight, its edges hard as stone, fell away, but only for a moment.

She broke off. "You'll come?" Her eyes captured mine. I longed to see if the feeling there mirrored my own—and it did! I wish I had paused before the world with all its weight, its edges hard as stone, fell away, but only for a moment. I wish I had taken and released a single breath. "I can't, and you know why."

Her mouth, sweet against mine a moment before, broadcast pain, frustration, and what I took to be collapse. Before I could think or react, she gathered her bag, turned, and walked through the indifference of the crowded café, through glass doors into the night.

Dedication

For Debbie,
who could see the world as it is and laugh

Chapter 1
Love American Style

I walked home through the rain and cried. I sat on the foldout couch in my studio apartment in the dark with my coat on and couldn't stop. I cried because in my heart I didn't want to solve my first case as the first female detective in the Portland Police Department.

I hadn't cried since they shot my brother at a traffic stop almost ten years ago. I cried for that and for the horrible way they treated me at work, for the meanness and venom behind the things they said, for being despised as a woman in a man's job. I cried for all the nights I spent alone wondering if I was worthy of love and all the nights to come and all the nights I wanted to cry but wouldn't allow myself.

But mostly I cried because of the heartbroken look in those infuriating, beautiful, midnight eyes of hers after I told her the job meant everything to me. I didn't say, "Yvonne, I've loved you since the moment we met in the park. Your unfathomable gaze, the red ribbon braided into your long, black hair, your dirty feet and dirty jeans and battered guitar case. The scar on your face looked like what I saw when I closed my eyes and looked deep inside. I leased an apartment overlooking the statue of *Rebecca at the Well*, hoping I would see you again." Because I didn't say, "I loved your fierce strength, your toughness, your gentle, tender heart."

We were the same, she and I, looking for a love beyond our grasp. I cried because she walked out, and I didn't have the courage to tell her how much I cared.

****

More than forty years ago, my first case, a murder among the young and wild, never made the papers. Both Clonch and Hardy have long since retired, but on the rare occasions we meet, their expressions question my integrity. For a long time, neither knew how angry this made me. The gall of them, those two in particular. Clonch gave up long before he left the job, and Hardy, well, I used to hold a series of grudges.

As a rookie detective on the Hennessy case, I interviewed witnesses, interrogated suspects, and lay awake nights, obsessed. It meant little to anyone else—a drunk poisoned in a bar, gone and forgotten.

They each believe in a different killer, Clonch in the logic of evidence and Hardy in the intuition of an experienced cop, but whatever their conclusions about Hennessey, they think less of me for it. I blew up at Frank Clonch one day, and we cleared the air, but Hardy would tilt his gray crew-cut head and slash a particular frown. But I understood one thing they didn't—this had been a murder for love.

I imagine it happened like this.

The officers who had been in the restaurant earlier that evening, certain of more trouble, parked in the lot and smoked, passing a pint between cars, waiting for another call about a fight at The Open Door. When the call came, they paused by tall red doors, faced with loud, slashing punk rock in a dark bar packed with people. Two officers pressed through the crowd while a third edged along a wall toward the emergency exit, and the fourth stayed to block the front door. Strobe lights jerked the action into staccato freeze frames. As officers penetrated the crowd, the band stopped abruptly mid-song, leaving a tense electric hush. Someone yelled, "Smash the pigs!"

A man wearing a bloody, white shirt staggered from the floor and fought his way toward the emergency exit, shoving people aside. Officers tackled him before the door, wrestling his hands behind his back to cuff him.

The band began a new song, way too loud, guitars savage and careless, stage lights flashing blue and red. The tall female vocalist with a wild mass of black hair paced the stage like a predator, supple and strong. She didn't sing but screamed, "He broke your nose with his big guns. You fought the cook, and the…" Her words were drowned out when the crowd roared. Another man struggled toward the exit and a cop pursued him out into the night. The singer snatched a beer bottle from an amplifier, guzzled it, and shattered it over a cymbal as if the law won, and I'm pissed and ready to wreak havoc if I can rip my way out of this fucking cage.

The killer acted. On a shelf under the bar sat a black coffee cup. Practiced fingers opened a paper bindle and poured white powder in blood-red wine, stirred two quick turns with the folded paper, tossed it in the bar trash—done in ten seconds.

****

Yvonne opened her apartment door to Charlie holding an empty box. He said between cocaine sniffles, "That's it, Yvonne, I'm done." His pale face set in a frown which seemed fragile and fake as if concealing a joyous occasion.

She flung the door open so it crashed against the wall and turned away, snarling. "Then get your shit out of here." Afraid her temper would cause her to do violence to his big, pasty face, she retreated to the bed and sat crossed-legged, taking refuge behind her guitar, pissed at herself for another stupid choice, another slice of life invested in what she'd sensed from the start would be a fiasco.

He avoided her eyes as he prowled her studio apartment, like he knew what he wanted and where it lay, taking most of the new records, even though she loved music and he was indifferent. When a man who didn't cook and didn't know how to clean them started stacking cast iron pans he had given her as if they were his, she imagined seizing one and driving him away with furious blows. She laid her guitar on the bed, rose, and stood before him, staring hard into his eyes.

"No," she said. He weighed a skillet in his right hand, glaring silently back. *You don't have the guts*, she thought. He set the pan on the counter, hoisted his box, and hurried out, slamming the door.

"Punk," she shouted after him as if she hadn't known from the beginning. Suppressing the urge to wield her guitar like a weapon and smash the things of her life, she sat on the bed in her studio apartment, bras and nylons drying on the bathroom door, rain roaring down. She leaned over her guitar, searching for something to play, hoping to conjure a vision of her future. She played a song all the way through, knowing the words but singing only the chorus. "You better come on in my kitchen, it's going to be rainin' outdoors." She rarely sang, her voice too soft to express her feelings, but in her head, she growled lyrics or belted them strong and proud.

When the last notes faded into lonely quiet, Yvonne watched rain drip from the fire escape, silver drops hanging suspended then falling free. For a long time, *she* had been hanging but now would be in motion, which sparked a flash of joy. She fell back on the bed, cradling her guitar like a lover, its brown body the color of her skin, its neck the color of her long black hair. Scratched and worn from years of playing on the street, the instrument still possessed a fine sound. She had stolen it as a teen. She'd seen it in the backseat of a car, smashed the window with a brick, and grabbed it. Almost new, it was the finest thing she'd ever owned. She pulled the E string, let it go, and felt its vibration in her core. In the dim, gray Portland light, she fancied she would one day sing a love song to a lover and mean every word. This seemed like a possible thing: people fell in love all the time.

She rose to get ready for work, oppressed by the idea of carrying drinks to drunks until two a.m. when the phone rang.

Djuna said, "Bangs."

"Five o'clock," replied Yvonne.

"Bangs at five," said Djuna and hung up.

The two women first rendezvoused at Captain Billy Bangs Pub years ago when they worked at Brasserie Montmartre because, feeling notorious in downtown Portland, Bangs was not on the circuit of their usual crowd. They reserved Bangs for dire situations; therefore, the recipient of a Bangs call stated only the moment of arrival, a matter of when not if. But Bangs had become less discreet because Yvonne and Djuna now cocktailed at a new restaurant, The Open Door, directly across MacAdam Avenue on the banks of the Willamette River. For a few years, the John's Landing Neighborhood styled itself as Portland's restaurant row along the river: Piccolo Mondo, The Wooden Horse, Quinn's Mill, The Rusty Pelican, Victoria Station, The Buffalo Gap, and down across the Sellwood Bridge, Salty's, all sharing an incestuous crowd of cooks and servers who drifted between them. Djuna and Yvonne had migrated upriver, hoping for respite from the craziness downtown, but they still lived chaotic lives.

****

Djuna secured their favorite, private, high-backed booth in the empty afternoon dining room and ordered a Manhattan up. She didn't order for Yvonne, who rarely drank before work. Besides, Yvonne vacillated between two choices: most of the time, Kentucky bourbon, Knob Creek, neat, water back, but when savoring life, Remy warm in a snifter.

Fishing a cigarette from her purse, Djuna glanced out the window. A bolt of sun shining through dark clouds set new spring leaves aglow like a moment from the first days of the world. If only life could change as quickly as the sun emerging, and you could run free of the million small decisions that transformed you into a person you had never envisioned and didn't particularly like. Djuna figured you could leave everything and move to a place where you knew not a soul and could be free of entanglements and expectations, where you could invent yourself anew. Such delicious thinking allowed her an unaccustomed moment of peace.

But she sensed Yvonne's presence—they shared a spooky connection that way. Yvonne stood at the bar, ordering, wearing the huge, ugly, gray, thrift store sweater which covered her short Open Door skirt. She made her way to Djuna's table with a double whiskey and a water, kissed Djuna lightly on the lips, a thing which did not quite satisfy, and slid into the booth with a grace Djuna envied.

Yvonne said, "Funny you should call. I thought about giving you a Bangs. What's happening?"

"Paul." Djuna spread her hands wide. "I can't decide. At least with Johnny, I know what I'm getting. I'm twenty-six. What would I do with a twenty-year-old, a cook of all things?"

Yvonne took a slug of whiskey. "Have some good, clean fun. Get a little lovin'. Isn't that what you've been hoping for?"

The sound Djuna made might have been a laugh or a sigh or a snort of derision, "I doubt there is enough of me left to fall in love. Besides, he's a boy."

Yvonne shook her head. "Not a boy, almost a man, and you can see bits of the man he's going to be."

"What bits?" Djuna urged.

Yvonne contemplated her whiskey. "Sweet, demanding, maybe in a hard way, maybe not. Hilton told me Paul is pretty much running the kitchen, and did you hear about his fight?"

Djuna leaned forward. "Tell me."

"During a basketball game with Hilton, some guy pulled a knife, and Paul destroyed him."

"Destroyed him how?"

"Like kung fu. His dad was some heavy-duty commando in 'Nam." She pitched her voice like Hilton's, *"Bet your ass, we got us a fiery grillman."* Djuna laughed; Yvonne caught her eye. "He navigated his way around the two of us okay. Few men could manage that so gracefully."

They shared a smile, Djuna peering into Yvonne's dark eyes and setting thin, pale fingers on Yvonne's long dark ones. Yvonne let them lay for a moment before reclaiming her hand to sip whiskey. Djuna reflected that the drink fit her perfectly: brown and beautiful, dangerous in large quantities. They had been best friends for years, occasional lovers, occasional rivals. She always seemed to leave Djuna longing for more.

"You know he's crazy about you."

"Lots of people like lots of people," Djuna replied.

"Admit it, you like him. He's handsome as the devil and that body." She licked a fingertip and shook it. Djuna couldn't resist a smile.

"I do like him, but he feels like yet another mistake." Djuna's romantic mishaps were legendary and now seemed to lie in an unsavory pile on the table between them.

Yvonne sipped whiskey before she spoke. "Maybe, but it might be a chance for you, and you can't keep on like you are with Johnny. What are you worried about? He's young. In a few months, he'll have his eye on some hostess or one of those hot bus girls Mitchell's been hiring, and you can bow out gracefully."

"Then where will I be?"

"Rid of Johnny. Seriously. You guys are poison for each other. If I were you, I'd jump at the chance. Paul would be fun to play with, and I can see why Raina is pissed."

Djuna sighed. "By the way, you were perfect. It wouldn't have happened without you. I don't know why I started crying. Maybe I wanted so much from my life and ended up with so little. Or maybe it's frightening to hope." Yvonne slid her hand across the table to cover Djuna's, who wanted to clasp those fingers in her own but knew you couldn't hold Yvonne.

After a moment, Yvonne withdrew her hand, pulled a thin, brown cigarette from her purse, tamped it on the table, but didn't light it. "I could feel the intensity between you two, which is why I backed off. Djuna, you weren't just a fuck to him; he made love to you." When Djuna didn't respond, Yvonne added with a half-grin, "I think he's afraid of me."

Yvonne could be intimidating. She bore a long, pale scar running from cheekbone to chin which looked fierce as the hard look in her eyes and her habitual scowl. She carried a quick temper, and the sense, often confirmed, that she knew no limits and might do anything.

"He's not. He said you were gentle with him," said Djuna.

Yvonne contemplated her unlit cigarette. "What else did he say?"

"We *snuck up on him.*"

"And pounced. We've wanted a threesome for years and got one with him. You underestimate him, and you underestimate yourself. How are you going to juggle them?"

"I'm not. He won't see me out of respect for Johnny."

Yvonne laughed and bolted her whiskey, wearing a satisfied, wolfish grin. "Respect for Johnny? That's a line you don't hear much." With one finger, she made a circular motion to the waitress, calling for another round. "By the way, did you notice how Paul kissed me goodbye? A respectful move. You could work with that."

Djuna couldn't help but smile. "I feel ridiculous, like I got him drunk and seduced him."

Yvonne said, "So what? Sometimes you're gettin', sometimes you're got. That's the game, and he wanted to play. After all, he'd been with Raina for a month."

"To think of him with her." Djuna gave a mock shudder.

"Does he know about her after hours, after a drink or four?" Yvonne asked.

"Johnny told him, then he found out about that construction guy, and that's why he quit her. He's innocent in that way."

"Innocent?" questioned Yvonne. "Nah, there's a devilish streak under all that shy quiet."

"Maybe romantic is a better word. But that's not right either." Djuna sucked a drag from her cigarette. She didn't know him well.

"How do things stand?"

Djuna exhaled from the corner of her mouth and crushed the remains of her smoke. "Dicey. He thought I left Johnny, and Johnny knows. At first, he said, *Ah, you got Paolo. Chalk up another one.* But now, he's figured out it's not just a one-night stand and gives me shit whenever I talk to Paul, and Paul gives me wounded puppy eyes when I'm with Johnny. It's gotten so I don't even want to go to work."

"You've got two. You'll probably end up with the one you should."

Djuna glanced out the window. The light had faded returning the world to tired and gray. Her six silver rings felt constricting, and she fought the urge to twist them from her fingers one by one. It would seem frantic and desperate to lick her knuckle to pull off the tightest of them, her amethyst, yet she found herself doing just that and dropping the lot of them in her purse. Yvonne watched her, rolling the unlit cigarette between thumb and forefinger.

Djuna hurried to fill the silence. "If I mess up, I could lose them both. Last time I worked, Raina sat down in the break room while I was doing my check out and blew smoke in my face. *I can't decide,* she said. *Should I go after Johnny or Paul? Seems like Johnny is getting restless. Maybe he doesn't like all your catting around. And Paul, he's single, right? What do you think, Djuna, the older guy who knows all the tricks or the kid who can go all night? Is one of them yours? 'Cause I'd hate to take your man.* Then she started talking about Evan. There would have been blood and ambulances if a couple of waiters hadn't come in."

The waitress arrived with their next round. They watched her serve, Djuna certain they both found things to criticize: her fingers touching the lip of the glass, how she dumped the ashtray instead of covering it with a clean one, then switching the two. "Anyway, Mitchell wanted me to make sure Paul goes to the employee party. Guys from corporate will be there; Paul wants to get into management. And here's the thing. If I leave with Johnny, she gets Paul, and if I leave with Paul, she gets Johnny."

Yvonne spoke with quiet certainty. "Paul will never go back to her."

"I wouldn't put anything past her, and Paul will be done with me if I drag him down there and walk out with Johnny. Johnny and I have our little affairs, but I don't think he'd take being jilted in his own bar, and Raina is just the kind of wench he'd use for payback. I've got two days to decide." Djuna shrugged. "To the idea angel." They clicked glasses and drank.

Yvonne drank deeply, reminding Djuna her friend had troubles. Yvonne's scar sometimes gave her a devilish, predatory air but now made her look sad, defeated. "What's up with you?"

Anger rose then fell in Yvonne's dark eyes. "Charlie came, took his shit."

"Why?"

"Our night with Paul and Dana Barber, that bitch he works with."

"Vonnie, I'm sorry."

Yvonne downed her whiskey. "It'll give me a chance re-think my pathetic life. I need to find a big strong man, get righteously laid, and blow the past right out the window."

Djuna lit another cigarette then immediately put it down. "I've got an idea."

"Oh, Djuna, no."

"My last idea worked."

Yvonne shook her head, examined her still unlit smoke. "If you mean jumping Paul, I'd have to say, sort of."

Djuna flashed an encouraging grin. "But you'll like this one. You sleep with him."

"Me?" Yvonne laughed, revealing the side of her Djuna liked best, wry, fun-loving, a hint of tenderness in her smile.

"It's perfect. You need to get righteously laid, so you sleep with Paul, who needs to get righteously distracted from Raina. It'll give me a week to figure things out."

"Why don't you?" Yvonne asked, eyes intent.

Djuna spoke with certainty. "Johnny will know and pay me back with Raina or someone worse. Come on, Vonnie, we've played tougher situations than this. I'll take care of Johnny; all you have to do is play the kid."

Yvonne considered the bare tabletop, scarred from heavy use. "I don't know. Playing the kid? Not what I'm looking for."

Djuna spoke enthusiastically. "You said it would be fun, and you'd jump at the chance. And like you said, he's young, no attachments. I'll make things easy. While you and Johnny are working, I'll get him all hot and bothered. You just step in at the end."

"Are you sure about this?"

Djuna loved her ploys and plans and wanted to sell this one. "Seriously, anything, as long as Raina doesn't get him. If she sets her sights on him, give him a ride home or take him to bed or beat the crap out of her, whatever. But you'll do it for me?" Djuna flashed the wide smile which opened doors wherever she went. Yvonne lit her smoke and nodded.

Chapter 2
The Open Door

In the months before the Hennessey case, both my personal and professional life were shit. In order to earn promotion to detective, I'd studied grueling hours and taken every crappy detail and all possible overtime— not a lifestyle conducive to friendships. I'm not a warm person. I'm independent, blunt, and don't suffer fools. Plus, competing with ladies who'd worked in the department for years and winning didn't make any friends. So I spent my free time reading, riding my motorcycle, wandering Portland, which I love, working out, or moping about my mother's place, sucking up whatever encouragement she and Alice could give.

In those days, I carried latent anger that often rattled its cage but rarely escaped. At work, most of us are quick to discover when we're getting screwed. First off, the Portland Police Department didn't pay me near as much as the other Grade One Detectives. Secondly, my lieutenant, Jim Hardy, boxed me off the flowchart, froze me out. I could not speak at meetings without snickers or ridicule, without sexual comment, or worst of all, without being completely ignored. For a while, men spoke to me only to hit on me. This eventually died down except for a determined few, certain I must have some use.

It would be easy to blame Hardy, and for years I

did, but I see now his choices were limited by both the tone of the times and the cast of his personality, caught as many of us were between a new era and the way things used to be. Conflicting issues must have kept him up nights—the press heralded my promotion, but no one wanted to be my partner. He didn't know what to do with me and set me to reviewing cold cases, stacks of files arriving daily. Joanna Reedy, Major Slaten's secretary, would shake her head and shrug when she delivered them without a word. Such were gender relations then. But I saw kindness and sympathy in her smile and the gentle way she set them on my desk.

The folders she brought in such generous heaps smelled of dust and old paper, their pages pecked on manual typewriter and onionskin by heavy-handed detectives or scrawled with every possible writing implement on a colorful variety of papers and stained with coffee and the whiskey which in those days still hid openly in desk drawers and coat pockets. So except for when they trotted me out to women's groups and elementary schools, I sat at my desk by my silent phone in a corner by the door, turning pages, watching, listening, taking in the essence of the bullpen.

In assigned futility, I learned how to read a case file, to tease passion from behind the pages: love, hatred, bitter disappointment, jealousy. We speak of crimes of passion, but even in the most calculated crimes, you'll find an overwhelming ardor; police see this as motive and the press as reason, but I began to see them as ends in themselves. We humans, stuck in this modern life, crave strong feeling and letting go of restraint, crave charging wildly over the edge. In yielding to our passion, the crime, if there is one, is byproduct.

I learned to let imagination have its say—so often we dismiss its rambling as fancy. I learned to set my feelings aside and accept what came. I learned, both literally and figuratively, to deal with my rage, my frustration, my humiliation—by turning the page.

I learned about my co-workers, those who viewed people charitably, and those who held them in contempt, those depressed by the work, those marking time until retirement. I could sit, calm as a spider in the chaos of the application of the law and dissect them all, see who had grown and who had diminished.

I learned the source of their resentment toward me, how they'd struggled for years to win a position handed to me by politicians.

I did solve a couple of cold cases, but I often wanted to quit and would have but for a huge stubborn streak. After a time, since it didn't matter, I began to skip files. Financial and property cases ended up at the bottom of the stack, murder on top. I got hooked on all that passion.

****

After the night of three, as he called it, Paul Tomaso fought through a week which longed for the past tense, convinced cosmic law dictated pleasure be counterbalanced by a double or possibly triple amount of torment. Raina worked an early shift Tuesday night and marched through the red front doors straight to the kitchen. "Ditched for the bitch. And you moved out while I was sleeping. A low blow, Paul, and a sleazy thing to do, just like her. But I could see it coming. Has she screwed you over yet? No? Well, wait for it.

Remember what I said, she comes off all smiley and sophisticated, but she'll stab you in the back every time."

An hour later, Djuna walked in through the same double doors, going straight to Johnny at the bar. Raina stood at the kitchen window waiting for appetizers. "I'm telling you, Paul, she's no good. I'll bet you the biscotti, the cannoli, and a frothy homemade cappuccino she goes home with Johnny." When Paul said nothing, she added, "No faith in your new girlfriend? Well, maybe she's a low-stakes kind of gal. How about a bottle of cheap Chianti? No? Well, at least you did one smart thing this week." Raina finished early that night and settled at the bar with Bags, her drinking buddy.

They designed The Open Door slick: chrome and black leather with dark ceilings and spotlights hanging low over each white-clothed table. The service staff, dressed all in black, moved like shadows through the dim light. "Our customers are stars," management would say, "and employees the supporting cast." In the main room, the bar stretched out along on the west side, and a display kitchen stood on the east with barroom tables in the middle. The dining room lay behind a wall to the south with windows along the river.

The firm originated in LA, Hollywood money, stores scattered in upscale beach towns, Santa Barbara, Malibu, Newport, Del Mar, all with water views and a vigorous bar scene. They owned two out-of-state properties, one recently opened in Scottsdale and the newest in Portland.

Paul Tomaso had done stints in them all. They used him as a troubleshooter because he was tough, smarter than he looked, kept his mouth shut, understood how things worked, and could figure out why when they didn't. At The Door, as everyone called it, he worked the grill on weekend nights, the man, because the menu featured dry-aged beefsteaks and twenty-one different cuts of fresh fish, most of them grilled.

From the kitchen, Paul could see Bags and Raina across the darkened room, silhouetted by spotlights. Whenever Djuna passed, Raina caught his eye and pantomimed opening wine with a corkscrew. Once, Bags roared loud enough for Paul to hear, "Wouldn't bet a bottle of cheap Chianti."

Of all the waiters, Paul liked Bags the least. He presented a round red face and a bulbous red nose and called himself a *lifer*, someone who would never be an actor, an artist, or an attorney but would always be a waiter. During training, he introduced himself to the cooks. "Randy Bogges," he said, "but my friends call me Bags."

"Bags of what?" asked Hilton.

This left Bags speechless, as if the question might hide an insult, but no sane waiter would tangle with the cooks on the first day, and few, sane or not, would tangle with Hilton, who stood six-foot-three, built like a cornerback.

"Good question," Bags said at last, but the answer soon emerged—bags of green bottles. After his shift, Bags would sit at the bar and order beer. "Johnny, line me up a couple of your green bottles." He favored German beer. "They got purity laws," he liked to say.

At The Open Door in a corner near the bar, two black leather and chrome sofas and several armchairs were arranged as a waiting area for diners. Known as

The Corner, it tended to be empty when waiters finished their shifts, so they gathered there for cribbage, backgammon or dominoes. As their numbers increased, swelled by cocktail servers and kitchen staff, alcohol flowed. Some customers complained the waiters laughed too loud and spewed too much profanity, yet employees provided a young, vibrant energy and left a substantial portion of their tips behind. Not yet twenty-one, The Corner was the only place in the bar where Paul could legally sit.

After work, Paul sat next to Hilton, watching him call his domino plays in rhyme. "Two and one don't make no fun."

Djuna brought Paul a 'ginger ale'—whiskey and lemon-lime soda disguised in a soda glass—courtesy of Johnny, who winked when Paul raised his glass in thanks. Djuna put her hand on his shoulder. "Yvonne asked me to close for her. Maybe I'll call you tomorrow." Paul would later brood she had slim talent for lying.

The clock told him he might still make his bus. As he rose to go, Bags called, "Is it love, Paul?" and roared with laughter. Raina clicked glasses with him, Johnny smiled; Djuna winced, and Bags roared again, "Johnny, how about a bottle of Chianti, cheapest you got."

****

The next night, both Djuna and the Grand Opening exploded in Paul's hands. The gala would take place on Sunday evening, and then Monday, a day the restaurant was closed, Management would throw a party for staff. The general manager, Mitchell, told Paul he wouldn't have to work either event in appreciation for "his fine work so far." To get Grand Opening week started, the corporate guys threw themselves a party. With select female staff members, they occupied tables one through five along the river. Comped food and wine flowed. During the rush, the line crowded with orders. One of the suits took Paul aside and gave him a to-do list for both events, saying, "This should have gone to your kitchen manager, Donny, but he's toasted, and I heard you're the guy who gets things done."

Yvonne, waiting by the kitchen window for appetizers, met Paul's eyes and said with a wry grin, "Well, that's one way to get screwed. I can think of some better ones."

At shift's end, Paul bummed a cigarette from Hilton and went out to smoke and ponder how events had left him doing Donny's job. Behind The Open Door, a floodlight illuminated the loading dock. If you were to take the kitchen rag hanging from this fixture and loosen the hot bulb, a peaceful darkness would descend, and you would be left with what Paul considered a fine view of Portland. He liked to sit, leaning against a wall, looking downriver at city lights and bright bridges arching over the dark Willamette River. Halfway through his cigarette, he heard heels snap against concrete. Djuna laid a cloth napkin on the ground and sat next to him with a tentative smile. "Paul, I know you're mad, and I'm sorry. Last night, with both of you here, I didn't know what to do."

"You picked him. I get it."

"I'm not sure you do." She touched his cheek gently. "Look at me. He's my bartender. I work with him, every drink I carry. Imagine if every time I ordered at the well, Johnny was angry or sulking. Imagine you two glaring at each other across the bar. I can't break up with him while I still work here. Too much drama. I'm working on it. I got out my resume; I'm going to retype it, add The Door and start looking."

"I'll type it for you," he said, firmly. "I type really fast. There's an electric in the office."

She took his hand, kissed it, leaving a ghost of her lips in red. "I'll bring it tomorrow, I promise. If I left with you last night, half the restaurants in town would be gossiping about it. We're kind of an institution, Johnny and Djuna. We've known each other a long time, been through a lot. To jilt him in his own bar, I couldn't do it." She kissed him one of her long, deep, slow kisses. "It'll work out," she said. "Trust me."

The next two nights, she traded shifts and didn't show.

****

Paul ended up working doubles Thursday through Saturday to prepare for the Grand Opening. On a hot Friday night, he got a dose of Johnny. The grill, the heat lamps, and some flaw in ventilation turned the kitchen into a sauna. Paul and Hilton made up extra verses to "Ventilation Blues" as they worked. They drank pitchers of ice water and wrapped frozen towels around their necks. Since Paul worked the closing shift, he took a break on the loading dock, the concrete wall cold against his back through a T-shirt soaked in sweat. A battered tug towed a barge piled with rubble upriver past The Open Door toward Quinn's Mill. He couldn't understand Djuna. She flirted with him constantly, flashed him her glorious smile, made love to him passionately, clutching him like she would never let go. Now, she avoided him.

Johnny emerged from the back door dragging a

chair. "Mind if I join you?" Johnny Urbino, in his early thirties, sported an immaculately barbered moustache and goatee and dark hair cut in a shag. He wore a white tuxedo shirt, a black leather vest, and a bolo tie built around a huge piece of turquoise. He arranged his chair to face Paul and sat, lighting his smoke with a flick of a Zippo lighter.

Paul and Johnny were friends of sorts. Johnny had warned him about living with Raina in Hell House and after that mistake counseled him about her drinking and her ways with men. They exchanged jibes in English and broken Italian, but since Paul couldn't sit at the bar, and Johnny worked late, they were not well acquainted.

"You and Djuna have a thing, don't you Paolo?" said Johnny in his quiet way.

"I guess," ventured Paul. "Are you mad?"

"Spread the love. People get upset but they shouldn't." Johnny opened his arms, palms up in the Italian gesture that means look at it and you decide. He smoked for a moment in silence. He smirked. "You two have a chance to talk much?"

"Not really."

"There's a lot about her you don't know. She isn't what she seems."

"Are you serious about her?"

Johnny considered, his expression changing to make him look older, discontented, worn. "We've reached certain understandings. I used to think we were perfect for each other, but things happen, and you realize you can only go so far with a woman like her." He studied Paul. "You don't believe me?"

Paul shrugged.

"You're hooked bad," sympathized Johnny.

"Listen, a friend of mine lives in this singles' apartment building. They have parties. Why don't the three of us go one night? It'll give you a chance to see what Djuna is really like and have a little fun besides." Paul must have made a sour face, for Johnny laughed. "Ah, Paolo, the look on your face. Now, I get what she sees in you. Naiveté is pretty rare in our crowd."

"It's not my style," said Paul.

Johnny laughed again. "It isn't? Raina. Djuna. Djuna and Yvonne together. You know how many guys have fantasized about bagging that pair? You don't go after the good girls, so it seems like just your style." He blew smoke rings into the hot, still night, one inside the other. "It's not the dark ages. It's 1979. Women are liberated; they're all on birth control, and penicillin is a man's best friend. The old rules are gone. Why not get some kicks?" He blew a last smoke ring. Black ankle-high boots ground his cigarette into the concrete. "My conscience will only let Donny make so many bad drinks. Come to the bar when you're done. I'll pour you a 'ginger ale.' "

After Johnny left, Paul put out his cigarette, picked up Johnny's butt, and tossed both into the dumpster. Carrying Johnny's chair in one hand, he reached up, grabbed the rag hanging on the fixture, tightened the bulb so the light came on, replaced the rag, and carried in the chair. He had no desire for whiskey.

****

Saturday night, he refused to look at Djuna when she came to the kitchen for appetizers, though he sensed her hoping for acknowledgement. After her check out, she approached the kitchen door, abashed. "I brought my resume. Will you still help me?"

He turned to face her, "I said I would," but felt defeated, thwarted wherever he turned. Raina, beautiful and funny, indulged in too much alcohol and too many men. He couldn't count on Djuna. His apartment had looked good but cost too much and required him to take two buses to get to work. He busted his ass for The Open Door, but they always wanted more. He worked listlessly and couldn't wait to be finished, defeated by three doubles in a row.

After his shift, he started to change into civvies but couldn't muster the energy. Djuna stuck her head in the locker room door and found him sitting on a bench, head in hands, dressed in jeans and white socks. She said, "I got worried about you."

"You don't care about me."

"It might seem that way, but things have been hard for me. Look." She handed him her resume. Under the yellow light in tiny locker room, he read through a list of cocktail jobs and got to education.

"You won these awards? And published?"

"Paul, you don't know me; I don't know you. I can't turn my life upside down."

He softened. "Why are you doing this?" He gestured toward the restaurants on the first page but meant much more.

She understood; she always did. "You'll have to get to know me. Listen, you were a surprise who fell all wonderful into my life. I wanted to grab you before you disappeared, but I don't know who you are, what we have. Can we take this one step at a time?" Her intriguing pale eyes and her smile dimmed by sadness softened him further.

"I guess. I've wanted you since we met. To have

you and lose you in so short a time," he shrugged.

"You didn't lose me. You wanted too much too fast. There's a job at this private club downtown. They're holding interviews on Wednesday. Come with me?"

She turned up the smile; he couldn't refuse. In Mitchell's office, they re-worked her resume with much laughter and a kiss or two. After rolling the last page out of the typewriter, he said, "Djuna, I'm exhausted. I've got to sleep."

She leaned over, wrapping him in her arms. "Paul, I'm going to stay. Johnny is a big part of my life. He probably shouldn't be, and maybe soon he won't be, but right now he is. Can you just accept it?"

"I'm too tired to know what I think."

"Don't think, just come. Here's my address. Wednesday morning, about nine?"

****

On Monday, the day of the staff party, Djuna called at noon, waking him. "Don't be grouchy with me, Paul. I know you're sick of the restaurant, but it's a career move. If you want to get into management, you've got to know the players. Besides, I'll be there with nothing to do because Johnny and Yvonne will be working."

"I'm tired. The suits have been on a weeklong party, and I've been working my ass off. They'll drive up in their Beamers, and I'll have to take two fucking buses."

He loved her voice, bright and filled with laughter. "I'll be your chauffeur. You can ride in the back seat."

Later, at his door, Djuna bowed low. "Your car, sir." She wore a short dress, beaded and sequined in silver with a net of silver chains covering her wild dark hair. She smiled with perfect red lips, kissing him long and deep.

"Come in?" he asked.

"I might never leave."

Djuna parked Betty Dorf, her aged powder blue sedan, in the red zone in front of the restaurant and walked around to open the door for Paul, bowing deeply. She escorted him in, then left him standing alone, running off to Johnny. The restaurant, lights on, tables stripped, looked naked and false, like a theater set in daylight. Paul intended to schmooze with Mitchell and the boys from corporate, eat, and head for home. Mitchell introduced him to a tall, tanned, bearded, redheaded man who handed him a card and shook his hand. "Hello, Paul, Bill Durling. I've heard about your work here and your interest in management. As soon as you turn twenty-one, give me a call." Someone tapped Durling on the shoulder, and he turned away, ending Paul's big meeting, the reason he had come. He shuffled awkwardly until Raina showed up with a 'ginger ale.' They assigned her to wait on the suits because, as Mitchell said, "Between sober and stunned, she has more personality than any five cocktail waitresses."

She said so all could hear, "Dave Fleming needs one more for dominos." He made a hasty exit, grateful to her for rescuing him. He sat on the sofa next to Hilton but didn't feel like playing. Yvonne handed him a 'ginger ale,' then another shortly before Djuna fell into his lap, put an arm around his neck, and started heckling the domino players. She made conversation in her bright way with whoever shared the sofa but also whispered love poems in his ear, a couple of lines at a time. She had a trick memory and knew dozens of poems. She started with *To His Coy Mistress*. "Now therefore, while the youthful hue sits on thy skin like morning dew, and while thy willing soul transpires at every pore with instant fires, now let us sport us while we may." Johnny glared from the bar.

Paul recited the only love poem he knew, Annabel Lee. She teased him, "If I love you, I'll end up dead?" "The Shooting of Dan McGrew" got her laughing as she whispered, "I Do Not Love Thee" between stanzas.

Johnny took a break and sat beside them, speaking low in a voice tight with anger, "Djuna, what are you doing? Everyone is staring; everyone is asking me." Still on Paul's lap, Djuna leaned over and whispered in Johnny's ear. Paul longed to hear.

When she finished, Johnny issued a satisfied smile. Djuna leaned back against Paul and said to Johnny, "When you're done, come sit over here." Johnny's shift ended at seven, but he worked late the night before and wanted to go. Djuna kissed Paul briefly, whispering in his ear, "Goodbye, my beautiful boy, and if the universe gives you a gift tonight, I want you to say yes. See you Wednesday."

Paul suppressed angry words. While drink numbed the hurt, he chastised himself for stupidity. Everyone was drunk. Raina had achieved stunned; she swayed, eyes dull, Durling's arm over her shoulder, her blank stare in sharp contrast to Djuna's wit and laughter, but once again Djuna chose Johnny.

A bus would come by soon, and he intended to take it, but then Yvonne approached, long black hair over one shoulder trailing down over a black leotard, red bra peering from under a strap. She wore very short red shorts, black cowboy boots stitched in red.

"Want company?" she asked in her soft Southern drawl.

"I'm not sure I'd be good company."

She sat beside him anyway and said, "I'm sorry about Djuna. Don't let yourself be hurt. She's kind of a mess." She laid a hand on his, her touch cool, long graceful fingers dark against his faded Los Angeles tan. He found sympathy in her eyes. "You must be sick of this place," she said. "Let's get out of here."

"Where to?" he asked.

"Wherever you want. I'll give you a ride home if nothing else."

As they walked out the door, Bags roared, "Grillman and the Ragin' Cajun. Any bets who ends up on top?"

Yvonne cruised dark backstreets, making restaurant small talk, rolling slowly in the ancient gray sedan she called The Battlewagon. She coasted to a stop on a dark, quiet road. The engine coughed to the restless silence of distant traffic, a breath of pine wafting through open windows. Paul had no idea where they were. She said, "I don't know what you want to do. We could get a drink or something to eat. I could take you home. Or…" Her gaze met his; her fingers found his arm. "You could come home with me. Djuna said…well, she didn't want you to be alone or me either."

"You?"

Her voice deepened with sadness that echoed his own. "Charlie dumped me for some barfly. Please come home with me. I don't want to be alone."

Djuna had set this up, given him away and

whispered her plan to Johnny. Again, anger rose and a yearning ache. Djuna's pale silver eyes sparkled but Yvonne's smoldered, and he found himself attracted to the heat. Djuna had said, "If the universe gives you a gift, say yes."

****

A streetlight, the off-white color of bone, lit Yvonne's small apartment. Tree leaves outside her window filtered it into shafts as though they were in the middle of a skeleton. He recalled Day of the Dead posters he'd seen in Los Angeles.

"Make yourself comfortable," she said. He sat in an armchair while she went into the bathroom. A yellow light briefly lit the room, banishing the bones, a harsh, debased light compared to the cool beams streaming from outside. He recalled Yvonne from the night of three, her lean brown body naked in this chair, legs open, smoking a long brown cigarette, rattling the ice cubes in her whiskey glass, watching him and Djuna. He had seen her as the picture of corruption. How did he end up here, in Portland, in this chair, waiting for this woman for this reason? He toyed with dueling ideas: it was either purely random or destined to happen. Desire and fear teetered in equilibrium. She emerged wearing a blood-red robe, open in the front, her body lean lines and generous curves.

"You're sitting in the dark," she said.

"The light is intriguing."

She approached, long legs swishing the robe aside until she stood before him, dark mound of pubic hair level with his eyes. In her soft drawl, she said, "I love that light. Sometimes it's like the nights of angels, and others it's like a full moon that never sets, and I feel like a werewolf."

He asked, "Tonight?"

"Definitely the werewolf." Her words provoked a shiver. She leaned over, entwined her fingers in his long hair, and kissed him hard. He let her, believing she wanted permission to have her way. She broke off the kiss, took his hand, pulled him to his feet. "Take off your clothes," she urged.

He moved as though hypnotized, under a spell. Djuna's courting and love poetry, alcohol, the dreamlike light, his fear of her, his lust and loneliness, the stern mastery she presented to the world, the lines of her body—these urged him to submit. He quickly undid the top button then the next.

"Slowly," she said, "eyes on mine." With each button, each piece of clothing removed, part of his will surrendered to her. When he stood naked, she gestured for him to turn in place.

"My stars, you're beautiful," she said. He didn't know what to do. "Lie on my bed," she ordered and stood watching him. He thought her the most beautiful woman he'd ever seen in person. She let her robe fall and straddled him. She kissed him hard and long, coming up for air, then kissing him again and guiding him inside her. Her long black hair covered them, smelling of cigarettes and flowers. She began to rock on him, slowly at first and then stronger, but when she was about to come and with him right behind her, she slid up his body until her sex hovered above his mouth, her knees on his shoulders.

She said, "Give me your tongue." He loved the taste of her, dark and musky, salty, rich and sweet, woman, earth and sea. She took pleasure from his mouth, once and then again, coming in moans and exclamations until he could taste blood from his lip. She treated him like a toy for her pleasure. Yet surrendering to her, submitting, caused something heavy inside to fall away. He understood why people served a god or a cause because then they too could be empty, empty of pain and loneliness, empty of *I*, of Raina and Johnny and Djuna and The Open Door. Once again, she guided him inside her toward his own sweet release.

Almost empty of *I*, after his climax, he said, "I love you."

She stopped, put two fingers to his lips, said, "No, Paul, don't go there." She rose, stepped to the kitchen, and opened the refrigerator. He closed his eyes against its harsh light, heard an ice tray cracking, ice tinkling in glasses. The refrigerator closed, and he opened his eyes, grateful for the silvery darkness. She sat on the bed; he edged away. She handed him a glass. He didn't want to drink because he relished the taste of her, while at the same time, he wanted to wash it away.

He put the cold glass against his bleeding lip. "You made me bleed."

She said, "Paul, I'm sorry. I didn't think. I made a mistake."

He said, "You fucked me just like Raina," but knew it wasn't true. Selfish, pleasure-seeking Raina made him feel a little dirty, but Yvonne's domineering anger made him feel bent and corrupted.

"Ouch," she said.

He drank because the taste of blood overwhelmed the taste of her. The bitter whiskey stung his lip. "I liked it, and I hated myself for liking it. A part of me resents you and another part would let you whenever you wanted."

She tentatively reached for him. The touch of her hand on his arm at first repulsed then soothed him. He didn't know what to think—everything contradicted itself. "I know that feeling. It's terrible and strong, and I'm sorry. I was pissed at Charlie and took it out on you."

Her words seemed honest and this comforted him. "It's my own fault. I let you. I liked it and that shocked me."

"Again, I'm sorry," she said.

In the tension-filled shifts after the night of three, she had quietly treated him as a friend, and he wanted to ramp down the discord. "Make it up to me and get me another drink?"

She refilled their glasses but didn't sit on the bed, choosing instead the big chair. She lit another of her brown cigarettes. In the light of the match, he saw kindness in her expression. "Have you had much experience with women?"

"You, you and Djuna, Raina, a girl back in high school."

She waited for more. "Tell me about the girl in high school."

"In my creative writing class, the teacher used to have these contests. He would read the stories he liked best, then the class would vote. Between us, she and I won them all. Before the last contest she said, 'Write a story about me, and I'll write one about you, and we'll see who wins.'

"One night, she knocked on my door and said, '*I got stuck 'cause I don't know anything about you. Care to help a fellow writer?'* I lied to my dad about the library, and she drove into the hills and parked so we could look out at the lights. We got together in the back seat. She wrote about it and made the sex awkward, the relationship hopeless. I wrote a romantic and magical story, but she won. We went driving a couple of more times, but the last time we were parked on a dead-end street, and a cop drove up. He delivered us home. My dad got pissed. He thought I'd taken advantage of her, but that's not how it happened. He made me sit in a kitchen chair and took off his belt. I wore shorts and he hit me across the thighs. He lost it and kept hitting me. He would have stopped if he hadn't been drunk."

"Did you fight back?"

"He taught hand-to-hand at Camp Pendleton. I couldn't. Nothing has ever hurt as much."

Yvonne exhaled smoke in a deep sigh, "You haven't been lucky with women."

"My night with you and Djuna was pretty amazing. You were gentle with me."

The familiar scowl clouded Yvonne's face. She seemed to decide something and returned to bed. On hands and knees, she moved between his legs like a predator. His body tensed. But she kissed his thighs, kissed where the belt had landed, up one leg, down the other, slowly, gently. She didn't speak and didn't stop, as his father hadn't stopped. He understood this to be both an apology and a wish to fix the past. Grief and anger he had never let himself feel rose within him; silent tears rolled. Still, she kissed his legs. When the tears stopped, her kisses filled him with desire and he stiffened. She took him in her mouth and kept him there until he opened and gave himself to her. She positioned herself beside him, cradling his head on her shoulder. "Yvonne, you've been so kind to me. Why?"

"I've been hurt, too. My scar."

She stroked his forehead, running her fingers through his long brown hair, kissing away the wetness on his cheek. "Paul, you shouldn't go out with women like me, women like Raina and Djuna. You should go out with someone your own age, someone sweet and innocent."

"Well, you're the gentlest one," he whispered, "the sweetest one." She held him until he lay still then rose, poured another whiskey, and sat in the big chair, looking at the young man in her bed, trying to understand her tenderness for him, an unusual emotion. She sought clarity from the light pouring in her window, which she thought of as pure, while knowing she was not. This saddened her. After the ice in her glass melted, she slipped into bed beside him, rose on one elbow, leaned over, and let her lips brush his cheek, wondering how it would feel.

"See, how sweet you are?" he murmured.

****

She awoke in the half-light before dawn craving the sex she wanted before Djuna got her mixed up with Paul—hard and practiced with a man who didn't care. She wanted this young man beside her in a different way, one she rarely desired. She caressed his chest and his lean stomach and then teased a nipple with her tongue until he awoke with a moan. She nudged him on top and guided him inside.

He didn't move but stayed still and solid and gave her soft kisses like she had given his wounded legs. He kissed her lips, her cheeks, and her neck, kissed her scar like it wasn't there. Between kisses, he whispered, "I used to think you were hard and tough. But there's a soft Yvonne, too, who nobody sees, who is gentle and kind. But you let me see her, and she seems just like me, someone filled with love with no one to give it to." She began to rock against him, but he stayed still, solid. He kept kissing, whispering. "You were in the chair looking at me, and the light coming through the window changed you and I saw soft Yvonne. Can I make love to her, to soft Yvonne?"

"Yes," she said, her voice tight. She began to kiss him back, to caress his face, to run her hands over the muscles of his back, his shoulders. And he moved against her, just a little, just enough. He whispered her name. He focused on her and nothing else.

Afterward, as they lay apart, she felt an undefined sense of panic, some impending horrible thing. She turned, put her head on his shoulder, and curled in a small fetal ball beside him. The night turned upside down; first, she had dominated him, then turned to him for comfort. He held her gently; she snuggled into his embrace; he stroked hair back from her forehead. She wanted him to protect her, and she wanted to protect him. He quickly fell asleep.

But sleep deserted Yvonne. She lay in his arms as the darkness receded to a sky filled with rosy light, wondering about soft Yvonne and the kind of man who would imagine a person like that.

****

The next day, she kept her distance as she fed him coffee, toast, and eggs. When these were finished, she approached him, kissing him, caressing his face. "It's nice to have a man to take care of."

"You took care of me last week at work, and Yvonne, last night was wonderful. I want to tell you…"

She put a finger to his lips, shushed. "I enjoyed last night, too, *mon ami*. Let's not spoil it with a lot of talk." When she dropped him off at work, he didn't get out but leaned against the door, a question in his eyes . "Okay," she conceded, "what's on your mind?"

"Does this mean we're boyfriend and girlfriend?"

She laughed, and the smile transformed her face to terribly beautiful. "Is that what you want?" she asked.

"I don't know how things are supposed to work."

"Things work how they work. You're a charming boy, but do you know how old I am?" He shook his head. "I'm twenty-nine."

"No way," he said.

"Almost ten years older than you."

He examined his hands before he said, "Does it matter?"

She stared over the steering wheel as if the answer lay on a sign too far down the road to read. "I don't know, but you belong to Djuna. You're in love with her; she has a crush on you; she's my best friend."

"Then why did you sleep with me?"

"She told me I could. She didn't mean to hurt you. She has some things to figure out about Johnny and didn't want you to be alone. Let's leave things like this. If you ever want me again, come and whisper in my ear. If things look like they'll work out, I'll say yes."

"What does that mean, 'work out'?"

She had never seen him in sunshine, his brown eyes flecked with gold. "If we won't get Djuna mad. If I don't have a man. If you're not using me to get Raina or Djuna jealous. If you treat me well. And Paul, one

36

more thing—thank you. If not for you, I would have spent last night mad, making stupid choices. You helped me, and I'm sorry if I treated you...kind of rough."

****

Yvonne ran the red light, crossing Macadam Avenue to swoop into the parking garage of John's Landing. She called Djuna on a payphone. "Bangs," she said.

"Ten minutes," said Djuna.

Yvonne chose their usual booth and ordered, "Manhattan up, Remy in a snifter."

Shortly after drinks arrived, Djuna sat, pale gray eyes alight. "So?"

"It worked like you said. Raina set her sights on him, so I scooped him up."

"He spent the night? Come on, Vonnie, out with it."

Yvonne's dark eyes held Djuna's. "I blew it, completely lost my touch. That's what years of mediocrity will do." She swirled the cognac in her glass, inhaled, smiled. "He acted shy and I just took him."

"Took him?" Yvonne explained the first part of the evening and his comment about how she fucked him just like Raina. Djuna feigned anger. "You were supposed to distract him from Raina, not remind him. The night ended badly?"

"I felt so fucking guilty; I gave him his first blow job. That seemed to help. Raina used him. You and I used him. Some girl in high school used him, too, and he got in trouble for it. You ditched him for Johnny. Then I used him again." She opened Djuna's purse,

37

took out a pack of cigarettes, pulled one from the pack, and tamped it on the table. "He's a sweet, beautiful young man, and you're a fool if you leave him for Johnny." A silence stretched between them.

"That's it?" wondered Djuna.

"Pretty much." Yvonne searched Djuna's purse for a lighter, fired her smoke. "Djuna, you shouldn't play with him unless you mean it." Yvonne's eyes burned, and Djuna remembered why she intimidated people. "I'm serious."

But Djuna had learned to stand up to her friend. "So you have your fun, blow it and then tell me, *Don't do what I did, that would be wrong.*"

Yvonne inhaled from her cigarette and blew smoke just over Djuna's head. "It was your idea. Look, this kid could go somewhere, be something like you could've once and maybe still can. He might end up being a man who gives more than he takes. Have you ever gone out with anyone like that? 'Cause I haven't. He wants to be in love. Go play with someone else and let this boy be."

But Djuna knew she would see him at least one more time.

Chapter 3
Costa Rica in Her Purse

Detective Frank Clonch cruised into The Open Door parking lot a little after nine a.m. on a misty Sunday morning. He didn't feel well. His bacon and egg breakfast at Denny's was fighting back. He attributed his heartburn to dread of his pending appearance in divorce court to learn the financial cost of years of unhappiness.

A small, blond man with a splotchy complexion and bloodshot eyes squinting against the brightness of the day met him at the door. A drinker, guessed Frank, with a certain sympathy having drunk too much the night before. He flashed his badge. "I'm Detective Clonch, this is Detective French. And you are?"

"Donny Brasco, kitchen manager. I found the body. Clonch? You from Baker?"

At the station, they ribbed Frank about the Baker Mafia, a loose association of economic refugees from the small town in eastern Oregon. To be a Bakerian far from home meant one owed courtesies and formed alliances with other wandering Bakerians. Years ago, a captain of detectives had taken care of Frank, given him choice assignments, promoted him a little too soon. "Yeah, I knew Brascos in Baker. Grew up with Peter."

"He's my uncle."

"Tell me, Donny from Baker, where is the body?"

"The banquet room. I figure she passed out and choked on her puke like Janis and Jimi."

Frank nodded as though he knew those people. "She's drinker?"

"Yep."

"Drugs?"

"Well, there's rumors," said Donny, licking his lips and examining his shoes.

He could delay no longer. Frank didn't like viewing bodies and considered the practice more ritualistic than helpful. He believed the forensics team to be far more skilled at deriving evidence from a situation than he. Donny led them to where she lay in a booth, skin pale against her black uniform and the black vinyl of the booth. Yet even in death, she retained her beauty, even with vomit dried on her hair, cheeks, and chin. Looking into her dead eyes, Frank's legs wobbled and his sweat glands opened. He spoke to break the spell, "Keep everyone out of here. Miguel, let's start interviews and phone calls. How many people work here?"

"Day and night shifts, about sixty," said Donny.

"Shit," said Frank. "How many customers last night?"

"Last night was crazy busy, packed, wall to wall, standing room only. We called the cops three times."

At four-thirty, when Frank and Miguel French finished interviews, they possessed many opinions and only a few facts. They spread out their paperwork on a four-top, and Donnie from Baker dropped off a couple beers which Frank insisted turn into sodas. Then, he read aloud through the highlights of his obsessively detailed notes, sipped his soda, and said, "We'll call it alcohol poisoning, then?"

"Yeah, for now. Crime lab will take at least four weeks to tell us for sure," said Miguel French. The victim's mother lived in Hood River, and Frank drove out to offer what comfort he could. Penance for whatever he may have done to drive his daughter near to a similar end.

"Alcohol and drugs have killed so many," Frank would tell me later.

But not this time. This one turned out to be poison.

****

Djuna lived in a small blue and white Victorian on NW 25th Avenue, a few blocks from Paul's apartment. A white picket fence surrounded a mowed lawn. Red roses grew in the sun and vibrant purple hydrangeas in the shade by the porch. When Paul rang the bell, a short, solid woman with a head of wild black hair streaked with gray flung open the door and cried, "You must be Paolo, come in, come in." She yelled toward the back of the house, "June, your friend is here."

From another room, someone called, "Ma, his name is Paul." It wasn't Djuna's voice but a bored, petulant, critical one in the same register.

Djuna called, "Damn, you're on time. I'll be ready in a minute."

Her mother said, "Let me get you something to eat. All you kids are so skinny. Aren't you a cook?"

The unexpected befuddled him, the three women. Djuna lived in a neat, conventional home with her mother and her name was June. The antiques matched; framed pictures hung on the walls; lace doilies decorated the end tables. Books covered one whole wall, floor to ceiling, fitted into every available space, overflowing into piles on the floor. He tried to pay polite attention to Djuna's mother, but his eyes kept drifting to the books. Because payday wasn't until Friday, he had skipped breakfast and ransacked his change jar for money to take Djuna to lunch.

The bored voice called, "Ma makes amazing crepes."

Djuna called, "Yes, eat. I'll be ready when you're done."

"Come eat," insisted her mother, seizing him by the arm and propelling him toward the kitchen. "You can meet my other lazy daughter."

She sat at the table and gave him a glance over her newspaper. "I'm the other lazy daughter. Some people call me April." She looked like Djuna with the same pale gray eyes but a thinner face and straight brown hair. She seemed his age.

"Sit," said Djuna's mother. "Coffee?"

"No, thank you, ma'am. Do you mind if I look at your books?"

"Go ahead. The kids call me Connie."

He spoke without thinking. "Is your real name Constance?"

"Yes."

"Could I call you that? Connie sounds like someone trying to pull one over on you. You seem more like a Constance." Nervousness had reduced him to babbling.

April lowered her paper. Constance Novak turned from the stove, studied him a moment, said, "Okay."

The bookshelves contained everything from opera scores to paperback romances. A thick old volume bound in dark blue cloth entitled *Classic Love Poems* caught his eye. The contents listed the poems Djuna had whispered in his ear. He would scour every used bookshop in town to find that book. The older books captivated him, dark with age, Dostoevsky, Tolstoy, and Chekhov. He found a book titled *Nightwood* by Djuna Barnes. His finger touched the faded paper cover at the same time a hand touched his shoulder. Constance stood with an appraising eye. "You like books?"

He began to gush. "When I'm older, I want a room like this, walls covered with books, and a big table in the middle and two huge chairs in front of the fireplace." He caught himself babbling again.

She looked at him oddly. "I've always loved books myself, and I'm blessed my daughters do, too."

Constance balanced the flavors in her crepes: strawberry, lemon, pastry cream, vanilla, an unfamiliar liquor. Along with them, she gave him a piece of her mind. "Paul, I appreciate what you're doing for June but help her find a real job. She needs to start a career."

"Ma, leave him alone," chimed in April. "Look at him eat. He's still hungry. Make him another crepe."

When Djuna walked in, he rose to his feet, not out of courtesy but in automatic reaction. Silver combs tamed her wild hair and matched her eyes. She wore a gray silk blouse under a black jacket and black linen slacks with a belt which accentuated her slim waist.

"You're beautiful," he managed.

"Shall we go, sir?" she said and took his arm. As they were crossing the porch, the door opened behind them, and Constance Novak stuck out her head.

"June," she asked, in a sweet voice, "could I have a word?" Djuna turned and slipped inside.

Her mother's anger shocked Djuna. "I don't know what you're doing with this boy, but if you break his heart, I'm going to break a broom over you. You've already got that worthless bartender, and now you're toying with this young man. Even your sister, who doesn't care about anyone, could see he's head over heels in love with you. What are you thinking?"

"I don't know, Ma. I…"

"You don't know? Well, figure it out. He doesn't need you playing ducks and drakes with his emotions. Two men at the same time? Did I raise you like that? Did your father?"

"I'm not seeing him, Ma. He's a sweet guy who needed a place to live when his shitty girlfriend cheated on him. I helped him move into Ginny's old apartment. We're going to a job interview. I'm not doing anything wrong."

"This is a young man. Guide him forward. Don't pull him down with you." These last words were a mistake. Djuna turned away. Constance frowned and sighed in apology. She paused for an instant before her face took fire again. "Is he in college?"

"No."

"Then I'll tell you this. If he's hanging around in September and he isn't in school, I'm going to throw you out of this house. No hyperbole."

"Yes, Ma, great idea. He'll like it."

Walking beside Paul, Djuna's mind was deliciously awhirl. She finally had him to herself, and things were becoming clear. Her mother's argument struck her as tangential to a point: two boyfriends in one place are too many. Time to exit The Open Door.

Getting hired at the Olympus Club filled Djuna

with what she believed to be excessive joy; the job was no better than her current one, but change made the world seem ripe with possibilities.

She ran down the steps of the club and launched herself at Paul, grabbing him and pecking him with kisses. "I did it." Then they were alone, nothing planned, an awkward moment. She guided them to a booth in the dark corner of a bar where they served a good burger. Shy, he seemed to have lost all conversation. Djuna lit the candle. "Tell me about yourself," she asked.

"You first," he suggested.

She figured then, he was too young. "Ask me a question."

He picked the hardest one. "I heard something happened to your father."

And suddenly, change and possibilities became illusion. You could not easily escape yourself and your life. "He died the night I graduated from college. Heart attack. He kissed me good night, happy and proud, and the next morning he didn't get up."

"I'm sorry."

Djuna spoke softly. "He was gentle and smart, and he cared about us more than anything in the world." To protect her make-up, she tried to hold back tears with a finger.

The waitress arrived to take their order and shot Djuna a look which said, "Young or old, they're all the same."

In the following silence, she rallied. "My turn for a question. What do you want to do with your life?"

He shrugged. "It's probably childish," he said, searching her eyes. "In high school, I wrote this story about consuming passion; I want that kind of love." She must have worn amusement on her face, for he seemed disappointed. She changed tack. "What do you want to do?"

She spoke without thinking, lines worn threadbare. "I don't want a conventional life, the job, the mortgage, the bourgeois values. Those feel like a trap. I want something more."

"You should go to graduate school. With your memory, you'd kick ass."

"My father would've agreed, though not in those terms."

She could see him get an idea, eyes lighting. It tickled her how he threw himself into things with joy and abandon. Like she used to do.

He said, "You know what's possible today?"

She failed to suppress a smile and shook her head.

He dug a scrap of cash register receipt from his wallet and slapped it down on the table. It said, *Costa Rica,* with a name and an international phone number. "This guy owns a resort on the beach. He said he'd give me a cabana, three meals a day, and a job cooking. It's pretty rustic but absolutely gorgeous. If you say yes, I'll sell everything, cash my check on Friday and buy two tickets. You and me, six months. The unconventional life."

"Is this real?" she asked.

He nodded. "Oh, yeah," like a determined man who knew what he wanted and how to get it. "Called him a couple of weeks ago to check."

A frightening idea caught her breath, *he may understand me better than Johnny or Yvonne or her mother, better than anyone.* While she would have preferred Paris or London, she held a dream of living creatively, exploration above routine, and every day an adventure, and now this young man offered her a piece of the life she craved, yet a wall of reluctance surrounded her, and she could not say yes. She closed her eyes, hating the degree of self-knowledge which allowed her to name the stones in the wall: habit, lack of will, ease, fear, practicality, the safety of living small. She now embraced everything she had once despised.

She opened her eyes and said, "I can't do it, Paul. I've got a new job."

He considered this. "It's not the job."

She sighed, tired and overwhelmed. "You're right. It's Johnny. People speak poorly of him, but after my father died, he helped me. He listened to me, took me out, got me a cocktail job at the Brasserie." Paul's face fell and Djuna's heart with it. He laid down his best card, and she had trumped him with every word.

"But Djuna, there's something between us every time our eyes meet. We could be perfect for each other."

If this were true, she would have to change. "You're spouting your hopes as truths. We barely know each other. Sure, I'm crazy about you. And I want us…" She stopped, uncertain of her desires.

"What do you want?"

"Be my lover," she said.

"I can't. I feel like shit every time I see Johnny."

She had expected this. "Wait for me," she said. "I can't promise anything, but things are changing, and I'll be out of The Door in two weeks."

On the street, the cool spring sun lightened their

mood. She took his arm and led him up the Park Blocks under the trees, by the statue of *Rebecca at the Well*. Passing the tower of the Hilton Hotel, she considered getting them a room, feeling if she nudged him, he would go. She didn't try. As they approached Portland State, she said, "My mom threatened me this morning."

"She didn't seem like a threatening person."

"Well, you rile up the both of us. She said if you're around in September and not in school, she's going to throw me out of the house, so we're going to the counseling office to see about getting you enrolled for fall."

"Does that mean you want me around?"

A difficult question. "Don't be presumptuous," she said to cover her uncertainty. After admonishings by both Yvonne and her mother, she didn't want to mislead him. She told him her best college stories as they strolled through the park, hand in hand, but red lights flashed. *No way am I putting this boy through school.* She wondered if this showed maturity of judgment or the death of romance and doubted she still believed in love, figuring Johnny for a symptom of that. She didn't much like the range of possible relationships if love was not the transformative elixir of poets but simply a feeling which left you vulnerable and a chain that bound.

After Paul met with a counselor, they sat over coffee in the student union. "Djuna, I could never pay for this. Maybe if I waited tables."

She gave him a mock wicked laugh and slapped a manila envelope on the table. "Ah, but this is filled with magic money, and I am the Dominatrix of Financial Aid."

"Where do I sign?" he said with a leer.

She thought The Hilton would have been a start, but said, "Come over for dinner Sunday night. Ma can gush over you, and I'll help with the forms." But alone in bed that night, she couldn't sleep. She kept coming back to The Hilton. She had plotted to get him there, but when given the chance, she held back, and didn't know why. With birds beginning to sing outside her window, she fell asleep clinging to one idea: If you cared for a man, you wouldn't press him to do a thing he believed was wrong.

****

The Open Door drew quite a crowd on Djuna's last night. Portlanders venture out on warm spring days, drawn to the sun like plants. The restaurant was hopping. Then, without warning, two buses of elderly tourists rolled into the parking lot. When the old folks shuffled in, Paul huddled his crew, prep cooks, dishwashers, and Hilton. "We're gonna get slammed," he told them. "But nobody freaks out; everyone helps each other, and no man is alone."

At eight-thirty, Djuna peered into the kitchen door. Paul, calm as a man at a Sunday barbeque, joked with Hilton, sipped his coke, and then put up fifteen plates, calling out, "Come on, people, orders up. You're crowding my window." He turned to her and winked.

After dinner service, Paul marched to the bar, face ruddy, long brown hair soaked with sweat. He smiled at Djuna as she garnished her drinks and said, "Johnny, thanks for taking care of my crew and, nobody else makes me those 'ginger ales.' " Paul put his hand out, and Johnny reached over the bar, and they shook, and then Paul's muscles surged and he gripped Johnny's hand. "But if you cheat on Djuna again, I'm gonna take her. Count on it."

"In the meantime, stay the fuck away from my girlfriend."

"Fair enough." He let go of Johnny and smiled. "Good night, Johnny. Good night, June." He put one hand on each of the restaurant's tall red double doors and strode through, pushing them wide.

Johnny said, "Dramatic gesture. Too bad he's now standing in the dark, waiting for a bus." Djuna failed to find a retort and walked away, but a cocktail waitress with her bartender for a boyfriend must always return.

At one a.m. after work, Djuna drove into the Thriftway parking lot where she could see the light in Paul's window. She imagined him reading or writing, maybe about her. She imagined going to him, holding him, making love, but after his promise to Johnny, he would keep his word. She imagined sitting across the tiny table in his almost empty apartment, but she would feel futile and desolate if she could not approach him. She imagined Costa Rica: a shack in the trees, exploring rutted roads in a car even older than Betty Dorf. She imagined that one day they could own a little resort between the beach and the jungle. Her imagination constructed a Victorian bed and breakfast where he cooked, and she kept books. They were both smart and hardworking and could build a life outside the world of nine to five. She took from her purse the piece of paper holding his Costa Rican dream and clenched it, silently asking the Idea Angel for help but could only imagine that ridiculous Victorian in the jungle.

An impulse not to lose drove her from the car onto

her feet. For the first time, Betty's dome light didn't turn on. The bulb must have burnt out. She hesitated, standing in the angle of the open door. She believed his declaration to Johnny was intended as a call for her to rise, to live at a higher standard, and wondered if she could do this. Yet, what did she have to offer a young man? She didn't know if she could truly love him, didn't know if she could be faithful, had abandoned all but the most functional of ideals, the most materialistic of dreams. And now she would climb those stairs to do what? Push him from his integrity? The lights in his apartment went off, one by one.

"Now it's dark," she said aloud as she folded herself behind the wheel and closed the door, reluctant to stay, unwilling to go home. She knew a club downtown where people went to find each other. It would be open for almost an hour. Before turning the key, she visited the hope that the car, like the light, wouldn't start, but it did, with a roar.

Chapter 4
Mannish Boy

I met Frank Clonch, my first friend in the detective's bullpen, by chance in an elevator. He nodded "Hello", ran his hands through thick, gray hair, looked at me with sad, blue eyes and said, "I can't stand when the stiffs are kids." This sudden revelation by a near-stranger took me by surprise. I didn't know what to say, and we rode four floors to the street in silence. But afterward, Frank treated me like a professional, called me Detective, and let me in the door on the Hennessey case. I wouldn't have gotten near it if not for Frank.

On a cold, wet afternoon, he invited me for lunch in the white-clothed dining room at the old train station, where he would explain his comment in the elevator. He had seen corpses for twenty-seven years, but kids and young people in their teens and twenties haunted him. He would wake up in a sweat, a dream image of the dead kid floating behind his eyes. He would turn on the light, get a drink, and sit at the breakfast room table to wait for the morning sun to burn away the ghost.

Drug overdose cases tormented him. Years before, he nearly lost his daughter to heroin. He found her in her apartment, entirely by chance, barely breathing. For hours, he sat in the hospital waiting room, shaken by desolation, guilt, and a sense of deep futility. She had lived, but every time he found a kid dead in some squalid room, this trifecta of emotions laid him low.

He tried to do right by them. If a dealer sold a product too rich or cut with something toxic, Frank tried to run them down. He spent time with the next of kin as penance for whatever he may have done to drive his daughter near to death, certain he must be in some way to blame. The OD work itself didn't bother him, if he could just get past the first view of somebody's child, a few years removed, spoiled and wasted. Everyone knew he couldn't wait to retire.

But things changed after Hennessey. He would, down the road, delay his long-awaited pension to be my partner. If I could choose my father, it wouldn't have been my old man, an A-1 prick, but it might have been Frank Clonch. Impractical and not a great cop, he possessed a gentle and evolved wisdom—for pain can guide us along the path. How often do you meet those kinds of people?

Later in the afternoon, he introduced me to the Hennessey case.

An hour before shift ended, the detective's bullpen was quiet. I sat at my desk trying to match mug shots with grainy black and white stills from the security camera of a convenience store. Frank Clonch sat at his desk, spinning a tale to his partner, "I get to Hood River, a doublewide way up in the pines. It's four in the afternoon, and they're sitting around the table with a half-gallon of whiskey and a liter of lemon-lime soda. I tell them we found her on her back, choked on her own puke. They're stunned and don't say a word. Finally, her mother says, *You mean she's dead?* And what have I been telling them for the last ten minutes?"

Frank sipped his coffee, looked at the clock, then at me, wearing an odd expression. At that point, I had been hit on, leered at, or put down by just about everyone. I don't get the lust. I'm not much to look at, freckles, chopped red hair, skinny and gawky, no butt, no boobs. Anyway, this look of Frank's didn't hold any lust, and he'd bought me lunch, so I kept the challenge from my voice when I said, "Can I help you, detective?"

"I have a troubling case," he said.

Not once since my promotion had anyone asked my opinion, asked for my help in anything but a clerical way, or spoken to me like an equal. "Want to talk about it?" I offered.

"Yeah," he said. "I do." He told me about the waitress who passed out and died. "A couple of things bother me. She was a habitual drinker. These are not the people who overdose. They crash cars, fall down stairs, get into fights, and hurt themselves. They make an infinite number of stupid mistakes but have a practiced sense of their alcohol limitations. People who drink themselves to death are despondent or new to drinking or frat boys with something to prove. She drank every night, kept a coffee cup of wine on a shelf by the bar, but timed her drinks so she wasn't quite smashed until after work. Yet the night of her death, she passed out, unable to finish her shift. This smells off."

I blurted in language elevated beyond the banter of the old boys of the bullpen, "Could alcohol and some other drug, in synergy, have caused fatal toxicity, perhaps heart failure?" Unlike most of them in 1979, I'd done a stint in college, but I would soon learn to keep my vocabulary in check.

Frank Clonch answered in a diction he knew from books on American history and a battered American Lit anthology he'd stolen from high school, a language he had always possessed but no one wanted to hear. "Well, she did use speed but crafted her equilibrium with that and alcohol, intimate friends she used every day." He flashed a smile. I'd made my first friend in the bullpen.

I said, "It could be medical."

"Could be. One witness, a cook, believed since she usually drank wine, shots of tequila did her in. A waiter suspected another cocktail waitress did the deed somehow. The problem is toxicology will take four weeks. And you know, Hailey." He spoke my name like I was one of the boys. "We weren't even thinking murder, but everyone we talked to suspected someone they hated did the coup de grace. I've never seen a place so filled with gossip and backstabbing."

Miguel French quipped, "Not even around here. Anyway, you stay late every night. Want to run names?"

"I'm working cold cases."

Clonch said, "What we're saying is, it might be murder, want in?"

I didn't know if they were motivated by laziness or charity, but they got me started on Hennessey.

****

Paul, the grillman, loves his job because cooking engages all his senses, lowers him from head to body. The kitchen is moist heat, rich with fragrance: roasting bones, caramelized onions, mushrooms sautéing in butter, a delicate scent of the sea. As he works, he tastes: trimmed bits of raw tuna, buttery sauce, and browned meat. His fingers discover messages in heat, texture, weight—smooth scallops, hefty steaks of swordfish and tuna, delicate sole. Bathed in the smoke of the grill, his senses unite to evaluate doneness: aroma, resistance, color.

He loves the heat, the way his sweat-lubricated body and heat-loosened muscles move, how sweat and pitchers of ice water cleanse him, washing away toxins both physical and psychic, how flames leap when fat drips, the transformative alchemy of fire, how things touched by it are forever changed, how the heat from the grill penetrates his chef's coat, apron, and jeans, hits him below the belt, how it fires the blood surging through his veins.

He loves how work lives in the moment, how the parade of tasks stifles memory, longing, and anxiety into one constantly unfolding instant so when he looks up, hours have passed, and he has lived in them entirely, moving and creating. He loves how the work has rhythm, how the cooks dance on the line, choreographing with a touch on the back, a sideways glance, weaving around each other, how they work alone, and yet in one instant, the order comes together, coordinated, complete, how if one fails and the other does not help, they fail or fall behind together. He loves how he comes off shift, empty and clean, feeling lighter, standing straighter, how when he steps away from the fire, the sweat dries, and the blood finds its degree. For him, work is meditation, the dance of the Sufi's, tai chi.

Early in the evening, Yvonne dawdled by the kitchen, waiting for an appetizer. Cocktail waitresses do this when the night is slow. Sometimes the cooks will feed them, and they, in turn, will water the cooks—

sodas on demand, beer charged to a big party who will never know. This pleases the cooks the way young women please young men. As they talked, he cut yellowfin tuna sashimi, mixed wasabi and soy, and offered the plate to her.

She stepped to the kitchen door so they could talk without heat lamps and the high counter between them. He set his offering on her tray, coming near enough to smell her musky perfume. She ate with graceful fingers. Her uniform revealed long legs and generous curve of breast. He remembered dark nipples, tiny areolas. She said, "Thank you," in her low tones, her slight drawl. Her black coffee eyes, large and almond shaped, met his, raising a question before she turned and walked away, his eyes following her. He remembered her saying, *If you want me, just whisper in my ear.*"

With him then in the heat and the sweat, she filled him as work emptied him so at shift's end, she surged in his blood and oozed from every pore. When he splashed water on his face, hoping to cool the fires, it had no effect. He sat alone near the hostess stand, apart from the others, trying not to devour her with his eyes as he remembered her lean brown body, her black hair falling around him, her cries of pleasure. When he could no longer bear to be apart from her, he approached the bar, touched her shoulder lightly, the energy within him jumping through his fingers. She shivered and turned. He whispered, "Yvonne, I want you. I've been thinking about you all night."

His right hand rested on the bar, and she drew one finger from his wrist over scars, scabs, and knuckles to the tip of his middle finger, then met his gaze and whispered, "I could tell," both warmth and laughter in her tone. "I should be off in an hour. Can you wait that long?"

He took a seat in The Corner, watching dominos fall and hearing Hilton slapping down his bone. "Now, I'm gonna make my move, double five. We're in the mood."

After her check out, she stood before him in a huge, ugly, worn, white, black, and gray sweater, clutching her purse, seeming smaller, as if diminished by his desire. He tried to counter that. "Do you want a drink?" he asked, hoping she would say no.

She shook her head.

Hilton slapped another domino down and called, "All I got is six and one. Guess ya'll gonna have your fun."

She took his arm as they walked through the bright red doors, from light to cool darkness. He turned to her, said, "Yvonne, I…"

She put a finger to his lips. "We'll talk later. First, we'll let our bodies talk and see what they can work out."

Her apartment felt smaller, nylons, bras, and panties drying on the bathroom door, bed unmade. A single light shone yellow from the ceiling. She closed the door behind them, kissed him then went into the bathroom and started water in the tub. She brought him a towel and a silver silk robe. "Take a bath, *mon ami*. I'll make some drinks." He wondered if the robe had been Charlie's, but it didn't matter. Nothing mattered: her age, his, The Door, Djuna, Charlie. If only they could make love like last time in the hour before dawn.

He emerged from his bath wrapped in another man's robe, alive with desire for her. She sat on the bed, back against the wall, wearing a white cotton nightgown, her black hair and brown skin rich in contrast. He wondered at her reserve. Her gaze met his and lingered, offering a question.

"I made hot chocolate and cognac," she said, gesturing toward a cup balanced precariously on the arm of the big chair. He sat and sipped his drink—chocolate, sweet over bitter, and cognac, alcohol bitter over rich liquor sweetness—a description of her tonight, even to the brown earthenware cup. Last time, he imagined her as whiskey, bitter with the ghost of sweet. She'd mixed this drink on purpose. He looked at her, amazed, and understood the silent question in her eyes: could he be a man for her?

This inspired a vision of the man he wanted to be. He stood, took three steps toward her, and seemed to cross a threshold. A voice he did not recognize as his said, "Yvonne, tonight, we will be perfect."

He extended a hand. She took it, rose from the bed, and waited. From her waiting, he knew he would have to be assertive. He took the last step toward her, put one hand on the small of her back, the other across her shoulders, and pulled her to him. He kissed her; each kiss he gave, no matter how strong or how gentle, she returned with a degree more tenderness until he understood the power and intimacy of careful attention. When he began to unbutton her nightgown and she stepped away to make his task easier, he knew that she would follow if he would lead. He intended to lift it over her head, but she slipped one side over her shoulder, leaving him to make it fall. He knew then he wanted a woman who would help him know his mind.

Her body, the color of dark liquor, left him

trembling, desire and tenderness warring within. Their eyes met. Her lips parted, waiting. The fiery grillman wanted to seize her, throw her down, and plunge into her, but her dark eyes were soft and curious. He backed her toward the bed and laid her down. In one graceful motion, she drew her feet toward her body, knees together, and then slowly opened her long legs for him. He thought of butterfly wings, of flowers blooming in time lapse, of double doors opening. Her hands guided his lips to hers. She tilted her hips and wrapped her legs around him. All the fires of all the shifts since their last encounter burned in him.

She took his face in her hands and said, "Come to me, *mon ami*. Don't wait." The grease flared and the cauldron bubbled. She held his eyes with hers as he poured himself into her.

He started to apologize, but she put two fingers to his lips, said, "Remember, we'll let our bodies talk because I think you still have something to say to me." She smiled and, with her legs still wrapped around him, began to rock, kissing him with gentle kisses. He found that their bodies had much to say.

Throughout the night, they loved and dozed. She would wake him with light fingers, her touch rekindling the flames. Twice he woke her, compelled to connect. The first time he took her with force and wild desire. Her response surprised him—she returned the same force, biting his lips and shoulders, calling out her orgasm loudly, and gripping his hair. The next day he would see bruises from his grip and would feel her scratches burn his back and knew she loved the passion of unfettered desire.

When he woke her with gentle caresses, she

responded with soft kisses and light fingers that played over his body. She wordlessly taught him to go slowly, as if each kiss, each touch could be a communication to be savored and understood. They found delight in each other's eyes. He saw pleasure and joy in her smile. In the light pouring through her window, she appeared for a moment as younger than he, innocent, a flower opening to the world. "My sweet man," she called him. "How do I deserve such a sweet, sweet man?"

Finally, she pushed him away and rose. She poured them each a cognac and sat in the big chair, bathed in elegant silver light. When he started toward her, she said with mock sternness and a huge grin, "You stay away from me."

He sat in bed, leaning against the wall, "If you'll tell me something about yourself."

She wouldn't say much. She had grown up in New Orleans and some small town. She had Cajun ancestry, among other things, a mutt of many stripes. Her father appeared and disappeared; her mother drank, struggled, made stupid choices about men. She ran away at fifteen but wouldn't say why. Got arrested at eighteen and wouldn't talk about that either. In jail, she read a National Geographic article about cleaning up the polluted Willamette River. She left New Orleans with her guitar, a hundred and twenty dollars, and a bus ticket to Portland. She wanted to live where things were clean. When he questioned her about details, she said, "I don't want to talk about my shitty past. I hate even thinking about it. Tell me about you."

He told her his father had been a Marine who served three tours in Vietnam, then come home to be a drill instructor at Camp Pendleton, a short, powerful man with a crew cut and Semper Fidelis tattooed on his right arm. He told her about life on base. She understood then his posture, his manners, his sense of honor. After retiring from the military, his father had drifted from job to job, each worse than the last, until he retired altogether to TV and Cutty Sark. His mother all but abandoned their home, taking refuge down the street at her parents'.

"Would you like to have a family?" she asked.

"I would," he said. "To be a good dad would be a fine challenge. Do you want children?

She laughed and said, "Me, kids? I wouldn't want to pass my rotten childhood to anyone."

****

He awoke to the smell of frying potatoes, onions, and peppers. She stood at the stove wearing only her long, straight black hair. Her lanky brown legs enticed him, the curve of her breast when soft Yvonne turned and smiled, "There's coffee." After breakfast, she bathed while he washed dishes. He also wanted to take a bath, but she said, "I want you to smell like you've been inside me all night," so he used her toothbrush, bound his brown hair in a ponytail, and they walked out into the sun. She wore jeans and a short-sleeved top in bold stripes of red and white. Feeling funky and sexy in yesterday's jeans and white T-shirt, he wanted to turn around and go right back to bed, but when she took his arm, a sense of completeness inspired a smile.

"Where are we going?" he asked.

"To the farm market. I'm going to make you gumbo." The sun warmed and brightened the morning, and rain overnight had left a scrubbed world and pristine sky. A transformed Yvonne walked empty

Sunday downtown streets beside him, full of smiles, laughter, tender caresses. Having her on his arm and kissing her at red lights filled him with pride.

In those days, they set up the market in Portland under the Burnside Bridge, where it rises to arc over the river because under the roadway is dry in rain and shaded in heat. Yvonne led him through booths and stalls, said, "There's someone I want you to meet, Fanny Mae, the only person I know here from New Orleans."

Fanny Mae wore a dress printed in blue and yellow and stood behind a table laden with boxes of fruit. She was stout, strong, older, with white skin and freckles, African features, short nappy hair streaked with gray, and a sad, lined face that whispered of a life filled with trouble, until she smiled, then everything fell away to joy. "Oh, Vonnie, I missed you, child," she said, wrapping Yvonne in strong embrace. She studied Paul. "This young buck with you? I got a hat older than him." She chuckled. "Got me a hat. But it's all right. Sometimes a woman needs to play the short game." Yvonne said words Paul couldn't catch, and Fanny Mae turned to Paul. "You, young man, use your fine body and stack those boxes in the van, and don't bruise no fruit. You wanna bruise some other fruit, go right ahead, but people still want to buy those." Her long laugh made him smile.

As he loaded boxes, the women spoke what sounded like French in animated conversation until Fanny Mae called him from his work. "You don't know, but my Vonnie is a witch girl, fill you full of enchantments. Be good to her, you'll be in for some lovin'. Be bad and the devil himself can't save you."

Her bubbling laughter made them both smile. "Let's do this how my grandma use to say. You, boy, come stand over here. Face each other. A little closer. He don't bite, and if he does, well, that's okay, too." She cackled again. They smiled nervously, face to face, drinking the sight of each other. "Now, you touch her. Wherever you feel."

He first wanted to touch her hand in friendship. She treated him gently, called him *mon ami*, took care of him and his crew in the restaurant. A breeze blew a wisp of hair across her forehead; he brushed it back.

"Oh," Fanny Mae intoned significantly, "good. Now, girl, it's your turn." Without hesitation, Yvonne put her palm on his chest, right over his heart. "Now you know what to expect. You may kiss the bride. You just got married by old Fanny Mae." She laughed her wheezing laugh, but he took Yvonne in his arms and kissed her solemnly.

Before they left, Fanny Mae and Yvonne embraced, and the older woman pressed something into Yvonne's hand, which she slipped into the back pocket of her jeans. Paul asked about Fannie Mae as they shopped.

Yvonne answered, "When I was on the street, she took care of me."

They were leaving the market, holding hands, when Djuna and Johnny stepped from behind a stall colorful with tie-dye and batik. Djuna's face brightened. "Hey, you two." The women hugged with uncertainty. Johnny smiled cautiously. Paul found himself full of smiles and offered his hand. He hadn't seen Djuna in weeks and searched inside to find she was not lighting fires.

Djuna said, "We were gonna poke around here, go see Fanny Mae, and then go eat. Come with us."

Djuna wanted no hard feelings, and he did not want to come between friends. He was about to say, "Sure," but Yvonne shot him a look, saying something with her eyes. "I don't know," he said. "Yvonne is gonna make gumbo." He held up a grocery bag. "How about another time?"

Djuna's face telegraphed disappointment. "Yes," she said, "another time. Come on, Johnny, we should go." The women stretched out their goodbye, gossiping about a waitress at Cassidy's. After they parted, Yvonne said, "If you want, we could find them."

"I'm just selfish, I guess," he replied. "I want to be with you, wanted to try some gumbo. Is that okay?" She pulled him to her, kissing him, biting his lips, hands gripping his hair. He had saved her feelings. He was amazed that overnight she had granted him power to hurt her.

He served as her prep cook, chopping onions and garlic, deveining prawns, coring, peeling, and seeding tomatoes. When everything was in the pot, she dug into her jeans and presented two folded bindles of paper, one red and one blue, which looked like packages of cocaine he'd seen in the restaurant. She said, "The witch girl is about to cast her spell. Should we have love or lust?"

"We've got lots of lust. Let's try the other."

She smiled and poured the blue envelope into the pot and stirred. A moment later, at the edge of sight, he caught her pouring in the red envelope before stirring again.

They carried red wine and brown earthenware

bowls to the fire escape. She asked him about living with Raina. He told of his adventures among the druggies and his dream one night of becoming a Buddhist monk, a tenzu, the monastery cook.

She laughed. "You could do the cook part, but when some woman comes to the monastery for refuge, you can't take her to your cell and fuck the shit out her."

"I would renounce all sexuality," he declared.

"It's easy to say now." They laughed together.

Paul asked, "Remember when I tapped you on the shoulder at the bar, and you said, *I get off in an hour, can you wait?* What would you have done if I'd said no?"

"Taken you to the banquet room so you didn't have to. I'm not the kind you bring home to Momma." Her familiar scowl clouded her face, and she wouldn't look him in the eye.

As he washed dishes, she took her guitar from under the bed and played flamenco, hard, fast. As she played, she watched him clean her skillet, wiping it with a paper towel drenched in oil until it shone black.

"You know how to take care of pans," she said, puzzled by how much his answer mattered.

"Yeah, my grandfather loved his pans. He said if you take care of them, they'll last forever." When she shivered at the sound of "forever," she knew for certain this relationship was a mistake and she would do it anyway.

He worked for a while in silence, listening to her play. "You're good. You could be a pro."

"No, professional is a whole other level. I used to play on the street for money. I had a boy who sang."

He wished he could sing and realized he brought nothing. His job, for all the "Hey here comes the grillman shtick" didn't pay shit. He could cook, but so could she. He had no car, no money. But he could work. He did a great job on the kitchen, cleaned the sink and the stove, swept the floor, and took out the trash while she played. When he finished, she put away her guitar and leaned against him, her eyes finding his, one finger tracing his lips. He had one other thing to give and whispered, "Teach me to make love to you. Teach me everything." Hours later, he would wonder what Fanny Mae had given her to put in the gumbo.

****

They awoke late on Monday. He made coffee, toast, and omelets, which they ate while reading the paper. After he had bathed, dried, and dressed, she sat him on the edge of the bed.

"The last time we were together, you asked if I was your…woman. If you asked me again, I'd give you a different answer."

"Why a different answer?"

"Because you didn't understand me the first time. When I said, *If you come up to me and say I want you,* I meant that night or the next or any night in the last month. It took you long enough, you little shit."

"Yvonne, I'd like to be your man. I don't have much to give. I…"

She put fingers to his lips. "You're not an always man for me. You're a for-now man. You'll be an always man for somebody but not me." He started to object, but again she raised fingers to his lips and shook her head. "There are a couple of things. I don't want cheating or drama or off-again, on-again like Djuna does. When it's time for us to go our ways, you come to me and say, *Yvonne, it's finished,* and then you give me the most passionate kiss ever, and that's how we'll end it." He nodded. Beginnings and endings smashed together stuck in his throat, and he could not speak the words. "And if I say it's over, there'll be no drama, no big scene. You promise?"

Again, he nodded.

"Also, I'm not your mama. You do your share like these last couple of days. And when fall comes around, you go to school like you planned with Djuna and let her help you."

He scanned her apartment. She had very little. Some feeling inside him itched to be recognized. "But that's not enough for me." He tried to explain. "When I cook, I don't just get food hot. That fish needs to be perfectly done. I go by color, by size, by pressure, and give. When I put my finger on this, no."

"What do you want?"

"To do things right. I've watched you work. You're organized and thorough. You pick up glasses by the stem every time. You always carry a full tray; never waste a trip. The ashtrays in your section are always clean, the dirty glasses removed. You like to get things right, too. I don't want to put my energy into something that will, in the end, be worthless. I want it so years from now, some night when I can't sleep and don't know what to do, I'll look back and say, *I want things to be just like they were with Yvonne.* Can we make something like that?"

"Even though it's temporary, you'd try that hard, make yourself that vulnerable? What if we fell in love?"

Paul answered firmly. "I'm already in love. I don't want to be used and discarded, and I don't want to spend myself on something shallow. I've done those things. How can I flip fish perfectly and have a shabby relationship? It's not forever? I can understand that. But half-hearted, careless? That's not you or me. I want us to give this our best shot. Serve from the left, pick up from the right, a napkin under every drink. Then, when it's over, we'll do what you want and calmly walk away. Yvonne, you're the woman I always imagined for myself, hard as nails and soft as flowers." The man he wanted to be smiled.

"Fucking hell," she said quietly. She couldn't look at him. Beams of morning sun slid in through the window, broken into shafts like golden bars. He filled her with tenderness and optimism. And doubt. He broke into her revelry.

"Yvonne, the truth is, I'm never going home. I need to create relationships that mean something."

She spoke in the barest whisper. "I don't have family either, except Fanny Mae. Maybe Djuna." Dust motes floated in beams of golden light, rising. She had lived in this apartment for two years but never seen the light in just that way. Maybe they weren't bars but strands of golden rope, which would lift her up if only she could grab one and hang on. She reached out, but her hand passed through the beam like she knew it would. "I've never done that with a man. I've always held back." She closed her eyes, fought a rising panic, and said to herself, *Please don't let me fuck this up.* She said to Paul, "I'd like to try."

He took her hand, kissed it. "I have a couple of other things. I play basketball on Sunday with Hilton.

And would you teach me guitar? I'd practice; I really would."

Yvonne rolled her eyes at a relationship with such a young man, then smiled and nodded.

****

On Tuesday, at 12:30, the earliest decent time amongst people who worked until two, the phone rang.

"Bangs," said Djuna.

Yvonne hesitated. "Let me see."

When Yvonne asked in an intimate voice, "Sugar, what time do you have to be at work?" Djuna understood Paul lingered a whisper away, and they had become a couple. "Bangs at four," Yvonne answered.

****

Yvonne drove Paul to his place for clean clothes. He had accumulated little: a tired sofa, a battered bookcase stuffed with books, a chair, and small table that held his typewriter. The wall held a promo poster of The Open Door, two red doors, one open, emitting a blaze of yellow light into indigo darkness. Next to it hung a photo of Djuna, black and white, unframed.

"I can take it down if you want," he said.

"No," Yvonne said, "I know you and Djuna have a thing. She and I did, once, too."

"Are you bi?" he wanted to know.

"I like sleeping with women, but for me, men are easier to be around."

"Have you had a lot of lovers?" he ventured.

She looked him in the eyes, hoping to avoid upheaval, wanting desperately to tell the truth. "Yes, does that bother you?"

"No, but nothing could now." He smiled with so much enthusiasm she felt sorry for him—a naïve kid in love with someone he knew nothing about.

At work, she dropped him in front. "I'm going to meet Djuna. We need to talk." She kissed him fiercely.

****

Hilton's cousin Ernie walked toward him, heading from lunch service toward her car. A tall, strong woman with a short Afro and huge glasses, Ernestine lived with Hilton, and whenever Paul came for dinner after basketball, she included him in the conversation, gave him work in the kitchen, made him feel part of the family.

"Far better choice," said Ernie.

"You know Yvonne? Ernie, what do you think of her? Tell me the truth."

"She's a lot of woman for a kid like you. I don't know if you have enough sand."

"Sand?"

"An expression of my father's. Sand means grit, stability, toughness. A woman like Yvonne is gonna have some storms. Do you have enough sand, enough steady weight to help her weather them? I don't know."

"I wish I did."

Ernie laughed. "You're a strange kid, Paul. Maybe I spoke without thinking. Hilton says you running this kitchen, Donny being useless and all. Just remember, Yvonne never really had anyone to believe in."

****

Captain Billy Bangs' was nearly empty, at slack water transition between lunch and dinner. Yvonne took their usual booth but had arrived early to collect herself. She ordered sparkling water and a shrimp salad and tried to examine her feelings. Paul had exhausted her. She dreaded talking to Djuna. She laughed at herself for the giddy feeling of being in love with a boy and felt a strong protectiveness toward him. Not drinking since wine with the gumbo left her oddly hopeful. Two ladies sat nearby, secretaries maybe, and she wondered if it would be a calmer life when sunrise came at the beginning of the day instead of the end, where one lived in sunshine instead of night.

She finished her salad moments before Djuna sat down with a drink from the bar. "Vonnie, you look different."

"I took your boy."

Yvonne feared her friend would be angry, but "I know," was all Djuna could muster.

"You had your chance."

"I know."

"Are you mad?"

Djuna lit a smoke, took a drag then crushed it in the ashtray. "Yes, no, sad, I guess."

"We talked about it. It won't be forever. Djuna, I didn't plan it. He kept staring at me. He wanted to get laid; I wanted to get laid, but when we got to my place, the chemistry. Djuna, he makes love to me, makes love, like I'm some precious, sweet, young thing."

Djuna was accustomed to feeling nothing, but the transformation of Yvonne surprised her. Instead of hard and beautiful, Yvonne appeared soft and pretty, and the scar seemed not the mark of a street tough but that of a victim. Her dead serious face hid a smile.

"You know I'm jealous, but if you guys are in love, well, we should celebrate." Even to herself, Djuna did not sound sincere.

Yvonne allowed a smile. "Let's hold the celebration. It's only been a couple of days. I'm sorry to hurt you."

"It's my own fault. I can't let go of Johnny. I used to think we might have a future, but now I know we don't, and I still can't let go. I come close, then some weakness in me, some fault which won't hold under stress, breaks, and I go running back. I don't love him. Maybe I'll never love anybody. Maybe I don't know how." She finished her drink. "I should order another." A tear snaked down her cheek. She put a finger to her eye to hold back the flow. "Shit, now my make-up. Where's the cocktail waitress? They're all incompetent, you know, every last one of them."

"Djuna, don't have a drink."

"But what else have I got to do? The club is a bore. Johnny is an ass. I lost Paul. You're in love. You'll take care of him, won't you?"

"Of course, and you will, too. You're going to get him into school and figure out the tuition. If you don't, he won't go." Yvonne fished her purse for money, said, "I've got to work. Promise you won't have another drink?"

"Sure. I've got to buy yet another fucking pair of nylons. I'll pay and probably see you in the parking lot."

Yvonne lingered near the door. The waitress walked from Djuna's table to the bar. When the bartender started pouring a Manhattan, Yvonne cursed and returned to Djuna. She stayed for an hour, drank with her, and put her in her car, hoping she would go home. Mitchell barked at her for being late, but she didn't care. Hauling cocktails in a short skirt and a low top was a shit job, and maybe she didn't want to feel like shit anymore.

Chapter 5
'Tain't Nobody's Bizness

I considered my work on Frank's case to be both an act of defiance and a chance to prove myself. I got to work early to call the east coast and stayed late writing up my findings. But then Frank and French were reassigned to a team investigating smuggling through the Port of Portland, so with mixed feelings, I took my information to Lieutenant Hardy.

Most people considered him to be a good cop, a straight arrow, perceptive, incisive, steady, the kind of cop I wanted to be, yet he had screwed me over, stuck me at a desk, and left me there. Also, a couple of the female staff handed me rumors about him, his divorce, his relations with women. It's not professional to listen to gossip. An officer is a citizen with a right to privacy, but the women who told me these things were trying to give me ammunition if I wanted to take a stand. I listened because I needed all the friends I could get. Besides, I entertained fantasies of lashing out at him and the system and had no qualms about a fight with dirty ordinance. Must have got that from dad.

Hardy's gray eyes unnerved me because every time we met, he checked me out, tits to ass. Rumor said this began around the time of his divorce.

When I knocked, he said, "Come, make it quick, press conference." Writing on a yellow legal pad, he looked up, eyes lingering on the meager assets of my chest before rising to meet mine.

I said, "Are you familiar with Hennessey? Waitress found dead. One of Frank's OD's." Hardy shook his head. "He thinks it maybe murder and asked me to run some names. Anyway, I might have found something."

"Frank is not your superior and doesn't assign you work. I do or Sergeant Croft. Not Frank."

"He is senior."

Hardy looked at me as though I were both annoying and stupid. "In Frank's case, that means nothing. Let him do his own legwork. Anything else?"

"No, sir. But I could use some real-time policework."

He kept writing as though he didn't hear. I had a hand on the doorknob when he called, "Give me the short version."

I couldn't. I'd worked too hard. "One of the bartenders, John Urbino, is connected. At least his family is. His grandfather ran things in a big way in New Jersey for a couple of years before a tax evasion bust. Johnny boy generated a nice little rap sheet in New York and Jersey: drunk and disorderly, three times; assault with a deadly weapon, dismissed on a technicality. He repeatedly rammed his Caddy into some guy's Porsche. His name came up in the investigation of a call girl ring. Arrested for possession of half a pound of cocaine—dismissed on a technicality. The family sent him to Portland to ice him out. He has a trust fund coming, over five million dollars if he keeps his nose clean. If not, he has to wait another seven years." Hardy continued writing.

"Also, one of the waitresses once killed her pimp."

Hardy looked up. "Tell me about that."

"She'd been a baby pro in New Orleans, the hottest thing going. A cop down there, Willard, remembered her and did some good work, running things down. One gal was still afraid of her and wouldn't talk. Another told stories. One of her rivals took a fall, ten stories from a hotel balcony with blood alcohol of over point three. With no evidence to the contrary, they listed it as accidental death. The gal had suspected who'd done it, but fear kept her quiet. Another rumor: A rival OD'd on a nearly pure morning shot of smack. And another: Girls would have dates lined up with musicians and sports stars, then they'd have accidents.

They arrested her for killing her pimp. He slashed her with a knife, and she slashed his throat with another. She spent six months in jail waiting for trial 'cause she couldn't make bail. She claimed self-defense, and the jury agreed. Willard also talked to a guy doing five to ten for armed robbery. He knew her and the man she killed. He called her ambitious, said she wanted to oust her pimp and take over."

"Write it up," said Hardy, a moment, treating me like a police officer. When I put the folder on his desk and said, "I already have," he didn't say a word.

****

Paul had captured Yvonne's interest from the moment Djuna dragged him to the break room to introduce him. He captivated her by the gentle way he shook her hand, the softness of his light brown eyes, and the sadness there, for how could she join with a man unacquainted with sadness? Paul, the mannish boy, enchanted her by the balanced contradictions of his personality: tough and gentle, intellectual and emotional, engaging and shy, stubborn but susceptible to being nudged. She saw him as a canvas on which an experienced woman could create.

Paul had never been in a relationship and exulted in her attention. He never imagined being with a woman so beautiful and saw her scar as the mark of a survivor who had transcended a difficult life. All the love songs were about her; she was the queen of his nights, of all his dreams, his "tippy-toed vamporator," his "wild love," his "junkyard angel." While she didn't keep "a .410 all loaded with lead," she did keep a .38, loaded, in a Crown Royal bag at the top of her closet. He cleaned the gun for her and convinced her to leave out the shells. She left him besotted.

They both loved to cook. His job flipping fish at the restaurant demanded volume and consistency, and his grandfather's cooking paid homage to tradition, but Yvonne's slow and improvised cooking filled him with joy. They liked to spend lazy days playing guitar, making love, prepping elaborate meals before work, and cooking them afterward. For his first gift, he bought her a used cookbook from Powell's, written in French.

Yvonne loved the blues. The first time they attended live music together, they stopped by her place on their way to Van's Olympia. He took a quick bath. When he emerged, toweling his hair, she had changed into jeans, high black boots, a red vest, and a gray fedora with a half-sized playing card, the queen of hearts, stuck into the black hatband. She sat braiding red thread into a few locks of hair next to her face. "What's with the thread?" he wanted to know.

"For luck," she said.

"Why do we need luck?"

"It's a crazy world, *mon ami*. We always need luck." A half a dozen stories cascaded through her eyes. He knew she wouldn't tell any of them, as both past and future were off-limits. They arrived between sets, found a table against the wall. When the music began, Yvonne came alive, swaying in her seat, marking time with her feet, whooping, and shouting for hot solos. She was provocative: the queen of hearts, her red vest, her long brown cigarettes, the way she called out. The scar made her seem thuggish, wicked, and wild.

A man approached, spoke in her ear. She shook her head no, downed the last of her whiskey, sat in Paul's lap, put her hat on his head, and kissed him thoroughly. She whooped loudly for a sax solo and watched the rest of the show there, shouting at the music and kissing him.

In honor of May Day, she procured him a fake I.D., and all the clubs opened to them. She knew people everywhere. When they went to Delevan's for jazz, Del came to their table, hugged her and found them a table near the front. When they saw Mose Allison at Jazz Quarry, he sat with them between sets, drinking whiskey and talking to Yvonne about New Orleans. Her persona at The Door and the way she appeared to the rest of the world were very different. At The Door, she kept to herself, stayed quiet and had few friends outside of Djuna. He believed she met him during a down period, the only time in her life she would have considered him.

When too tired to go out, they would bathe in her big tub, make lazy love, or just spoon in bed, talking. Sometimes Yvonne would put a record on the turntable, always just one, and they would lie in bed and listen. One night, Paul came home exhausted from working a double. Yvonne cued up a jazz album.

"Yvonne, I'm beat," he said in apology and lay on the bed, arm over his eyes. She put the record on, lay beside him, guided his head to her shoulder, and stroked his forehead. With the muted horn of "Blue in Green" behind her, she asked, "Paul, how come your father beat you?"

He spoke softly. "One day, walking home from school, a couple of kids beat the crap out of me. After that, every day after school, he made me take a fighting lesson. We would go out on the lawn to spar. If I learned, it would be a short lesson. If I didn't, I'd get my ass kicked until I figured it out. Sometimes, his buddies would come so I'd learn to fight two or three. I hated fighting with him and hated him for it. Eventually, I knew all his tricks. One day, he made a mistake. I got in one shot to the solar plexus, one to the groin, which left his throat vulnerable; I could have killed him. He had taught me how. My hand stopped right at the spot. That's why he beat me."

"So you could have fought back," she said.

"I couldn't beat up my father. Semper Fi." He raised a half-hearted fist.

After a long moment, Yvonne asked, "What did your mother do?"

"When he took off his belt, she went to her room and closed the door."

Yvonne almost said, "I will never close the door on you, Paul," but feared such a promise and said nothing. They lay in the silvery, almost-dark of the streetlight, the piano playing with the horn at the beginning of

"Flamingo Sketches," the music carrying them away like a slow river. Yvonne said, "Paul, I love you," but he had fallen asleep.

****

One night Yvonne stayed home sick. When Paul got home after work, they lay together in a tangle of legs, feet caressing feet. She asked, "Any gossip?"

"Jazmin is training to work nights."

Yvonne chuckled. "I'll bet the waiters were in an uproar."

"Why does everybody hate her?" wondered Paul.

"Don't you know? She's a call girl, an expensive one."

"No shit?"

"Paul, be nice, no vulgar comments with the boys, no leers. She used to be married. When her husband's business went under, he left her with no money and a seven-year-old. Plus, he hadn't paid taxes in years. The IRS garnishes her wages. Whenever she works, she has to pay a sitter. I want you to be respectful, Hilton, too."

****

One night after work, on his way to the bus stop, Paul saw shades of people through the rain spotted windshield of Raina's car. Since he and Yvonne were an acknowledged couple, Raina had been distant. He angled toward the car, thinking they could be friends.

When Raina yelled, "Damn it, Randy, let me go. Get off me. No, I said, no!"

Paul pounded on the roof of the car. In his father's voice, he bellowed, "Hey, what's going on?" Shadows within rearranged themselves; the dome light came on, the door opened, and Raina emerged, drunk, sweater twisted, belt undone, hair a mess.

"It's Gianni Wayne, the junior Marine to the rescue!" She clutched his arm. "Just in time."

"What happened?"

"Bags kind of forgot himself."

"Want me to get him out of there?"

"Let's not make this a big deal. I'll go in and have someone walk me out later." She kissed him on the cheek. "Better hustle, Sergeant, there's your bus."

****

One night at work, Yvonne gave him a battered, much-notated copy of Lao Tzu's *Way of Life* with a note from Djuna. "Read it. We'll talk—Sunday, Dim Sum. The notes were made over a period of years, so I want it back." It would be his first sight of Djuna since the market. Knowing Yvonne, relations between he and Djuna were covered by arrangement.

Djuna planned to grill him about the book as preparation for college. With Yvonne acting as courier, Djuna had been helping him with his application essay and financial aid forms. She was a demanding editor. As they ate that Sunday, Djuna quizzed him. She could quote the material extensively, follow arguments past the writing, and apply counter-arguments in detail. She could apply these lessons to anything: politics, art, The Open Door, Yvonne.

The very the first lines troubled Paul.

"The secret waits for the insight
Of eyes unclouded by longing;
Those who are bound by desire
See only the outward container."

He said, "But I'm full of desire." Yvonne pinched his leg. "I'm ambitious and filled with longing. This seems like a book for saints or old men." He read her a list of puzzling quotes.

Djuna got frustrated. "You're getting hung up on words."

"It's a book; what else have I got?"

"Some concepts are too big for words, like God and love. *The Tao that can be named is not the Tao.*"

"Well, I've missed the point," he said. "Maybe I'm out of balance. What happens when yin and yang are out of balance?"

Djuna spread her hands to include the dining room, "Look around." The instant Johnny and Yvonne turned their heads, with the timing of a magician, she caught Paul's eye, and wearing an expression of profound sadness, pointed toward herself. "Excuse me," she said and nudged Johnny to let her rise, "I have to powder my nose."

Walking home, Yvonne said, "Djuna needs someone to care for her the way you care for me."

"She didn't look too good, but then neither did Johnny."

"You know *powder my nose* means cocaine, right? She's doing way too much. Fucking Carriage Room." It's funny. She knows all this shit I will never understand but ended up with Johnny and cocaine. Sometimes it's hard to do what you know is right."

****

One night, Paul drove home after a show at The Last Hurrah, Yvonne beside him, a little drunk. "You could force me," she cooed. She liked to play games, and Paul imagined this one. He would try to seduce her; she would let him to a point, then resist. He would force her; she would object. He would get rough; she would fight him, plead. He would take her anyway.

She shouted, "Asshole. Look." Johnny's red Italian sports car turned left in front of them, Raina in the passenger's seat. "What a bastard. I'll cut his balls off. Follow them."

"What are you going to do?"

"Fuck him up."

When the light changed, he drove toward her apartment in Goose Hollow. She glared, steaming with anger. He asked, "Are you going to tell Djuna?"

"If I do, she'll just do something stupid. Their cheating games are mean enough, and whenever he hurts her, she hurts herself, but the one line she's drawn is Raina. She can put up with a lot but not her." She sighed like breathing fire. When Paul parked, she turned to him suddenly, lacing her fingers through his hair and glaring into his eyes. "Don't cheat on me, *mon ami*. No telling what I'd do."

****

A week later, Dave Fleming, the waiter, threw a party at his parent's house. People from restaurants all over town attended. Shortly after they arrived, Yvonne left him to greet a woman she knew, so Paul grabbed a beer from the keg in the kitchen and sat on an empty sofa.

The party gathered around him. Janie, a busser at The Door, sat next to him and began the story of a dine-and-dash. A table of prom kids had disappeared without paying. Janie and Bags jumped into Janie's car and gave chase, screeching around corners and running red lights, hoping to get a license number. Paul bummed a cigarette, and Janie offered a light. Paul cupped his hand around hers, lit his smoke. Yvonne glared. Janie looked at Paul, puzzled and worried.

Paul rose and urged Yvonne aside. "What's wrong?"

Yvonne looked furious, grabbed his arm, and dragged him to an empty bedroom. She slammed the door and reached for his belt.

"Yvonne, no."

"No?" she questioned, voice dripping with sarcasm.

He took her point. She had never denied him, no matter what he desired. This didn't feel the same. "Talk to me, Yvonne. What's come over you?"

"I told you: no cheating, no drama."

"You're the one making drama. We weren't doing anything wrong."

"Don't defend her. I've seen her sniffing around the kitchen."

He got mad then because once or twice, he had flirted with Janie. "You're full of it." He turned toward the door.

She dug her fingernails into his arm, spun him around. "Don't you walk away from me." Her eyes were venomous. If he were to stand up to her, they would brawl, yet he did not intend to back down. The Tao had taught him anger was a shadow of her love for him. He softened his face and eyes, looking at her with affection. Slowly, she returned , eyes cooling to a softer Yvonne.

They were quiet as Paul drove fast along Skyline Boulevard, accelerating through corners, slowing only a little at stop signs.

"I behaved badly," said Yvonne. "I'm sorry."

Paul swerved into a turnout, hit the brakes hard, tires sliding to a stop in the dirt. In the dark and sudden silence, he demanded, "Yvonne, what happened?"

"I got jealous. I get jealous at The Door, too, but try not to show it. I've always been that way, but it's worse with you. I'm just not ready to let you go."

"Damn it," said Paul, "I'm not going anywhere." He opened the car door, got out, and slammed it hard. He strode around the Battlewagon and flung her door open. In the yellow dome light, her expression broadcast fear. He turned away, staring at the dark forest, hoping the words he wanted to say were true. He crouched before her.

"Yvonne, I've been thinking about this."

"Paul, no. Let's go home." He grabbed her wrists in both hands, compelling her to look him in the eyes

"No?" he questioned, mocking her tone in the bedroom. "You're the first woman I've ever loved. If you were mine forever, I'd have all my dreams come true. I feel, in all my soul, that you are the woman for me. When I'm with you, I feel complete. When I'm not, I feel broken. I think I'll always feel this way." She looked at him with resistance. "Yvonne, I will never want anyone else."

"Paul, it's been two months. You're twenty. How can you know what you're going to want at thirty? You don't know me, who I am, where I came from."

"Tell me."

She made a sound like a sad laugh and shook her head.

"I love you, Yvonne."

"I know, and it's the sweetest thing in my life. I'm sorry about tonight. Please get back in the car."

He got behind the wheel, feeling defeated. A car sped around the corner; its bright lights set shadows running, blinding them for an instant before it passed, leaving shadows dashing into darkness.

She slid next to him, put her head on his shoulder, her hand on his leg, and said, "Paul, you know how I feel about you." They sat for a long time before he started the engine.

Walking to her building, she leaned against him as she did when she wanted a hug. He put his arm around her. She stopped, held him and said, "Our first fight. You saved me, Paul. No one has ever brought me back like that, with just a look. I felt you were going to take care of me."

"I'll always take care of you. I promise."

****

One night at work, Paul got sick, the heat of his body exceeding the heat of the kitchen, his head throbbing. During a lull, he said, "Hilton, I gotta take a break."

"Take some aspirin and hurry back."

He retreated to the banquet room and found Raina sitting in dim light, smoking, a coffee cup on the table before her. "You look pale for an Eye-talian. Your noodle going soft?"

He grinned weakly. "I feel terrible."

"I got speed," she offered. "It'll get you through."

He desperately wanted to get through. "I guess I'll try it."

Yvonne was covering Raina's section and knew where she was. When Paul headed toward the banquet room, Yvonne vowed that if he didn't come back in two minutes, she would go after him. A minute later, she did, at a pace exceeding profession decorum.

A waiter lounging against a wall in the bar waiting

for his last table to pay saw the scene unfold and motioned to one of his buddies. "Dude, come on. Yvonne's after Raina." Both waiters sped across the bar, and Mitchell followed.

Raina stood and said, "Here, this will fix you." She dropped a black pill into his hand, picked up her tray and found herself propelled to smash against the wall, tray crashing to the floor, tip cup shattering, money scattering. She gained footing, poised to fight. Tall, Nordic Raina against thin, dark Yvonne.

Yvonne got in her face, shoving her shoulders as punctuation. "You tried to give him speed? Speed? You poisoned little tweaker. Nobody cares if you fry yourself, but if you give him anything again, you'll regret it. You hear me?" Raina nodded. Yvonne pushed her again. "I said do you hear me?"

The two women locked eyes before Raina answered, "I hear you."

Yvonne turned her back on Raina. "Let me see." Paul opened his hand, and Yvonne slapped the back of it, sending the pill flying into the dark. "You start taking that shit, I'll cut your pecker off." Then she said to Raina, on her knees picking up money. "Stay away from him, or I'll fuck you up, bad."

Yvonne turned back to Paul. "Speed?" She slapped him a gentle slap across the face. "Speed?" She hit him harder. "What the fuck are you thinking?"

"I'm sorry."

"Not as sorry as you're gonna be if you start doing that shit. We agreed, 'cause of Djuna: no pills, no powders. We're working out, walking, eating fucking expensive organic food, and you want speed?"

With no argument, he tried for pity. "I'm sick."

"Go home."

"But The Door," he said, as if those words explained everything.

"You want to give germs to all those people you serve? You know, for a smart kid, sometimes you're pretty stupid."

****

Late one Saturday night, the bar empty, Raina sat near the well nursing a white wine spritzer. She wore an off-white, corduroy dress. Her strawberry blond hair had been permed to light curls which framed her face, lending her an angelic look. Johnny cleaned, taking liquor bottles off the shelf, wiping the shelf, wiping the bottles, and putting them back.

Raina asked, "So what's next after bartending?"

"I don't know anything else. Maybe I'll switch to days, some quiet place, a quiet life. Too much craziness at night."

"I've been thinking about days myself. How are you and Djuna?"

Johnny stopped working. "I should have let Paolo have her. She's not right." He shook his head. "I'm too old to do drugs all the time."

"The joy of cocaine not for you?"

Johnny shook his head. "Not every day, all day. No secrets in a restaurant. I guess."

Raina sipped her spritzer. "The whole Paul thing knocked her sideways. She got strange over him."

"She did. And when Yvonne ended up with him…" He shook his head and began clearing another shelf. "All those affairs we had, the only people she might have left me for were those two, Paul and Yvonne. She's wanted to be with Yvonne since day one. Story is: Yvonne likes her women strong."

Raina said, "I didn't know," and sipped her spritzer. "You haven't talked to Paul much. You work late; he can't sit at the bar. You know what he said to me one day? *If you'd quit drinking and the drugs, you could do it.* I said, *Do what?* And he said, *Whatever you want.* I keep thinking about that. *You could do it.* Not words I heard much as a kid. A high school teacher, a couple of professors. I say it to myself every day now when I put on my make-up."

Johnny put down a bottle. "You look different, calmer."

"Mostly sober. I'm gonna do it. Don't know what. Marketing, maybe real estate. Like Paul said, I can always think of something to say. A two-spritzer limit might work."

Johnny smiled, not his usual faint half-smile but a broad grin. "I wondered what had changed for you. Spritzers, of all things, and no wine in the coffee cup. What's it been, two or three nights now?" He raised a clenched fist, "You can do it," and returned to cleaning bottles.

"I wish I would have known you before Djuna. Because I think deep down, you're just a nice Italian boy."

Johnny laughed. "When I was ten."

Raina didn't sip her drink, didn't light a smoke, spoke softly. "I have an opportunity for you, might give you a purpose. It helped me."

"Oh? Tell me about it."

"I'm carrying your baby."

"How do you know it's mine? It could be a lot of people's. It's probably Bags'."

She still spoke softly. "It's yours, Johnny, has to be."

Johnny's voice rose. "I'll pay for an abortion, arrange it, take care of the whole thing."

"I'm having the baby."

Johnny tightened his bolo tie. It's like he's strangling himself, Raina thought, at the idea of being a father, of being connected to me. He probably found relationships suffocating and could only manage ones like that mess with Djuna.

"Raina, if you want a baby, find someone who wants to have one with you. I'm not going to play daddy."

She wanted to grab him by the bolo tie and shake him yet made sure to speak in calming tones. "It could be a good thing. Get you off the cocaine, out of the wild life."

"How do you imagine this is going to turn out? You're going to ruin my life, the kid's life, whatever pitiful shit of your own is left. Damn it, Raina. You've been drinking up until the day before yesterday, taking speed. The kid is probably fucked up already."

She bit her lip, sat silent, then spoke in reassuring tones. "We can do this any way you want. No preconceived ideas. We'll make things up as we go."

"If you're planning to look in the mirror and say, *I can do it* and think about me, it's not going to happen. End it."

It would be ridiculous to cry over Johnny, yet she could feel her face flush and tears well.

He softened. "You were going to start a new life. How can you do that with a baby? You can barely take care of yourself."

Raina took a ten from her purse, slapped it on the bar. "Tequila. Three shots. Line 'em up."

"Raina, no."

"No? You actually give a shit about someone besides yourself? Don't want to poison your baby? Tell me you care even a little, and I won't drink." He looked away. "Pour the drinks, Johnny."

He set three shot glasses on the bar, filled each to the brim. She picked up the first shot and, staring him straight in the eye, drank it down like water and slammed the glass upside down on the bar. She took the second shot the same way, eyes locked on his. When the third glass hit the bar, she said, "You know what's going to happen?" She put her purse over her shoulder. "Your child. With you or without you. And if you think you can look in the mirror and forget about me, think child support."

Chapter 6
Everything's Jake

I got hired because the powers that be decided the detective's bullpen in the Portland P.D. had need of a heifer. They advertised; I wanted to be a detective. I applied, not because I wanted to break new ground for women or lead a movement but because I wanted to get ahead. Truth be told, I looked at the men around me in the Oceanside Police Department and knew for certain I could do at least as well as those old boys. They tested and screened me, interviewed me, and interviewed me again. My superiors were called and recalled. Upon entering the program, I agreed to extra reviews and evaluations. I beat all comers. I was a good cop, a real good cop, and I say this now because later, you might not think so.

Anyway, administration wanted me to walk a beat and "learn the department from bottom to top." Travis, my partner, and I patrolled an area along Broadway and The Park Blocks from Portland State past the library, past the vulturous pimps at the old Greyhound station, all the way to the sex shops between The Benson Hotel and Burnside. We practiced community policing, which I believe in. I was on a fast track and loved strolling through the city on bright summer days. I fell in love with Portland. A few glass towers were starting to emerge on 6th Street and on Broadway from a town built of aged and weathered brick. Portland seduced me with a cutting edge in attitude and ideas and its sleepy, gray days, its old Victorians and tree-lined streets, and its ease with great buses and a little bit of everything concentrated downtown.

We were walking The Park Blocks at the statue of *Rebecca at the Well*. The woman I would later learn to be Yvonne sat on a bench in the sun, cradling a guitar, an open case at her feet. She wore a red silk vest, no blouse, no shoes, bare feet, the hems of her flared jeans frayed. She had a body like a sports car, lean lines with curves in all the right places.

In profile her stunning face might have been carved and polished from some dark wood by a sculptor who loved strong women. I couldn't tell if the strength originated in her eyes, black and intent, from the chin and jaw, from the sharp cut cheekbone or if her strength projected from inside. Yet her smile broadcast an impish delight and a glint of mischief. She was talking with a hobo I'd come to know as Mountain Max, big as a mountain. She said, "Like I told you, I got a regular job now, an apartment. Things are different. Take what you need."

"That wouldn't be right," said Max, "It's yours."

She flashed me a smile. "Okay, you take the bills, and I'll take the change for laundry." She plucked bills from her case and handed them to Max. He didn't know what to say and shambled off, enthralled by good fortune.

"Good morning, officer." Both Travis and I knew her greeting had been directed at me. He gave me a look and wandered off to investigate an old man sleeping against a tree, a bottle in a bag between his legs. She gestured with her guitar. "Did you know Max calls you Officer Honey?"

"He does? Why?"

"The color of your hair, though I think it's redder than honey, Officer." She gave me an impish grin.

"Pretty good haul," I said, pointing to her case.

"In less than hour, and I gave Max my bills. He saved my ass once, but I don't think he remembers. Anyway, the worker drones like flamenco, enlivens their dull lives."

"Go ahead, enliven my life." She did, played fast and hard, bare feet marking time. When she finished, I clapped and took a money clip from my front pocket and loosened a five.

"You're easy to please," she said with a grin, quick fingers making my money disappear. I long remembered the way she caught my gaze and held it. "You like music?" she asked and played a few bars of "You've Got to Hide Your Love Away."

"I do but can't play a lick. My mother got all the talent."

"She plays?"

"Jazz piano, attended Berklee for a while."

Yvonne faked a little of "That Old Black Magic," mumbling the words. "I'm not much of a singer." The scratches in her old guitar revealed light wood under dark stain. She rested it against the bench and crouched on her haunches, gathering coins from her case and putting them into a red cloth purse.

"Well, Officer Honey, I gotta go. I got a date, and she's beautiful. But not as beautiful as you." She turned and I caught first sight of the scar, an ugly wound, poorly mended, a pale slash in her brown skin, curving from the cheekbone beneath her right eye down the edge of her jaw to below the corner of her mouth. I gasped; her smile vanished.

"See something you didn't like?" She faced me straight on, a picture of contained fury, the flawless and the marred juxtaposed. Voice full of contempt, she said, "The biggest difference between you and me is I wear my scars on the outside." She glared, exquisite mouth twisted in a scowl which then softened. "It's not true," she said. "I have scars on the inside, too." A hand rose to touch her damaged face. "Worse than this."

Then she looked at me, studied me for a long while, too long, longer than anybody ever stares, straight on and open, long enough, perhaps, to see past the veneer we wear to hide our true selves. She said, "I'm a little too much for you now, Officer Honey." She gave me a wink, picked up her guitar, and walked up Yamhill toward Goose Hollow.

I loved the way she engaged me, her joy, her generosity, her strength, the way she saw inside me and knew what I desired.

Though I looked for her the rest of the summer, she never returned to the park, but she became an image in my dreams and fantasies.

****

I encountered Yvonne again, a month or so before the murder. She and Paul were in the Japanese garden—a place cultivated to appear wild. I was walking in the long shadows of late afternoon on what promised to be a hot, uncomfortable night, wrapped in a familiar loneliness and oppressed by dread of Monday's certain indignities. The trail looped around a large rock. My woman from the park sat on a bench before a pool.

Her scar made me remember the world outside the garden: concrete and brick, glass and steel, hard and dangerous, yet she seemed at peace, a waterfall spilling gracefully behind her.

I paused, my hand on the rough bark of a pine. On the path in front of her, a young man flowed through martial arts forms as fluid as dance, fast, balanced, powerful, and graceful. It thrilled me to watch him. He wore faded blue gym shorts, no shirt, no shoes. He seemed young for her, an unquenched enthusiasm about his handsome face, his brown hair tied in a short ponytail. He was lean and strong, "muscle and blood and skin and bone," as the song says. They were certainly lovers, the hungry way her eyes followed him, her dark, full lips parted. The woman of my fantasies adored this young man. I imagined a scene from ancient ages, knight and lady or samurai and geisha. Soon, she would light a lantern and lead him to a cottage in the shadows of the trees.

A small older man strode down the path toward them, a gardener in a tool belt, a floppy green canvas hat, and glasses. I figured the gates were closing, and he would run them off. Instead, he put his hands together and bowed to her young man, who bowed back deeply, and the two shook hands. They spoke for a moment, and then the gardener took off his tool belt and work boots and followed the young man through his forms. They danced, young and old, almost as one, the elder following, a heartbeat behind. Yvonne grinned with pride.

I wanted to approach, but I have always been shy of relationships, a couple of high school dalliances with boys who considered me worth pursuing, and a more mature affair in college which left me bruised, feeling somehow both victimized and guilty.

Upon finishing, both men bowed low. The young man turned to her and guided her into his arms. She wore very short cut-off jeans, a puffy white blouse embroidered with red flowers, her mane of long black hair. Their kiss took my breath away. They were beautiful, their faces, lean bodies, obvious affection. She kissed him again. Then he donned his shirt and sandals, and they started toward the gate.

The gardener looked at me, gestured to a watch he wasn't wearing, and waited for me in front of the waterfall, a short and thin man, with a deep tan and large dark eyes. As he spoke, he waved brown, gnarled hands. "Quite the tableau, the four of us, me intruding on their love scene, you behind your tree." He laughed a little. "Don't get me wrong, I understand the impulse to be involved from afar—like an audience. But for me, the young man had been exquisitely trained." We walked for a while in silence, until he added, "But perhaps, I was closer and saw something you didn't. His eyes were sad, quite sad. I wondered about that. A young man, talented, disciplined, loved by an attractive woman. But if all things are in balance, where, I wonder, is the ugliness?" When we arrived at the black iron gate, he opened it for me. "I hope your evening continues to be beautiful."

It wasn't. I roasted in my small apartment and tossed in my bed. Yet when I slept, I had a dream where I was him, a knight with a sword practicing arms, and she held a lantern and led me to a cottage in the woods, which became the setting for my fantasies about her.

After a day when the leers and snide comments and

sexual innuendos overwhelmed me, when the boredom and futility and second-class status of the cold case files laid me low, when I lay in bed at night, wounded and lonely, desperate for connection and someone to care for me, my fantasies would put me to sleep. I would be the soldier, the warrior, the protector with gun and badge, and she would be my lady and lead me to a place away from the world and bathe me with tenderness and kindness and passion.

But the next time I saw Yvonne, she was in an interview room, handcuffed to a table.

****

One afternoon while walking downtown, Yvonne gestured toward a black-glassed office tower and the bar in the lobby. "I have to piss."

A brokerage firm occupied the space next door, and Paul wandered over to ponder the stock ticker: the Dow, the S&P, the price of gold all shone green. Would college lead him to a place like this—moving other people's money for a share to call his own?

Yvonne emerged from the bar excited, "I just got a job. I saw a help wanted sign, and the manager hired me on the spot." Seeing Paul about to object, she added, "It's business, Paul. The Door isn't busy anymore. You get wages, but I live off tips. Remember Thursday? I got off at eight-thirty. I have to go where the money is. Places come and go, get hot, then fade. Besides, it's a businessmen's place; they close at ten. I'll be done when you are."

Green still dominated the symbols on the ticker. The market was up, and Yvonne would make some small percentage of that money hers.

****

Around midnight, the restaurant empty, Mitchell closed the bar. Paul had long since gone home. Yvonne sat in the break room before a ten key, working on her checkout, when Raina marched in and sat without a word. Since their fight, the two women had kept their distance, talking only as the job dictated, yet Yvonne sensed Raina had been calmer and was drinking less. She wanted to lower the tension with a woman who had been Paul's friend. "Not much money tonight," she said.

"Nope," said Raina.

Yvonne took a chance. "Seems like you're doing better."

Raina's voice held an edge. "Better? You mean I'm almost as good as you?"

"That's not what I meant."

"But you *do* think you're better than me. You think you're prettier, a better waitress, better for Paul."

"I am better for Paul. I love him. I care what happens to him. You never did. You just used him."

"Come on, Yvonne. Who are you kidding? I'll bet you three months with Paul Tomaso, you dump him before the first of the year."

Yvonne said nothing. Raina began separating her checks and charge slips.

"Janey overheard you talking to Jazmin." Raina impersonated Yvonne's drawl, "*Should I let him go now or wait and hope he finds someone his own age?* Ever talked to Janey? Course not, you're too good for her, too. She's had a crush on him since day one. She's perfect for him: works hard, reads, goes to City College, just a little wild. You shot her down, and for what, a couple more months?"

Yvonne's adding machine fell silent while Raina's tapped and whirled as she spoke. "At least I didn't make him love me and then break his heart. I could've. One night, I made a choice. I drove him away for his own good. You didn't. What's the matter? Cat got your tongue? Come on, Yvonne, prove me wrong." When Yvonne said nothing, she kept talking. "You and me aren't so different. You're a poor girl, too. Drunken mom. Strange men around the house. Where was your hell house? Mine was a trailer in the pines."

Raina stapled her checks, started counting money. "Don't be surprised if I grab him when you're done. Like you said, I'm doing good, and I could do even better with a little help. Nothing to say? I was hoping for some repartee, a little more fight." She ripped the tape from her adding machine. For the first time, she looked at Yvonne. "So new job. How much longer do I have to put up with you? A week?" Raina began gathering her things. "Still working on your checkout? Oh, that's right. You didn't even finish high school."

Raina walked past Yvonne toward the door. Yvonne sprang from her seat, grabbed Raina's hair, and pulled her head back, hard. "You don't know anything about Paul and me. Touch him, and you're dead."

Mitchell stuck his head in the door. "Hey, you guys okay in here?"

Yvonne let her go. "I found a bug in her hair and killed it for her."

Raina said, "One week, bitch," handed Mitchell her checkout, and left.

****

Yvonne took Paul thrift store shopping for clothes. He had never owned dress clothes as an adult. She bought him brown wool slacks, a fawn shirt silk, and a brown leather jacket, said, "I want to show you off at a place I used to work."

Walking from car to bar, Paul caught a glimpse of them in the dark window of an empty shop. Yvonne wore a red dress, cut high up her long legs, low at the breast. Proud of their elegance, he said, "I wish I had a picture so, years from now, we can remember how we were once young and beautiful." She kissed him in the firm way she sometimes did.

Brasserie Montmartre sported white plaster and black wrought iron with high ceilings, intricate molding, and a black and white checkerboard floor. Yvonne's presence caused a stir. A bartender with long, steel-gray hair in a tight ponytail called out in a French accent, "It's Yvonne," and came from behind the bar. Waitresses found their way over for hugs. At first, Paul tagged along but soon saw he was cramping her style. So when a couple left the bar, he claimed two stools, ordered drinks, and bummed a cigarette from the man beside him. A quintet called "Everything's Jake" played swing jazz with string instruments. Paul recognized tunes from his grandfather's records and considered these versions effete, lacking brass and punch.

A woman hurried toward Yvonne shouting, "Vonnie." They shared a hug and a kiss. Yvonne introduced her as Valentine."

Valentine offered her hand. She was a tiny woman, perhaps mid-thirties, with short, spiked blond hair and large, blue eyes. "Vonnie, is this handsome man with you? Kiss the people who want to kiss you while I steal his heart." Yvonne winked and turned to go. Valentine called after her, "Did you know Dahlia is in town?"

Yvonne didn't seem to hear.

Valentine swayed, well on her way to drunk. She sat next to Paul, took his hand and said, "How did you two meet?" She drank the whiskey intended for Yvonne, keeping hold of his hand as she quizzed him. When Yvonne returned, Valentine sat between them, sharing both stools.

"Are you seeing anyone?" Yvonne asked her.

"No one," she replied, eyes fixed on Paul. "Just this big, strong man."

A cocktail waitress with bangs and wavy brown hair long as Yvonne's put her tray down by the well and sighed. She glanced down the bar and smiled at Paul. Yvonne had taught Paul to read character in faces. Her smile and big brown eyes radiated gentleness and a fundamental happiness. He smiled back. Hers widened. Her eyes turned to Yvonne, who looked at Paul with a mischievous smile and a question in her eyes. Paul considered himself in the midst of an abundance of beautiful women.

Valentine began squirming on the seat beside him, shouted, "Dahlia!" and pointed toward the door where a tall woman stood, surveying the room. She wore gray slacks, a matching jacket, and pointed black boots. She looked rugged and assured, blue eyes, dark hair short, swept back, and slicked in a style Paul recognized from barbershop menus. Valentine said to Yvonne, "Both of you here on the same night. You must be thrilled." Then she motioned for Paul to stand so she could rise. She crossed to the newcomer and threw herself into her arms, much as she had done with Yvonne. Paul watched Yvonne watching them.

The woman in gray discarded Valentine and

beckoned Yvonne, who turned to Paul, touched his arm lightly, and said, "I'll be right back." The woman projected personal power, as tall as he, thin yet muscled, confident in her stance. She exuded a magnetism he couldn't match and compelled Yvonne in a way he envied.

Dahlia embraced Yvonne then bent to kiss her, passionately. Valentine appeared at his side. "You can't blame her for Dahlia. She's like a drug. Once she gets under your skin, a woman will do anything for Dahlia."

Dahlia broke off the kiss, leaned against the wall, pulling Yvonne toward her. Yvonne whispered something and put her head against Dahlia's shoulder. Dahlia turned her gaze to him, her blue eyes filled with challenge. Their eyes locked until he turned away, seeking refuge in his drink. Drunken conversation roared, and jazz filled the crowded bar with joyful noise. He almost bolted but held his ground while making ready for retreat. He paid his tab, laid his change on the bar, feeling empty. Without Yvonne, he had nothing but a hard, low-paying job. He had no purpose in this bar, in this town. Yvonne returned to sit beside him. "We can go," she said.

"Is that what you want?"

"Yes," she lied, eyes evading his. "Paul, I." She could find nothing to say, and her gaze turned again to the woman in gray.

Hating the man he wanted to be, he took Yvonne's arm and walked her to Dahlia. Dahlia, a hand on Yvonne's hip, pulled her close. In Yvonne's face were strong emotions he could not read. He spoke in Dahlia's ear. "She is very dear to me. Be good to her." Then he walked out of the bar to soft rain dancing in the puddles under the streetlight.

At seven in the morning, Yvonne shuffled through his door, dress wrinkled, hair disheveled, carrying her shoes. She sat on the bed, waking him. "Did I hurt you?"

He nodded. "Are you going to leave me?"

"No," she answered. "Are you going to leave me?"

An action he hadn't considered. "No, I love you."

"I know," she said. "I promised I wouldn't cheat, and I didn't."

"But you chose." The calm in his voice surprised him. "Why?"

"I've been up all night. What do you want me to say?"

"The truth."

Her anger flared. "What truth? What choice? Take your pick. I'm here because I'm sorry. Because I'm not ready to give us up. Because when I'm with you, I'm a better person. Because at one time she was the most important person in the world to me, but now you are. Because I feel guilty. Because I thought of you all night. Because you're my family. Because the only person I've got to talk to is Djuna, and she'd tell me I'm a shit and an idiot, too. Is that enough truth for you? And speaking of choices, why did you leave me with her? I said I wanted to go."

Paul wore Yvonne's hard and scowling face. "Because I don't want to be with someone who wants to be with someone else."

"Or because you didn't have the guts to just take me? I picked you, then you delivered me to her." Yvonne gave up fighting and slumped on the bed, eyes down. "It wasn't like you think, romantic or sexy. We fought most of the time. Another woman had been staying there. Things needed to be resolved. Now they are."

She had circles under her eyes, a fan of wrinkles in the corners, the first signs of age he'd ever noticed. "Dahlia is an interesting and, I think, dangerous person. She's international, arms deals, black markets, industrial secrets. She was pissed to learn a kid cook from Portland had beaten her."

"Portland?" he said in a cholo accent and raised a clenched fist, "No soy de Portland. Soy de East L.A."

That night, after dinner, they took a bath, facing each other in the tub, feet by each other's shoulders. Yvonne said, "Can we have a short conversation about last night?"

"Short sounds good."

"What would you have done if Dahlia had been a man?"

"I'd have kicked his ass. Look, if you want to have a woman lover, too, I could live with it. But a man, well, I just couldn't."

"That's very generous, but one lover seems complicated enough. But if you and I ever wanted to pick up a woman, we'd be quite a team. Remember the cocktail waitress with the long brown hair? She saw us together at Delevans and thought you were hot."

"Damn, we should have done that instead."

Yvonne said, "Sometimes, the best-laid plans don't get you laid," then splashed him, knowing what would follow but wanting, more than anything, to see his face cast in joy.

Chapter 7
Here Comes the Night

On stakeout the night of the murder, the only thing resembling actual police work I could get, radio calls about fights at The Open Door made me long to be in a squad car in the thick of events. The second fight sounded like a riot, and I considered offering back up but was far across town.

When the radio chatter passed, I sat in my car in the dark, brooding about Hardy screwing my career, cussing him, and pounding the steering wheel. I suppose all leaders inspire enmity, but sitting there, I decided I would beat him, make him hurt. Nights are long on stakeout alone. Sitting makes your ass sore. The nothingness deflates you and sets your mind racing. I imagined quitting the police to finish my degree. Maybe I could be an English teacher, but my stubbornness wouldn't let me. I stuck with plotting acts of rebellion and revenge so outlandish they'd be forced to fire me.

****

Yvonne's last night at The Open Door turned into a fiasco. In an effort to coax business to the bar, Mitchell had hired the hottest band in town, Devious. Their promo picture showed a sexy female vocalist, and Mitchell said they performed rock cover tunes. He prevailed upon Yvonne "to work one more night—the money will be great."

When Yvonne and Paul walked in, the band had assembled on stage for a soundcheck. "Wow," said Yvonne, pointing toward the singer, "she's hot." The lead singer stood tall in high black boots above the knee. She had strong shoulders and a body wiry as a predator, punked out from spiked black hair to a Black Flag shirt with the sleeves and neck ripped out. She saw them watching her and flashed an entertainer's smile.

Yvonne turned to him, eyes alight. "Let's try for her, Paul."

"Okay, how?"

"The first move is mine." Paul watched from the kitchen. With a bar rag, Yvonne strolled to the tables near the band. She looked different there in daylight wearing jeans and a black leotard. She worked with the grace Paul loved, wiping tables and arranging chairs. She kept her eyes down and her back to the band. In front of the stage, she glanced up and began a conversation with the singer.

Yvonne reported back. "Her name is Nikki, and she caught on immediately. She kept saying, *I like to be in charge.* When I told her I'd get them drinks during the show, she said, *I'll tell you exactly what I want.*" The look in Yvonne's eyes made Paul jealous. "But I feel bad juju tonight. Let's keep an eye on each other."

The crowd gathered early. Raina, Yvonne, Jazmin, and two other cocktail waitresses kept Johnny and another bartender busy. Craziness may have slipped across the full moon's reflection on the river to sneak in the windows. Before Devious even started playing, Mitchell and Bags combined to coax a staggering man out the door.

Hilton said, "Imagine Bags tossing a drunk."

Later, someone shattered a window near the front door. A few minutes later some kid in heavy black boots kicked in the other. Police were called. After they left, two women got in a fight. One of them ripped out the other's hoop earring, and blood sprayed the floor. Police were called again.

At about nine, Djuna stopped by the kitchen. "Yvonne called, said things were poppin'." Her strained smile made Paul think about cocaine and things out of balance. She found a seat near Johnny's well.

As the dining room emptied, the bar filled to overflowing. Suddenly, the stage lights blacked out, and in the dark, Nikki issued a series of orgasmic screams. When the spot came on, Nikki whirled about the stage, swinging her mic with one hand and its stand with the other, the music primitive with drumming and frantic bass, guitars out of control, lyrics more snarled than sung. A Bowie cover disintegrated into wild drumming which transformed into a manic song about devils.

Anxious to watch, Paul worked hard cleaning the grill. The crowd roared behind him. The shouting grew louder, then a woman screamed, then another, and Hilton spun him around.

"Your woman," he yelled, pointing.

Yvonne stood in front of the bar, hammering blow after blow with an empty tray on a tall, redheaded man who held Jazmin by her ponytail with one hand, and tried to ward off Yvonne with the other. As Paul fought his way through the mass of people, Yvonne broke a wine glass against the man's head and begin to slash with the shards of the stem. The man charged forward, bowling her over, and even as she fell, she slashed.

****

Violence cleared a space around her, and from where she lay on the floor, Yvonne watched as Paul drove the heel of his hand into her assailant's chin, knocking him from on top of her to crash into now empty barstools. He started to rise, but Paul kicked him in the solar plexus. She screamed his name.

A man grabbed Paul from behind and another charged him and drove a fist into his eye. His second blow hit Paul on the cheekbone. Paul's speed amazed Yvonne. His right leg shot up and staggered the man in front with a blow to the groin. The leg swung back, and Paul's heavy kitchen boot crushed the knee of the man behind who released him, bending in pain. Free to maneuver, Paul stomped hard on the foot of the man in front, then with a hard right broke his nose, spraying blood. Paul turned, surveying the scene. In the space the crowd had cleared around them, Jazmin helped Yvonne to her feet. Three men were down.

A stillness settled over the bar until Nikki growled from the stage, "Anybody else dig fucking savage men? This song is for Paul, the cook."

The band quit mid-song and ripped into a song about a street fighter. Yvonne, on the ground, blood on her hands and arms, had the thought that Paul was not primarily a lover, a worker, a thinker, or a cook. He was, at heart, a soldier.

The police arrived quickly. An officer interviewed Paul on the loading dock and listened to his story. "You did all this damage?"

He nodded, wanting to protect Yvonne whose past, he feared, wouldn't bear scrutiny. Recognizing something in the policeman's bearing, he took a chance.

"My father, sir, was a drill sergeant at Pendleton, taught hand to hand. I got beat up one day, and he worked hard to make sure it wouldn't happen again."

The officer considered this. "Well, tonight, he would have been satisfied with his work. I was Rangers. My partner was a jarhead." He finished writing in his book. "Don't make a habit of this."

"No, sir, I won't."

The brawl blackened Paul's eye and left his face red and swollen. Mitchell told them to go home, but Yvonne said, "I'll stay. I'm not going to let those bastards beat me." Paul positioned himself against the wall by the well. She put a hand on his chest and whispered, "Stay close, babe. Bad juju here still." An odd contentment filled him. "Your woman," Hilton had said. He had defended his woman and The Door, his place.

For a while, Raina performed at her best, drunk enough to be expansive but not yet dulled. When the band took a break, she slid her tray of empties up to the well and spoke to Paul. "Kindersection full? Well, tonight, please join us in the real bar. More 'ginger ale?' A Shirley Temple? A straw?"

Bags sat at the bar, a few stools from the well, drinking his green bottles. Alcohol would first make Bags eloquent, much as it did with Raina. Together, they were a conversational onslaught, but at the point where Raina quieted, Bags grew loud, sarcastic, insulting. When Bags began buying tequila shots for Raina's coffee cup, Paul grew angry and gave Johnny a look. After the third shot, he caught Johnny's eye, and commanded, "Basta," and Johnny refused to serve Bags.

"Cut me off? After all the money I tipped you? Hell, I throw cash at you, enough to buy your vest and that turquoise."

While Bags harangued Johnny, Raina and Yvonne arrived at the cocktail station at the same time. Raina slid in next to Paul and said to Yvonne, "I hope you don't mind. I used to like just rubbing against him."

Yvonne shot her a what-the-fuck look but at a glance from Paul, shook her head and called her order. Raina's flushed face revealed she was deep in her cups. Soon, she would get quiet and cease to speak at all, but not yet. "I'm going to get those easy opening shifts when you're gone. And when Paul gets tired of the dark meat, maybe I'll get him too." Yvonne garnished her drinks and left without a word.

This impressed Bags. "Rain! Messin' with the ragin' Cajun. I'm gonna take your shifts and take your man. And you're still alive."

An hour later, Mitchell approached Yvonne. "I know it's been a hell of a night, but could you stay? I'm going to let Raina off. Too much wine in the coffee cup. She fell and we had to help her up. Liza will close, but Jazmin's too freaked out to work and I need you. You can go when the band is done." After the show, Mitchell kept his word, and Paul followed Yvonne to help with her check out. When they returned to the bar, the room had cleared. Bottles, butts, and broken glass littered the place. White stuffing hung from a rip in one of the sofas in The Corner. Nikki paced like a caged lion by the hostess stand, her dark hair and ripped T-shirt drenched in sweat, blue eyes gleaming. "There you are. Let's get out of this shithole."

"We're not going," said Yvonne. "My man fought

for me, and tonight I want to take care of him."

"You're fucking kidding me," said Nikki and grabbed Yvonne's arm. To Paul's great delight, using a tactic he taught her, Yvonne knocked Nikki's hand away.

"No, I'm not," said Yvonne.

"Tease," hissed Nikki and stomped off.

Mitchell called to them. "Have you guys seen Raina? She left without turning in her money." When they shook their heads, he added, "Go home, get some rest. I'm sure you'll be in to see us, Yvonne, so I won't say good-by."

Johnny shouted from the bar. "Hey, Mitchell, the dishwasher is overflowing."

He hustled off. "He's a good guy," said Yvonne. "I hope he doesn't lose his job over this." They looked for Djuna, but she had gone. As Yvonne and Paul crossed the parking lot to the Battlewagon, a car door opened and a dark form emerged. Yvonne clutched his arm. "Shit, what now?"

Jazmin called, "Hey, can you guys give me a ride? I'm so shaky I don't trust myself to drive."

"You've been sitting in the car this whole time?" asked Paul.

She nodded. "I've been lying down on the seat, hiding. I kept telling myself to just go, but every time I think of getting swung by the hair, of being powerless, I start shaking."

Yvonne said, "Come with me, and Paul will follow in your car."

Jazmin's building stood alone amidst empty lots and the ancient warehouses by the train station. Its sooty red bricks were tagged with graffiti, the white trim peeling paint. Paul idled, and Yvonne pulled the Battlewagon up.

"Walk her to the door," Yvonne suggested to Paul through the window. Paul parked her car. He offered Jazmin his arm, as Yvonne had taught him. *Look at my boy. He's worked a full day, been drinking whiskey, been in a bar brawl, has a whore on his arm. If he kisses her goodnight, I won't know whether to laugh or cry.*

At the top of the stairs, Jazmin hugged him, then he bounded back to Yvonne.

"I've never been as ready to go home," he said, sliding beside her. "Listen, if you want another woman, I'll go along for the ride because I'd go anywhere with you. But if there were no other woman until the day I die, I'd have everything I wanted."

Yvonne stared out the windshield. "Teach me to fight. That fucking tray was useless. I want to do some damage."

"I got a lot of bruises learning to fight."

"Bruise me all you want but teach me. I hate feeling weak." Paul recalled her slashing with her broken wine glass and realized Jazmin had already been released. Yvonne had been on the offensive, moving forward, fighting with the rage she struggled to control.

Yvonne's voice rose with excitement. "I saw you coming, but I couldn't imagine. Wham, bam, pow, like a comic book, bad guys dropping like dominos." But he, too, had been possessed by an exhilarating anger and could find no shame in her savagery or his own, in the gleaming shard of glass in her hand or the blood spraying or the men he'd broken. He had one glorious thing in the world, Yvonne, and no one could hurt her without a fight. On this, Yvonne and his father would agree.

"I'll teach you if you take care of me like you told Nikki." With two fingers against her chin, he turned her head to look into his eyes. "I'll tell you exactly what I want." Her expression set his heart to pounding.

Chapter 8
So It Goes

Each day after an eternity at work, I'd come home to whatever I could find, a can of this or some frozen that, and eat at my rusty yellow table. Then, I'd do what needed to be done, laundry, bills, cleaning, and finally, I'd take a bath. One of the perks of living in an apartment older than my grandmother with no shower was a gloriously deep, ancient, clawfoot tub. Caressed by warm water, I'd relive the day's humiliations while also trying to forget them. Sometimes, I'd feel a rise of tears, a swelling near my heart, or maybe a collapse or both at the same time. But I always suppressed the urge to weep.

After my bath, I'd open the ugly, brown fold-out couch and crawl into bed. I always read before going to sleep, for five minutes or when my anger at the day wouldn't quit, for five hours. Reading had always been an essential part of me which existed before I was a cop or a detective or even an adult.

If I didn't fall asleep with a book on my chest, I'd ease my restlessness by imagining detailed fantasies of *her*, a woman I'd met once whose name I didn't know.

One of my fantasies began with us standing in the park in the middle of the city under blue skies and green trees, but instead of walking away, she would step close to me, her lips brushing mine, and a spark would shoot through my body, every cell of it, lighting and awakening. I imagined her breath tasted of peppermint. I imagined vulnerability and tenderness in her dark eyes. I imagined she found something about me beautiful.

After another kiss, she would take my hand and say, "Come with me. There is something I want to show you."

"What?" I would ask.

There would be laughter in her eyes when she said, "Everything you want me to."

But one night, my imagination twisted. After our fantasy kiss, she picked up her guitar and, in 1980, the year Ronald Reagan got elected, in the middle of the park with people walking past, she took my hand with her long, graceful fingers and we walked away. Away from being a policeman, away from any reality of my life. But soon, I got nervous. I was in uniform. My hand got sweaty, and I wanted to pull away. People would know, would form conclusions, pass judgement. A squad car could cruise the park. Beat cops could appear at any intersection. The department would find a way to take my job, and all the shit would have been for nothing.

Suddenly, in my imagination, she stopped and turned to face me. Her fingernails dug into my hand. Her eyes glared, and the scowl I would come to know darkened her face.

She said, "I'm sick of people looking down on me. You can't be ashamed of me. You can't be ashamed of who we are together. You can't be ashamed of yourself."

In real life, Yvonne stood at five foot eight, but in

my fantasy, for an instant, she looked mighty, ten feet tall, and determined as hell. I wanted to tell her no, I would never be ashamed, but my mouth wouldn't function to form the words.

And then the phone rang, and the fantasy disappeared. They needed me at work. A mob had beaten a man outside a gay bar downtown.

The next day, exhausted after being up all night, I bought a bag of those round, red and white striped mints they gave out at restaurants, and afterwards, I always carried a few in my purse. When the work seemed overwhelming or discouragement brought me down, I would slip one into my mouth and imagine, for a moment, that I could live without shame.

****

The morning after Devious tore up The Open Door, the phone rang early at Yvonne's. Paul answered to Mitchell. "Hello, Paul. How's the face?"

"It hurts. Haven't looked in the mirror yet. What going on?"

"I need to talk to Yvonne, and Paul, it's important. I wouldn't have called this early. Hell, I wouldn't be up this early."

"Good morning, Mitchell," said Yvonne, her voice husky with sleep. Paul loved her first low, rough words in the morning and hoped they would spend the day in bed, sleeping and loving. "That's terrible," said Yvonne, sleep gone. "No, I'll tell him. We'll get there as soon as we can."

Yvonne put down the phone. "They found Raina dead in the banquet room. Mitchell thinks OD. The police are there. They want to interview everyone."

At The Door, they sat on the ripped sofa in The

Corner. Paul had been quiet since news of Raina's death. Yvonne held his hand in both of hers. Out of uniform employees sat huddled in knots of three or four, talking low. The bar seemed surreal, all of them there, but no cocktails, no cribbage, no backgammon, no laughter—eleven o'clock, and brunch would not be served. Crime scene technicians were working in the banquet room. Detectives sat at tables on opposite ends of the dining room and were conducting interviews.

Paul and Yvonne had stayed up until five in the morning, loving and whispering. She spoke at length about them as a couple in future tenses, something she never did. She wanted to own a duplex. A realtor had told her prices might rise, and she wondered if together they could swing it. In the corner, Paul nodded, drowsy, wrapped in memories of intimacy in her arms, when Bags shuffled in, his face almost as red as his eyes, wearing the fragile look of someone still drunk the morning after. He weaved over to Yvonne, stood before her. "I said she was lucky you didn't kill her, and now she's dead."

Paul exploded off the sofa and shoved Bags who staggered back against a table. "You're full of shit. You killed her. How many shots did you give her? I saw three." Hilton got to him first. Even as Hilton held him and Mitchell hustled Bags away, Paul continued to shout. "What were you gonna do, get her so drunk she'd fuck even you? You killed her, Bags! You!" Two waiters aided Hilton, but Paul struggled to get free until Yvonne stood before him.

"Let it go, Paul." She put her hand on his chest, and the softness of her eyes soothed and settled him. She led him to the sofa and sat on his lap, intending to stay there until they called him for an interview. She whispered, "I like the lover far better than the fighter." He didn't get a chance to answer. The police wanted him next.

****

Paul and Bags didn't work together until Thursday night. Bags held one of the coveted sections next to the windows overlooking the river. Before shift, he approached the kitchen door and said to Paul, "Hey, man, no hard feelings," offering his hand.

Paul turned away. "No problem, Randy."

At The Open Door, to time meal delivery, cooks did not begin an order until a server issued the command, "Fire table two." Bags fired his first order after delivering salads, yet fifteen minutes later, his food had not come up. He approached Paul, "What happened to table two?"

"I'm waiting for you to fire it. You said, *Don't fire two.* I'm waiting."

The next ticket Bags fired contained a very well-done steak. When he picked up the order, the round baseball-cut steak quivered. "It's supposed to be very well," said Bags, "Not very rare. I can't serve this."

Paul held up the ticket and pointed to the clearly written *VW*. "My mistake, Randy. I guess this isn't my night. I'll put it back on the grill, but it's going to take a while."

Bags told Mitchell, and Mitchell marched to the kitchen, furious. He chewed out Paul. "You can't do this. You're sabotaging my customers. If you guys have issues, we'll talk after shift, but if you can't do your job, I'm sending you home."

The next order Bags picked up consisted of three

plates. He put two of them on his tray and grabbed the third, which was so hot he dropped it instantly, shaking his burned fingers. "You fucking asshole."

"Randy, you killed Raina with tequila. And I despise you for the shit you tried in her car. I think you should find some other place to work."

"You're not management."

Paul shrugged. "How much money do you think you're going make here?"

"You can't do that."

"Anytime you'd like to try and stop me," said Paul quietly.

Again, Bags told Mitchell, who burst into the kitchen, face red, roaring. "Damn it, Paul, get out! If you want to work tomorrow, be here at nine sharp with a whole different attitude."

Paul believed he held an unassailable position in the restaurant. He strolled across the bar and waited for Yvonne at her well. Mitchell glared at him. Bags glared at him. He smiled at Yvonne who rolled her eyes. "Bangs," she said.

"I'll sit in the corner until you get off."

"Bangs. And you better be sober." Paul understood the concept of a Bangs call, but this seemed like being called on the carpet. In the heat of the kitchen, a certain pride rose within him. Nobody could kill a friend of his, however accidentally, and get away with it. But in the dark, standing on the curb on MacAdam, waiting for the light, traffic roaring past, he began to reconsider. He could recall Mitchell's face, Yvonne's. He figured he had squandered some capital that was about all he possessed in the world. Yvonne once considered him a man worth investing in. Mitchell built his restaurant around him. What did they think now?

He was shooting pool with a waiter from Piccolo Mondo when Yvonne arrived. She glanced at him, strode to the bar, ordered two beers and carried them to a booth in the now darkened restaurant.

He sat across from her. "I messed up?"

"No. You just looked immature. Paul, Mitchell is like family. You could have gone to him and said, *Can we do better than Bags?* He would have heard you out." Her dark eyes were soft. "You're a good man, *mon ami*, the best I've known. Whatever happens, remember it. Come on, I'll drop you home." She saw his disappointment. "Not tonight. I have a lot on my mind."

Chapter 9
Good Cop/Bad Cop

Major Slaten of the Violent Crimes Division sat at his desk flipping pages of a folder resting on a stack of folders. He wore a charcoal gray suit, had a full head of steel-gray hair, and, unaccountably, a nearly unadulterated black mustache. He wore a wide yellow tie and a blue shirt and mouthed a huge cigar, unlit. "Okay, now Hennessey. Frank fucked this up."

Lieutenant Jim Hardy sat opposite him, writing on a yellow legal pad. Slaten knew Hardy as a twenty-year veteran on the force, ten in homicide: a short, wiry man, a fierce competitor at handball. Slaten considered Hardy a master at the quality of keeping drive and restraint in perfect balance, a valuable trait in a detective and an officer.

"Not his fault," said Hardy, looking up from his pad. And when we transferred him to narcotics, well, it fell through the cracks. "It's the crime lab problem, four weeks for toxicology. How the hell can we gather evidence four weeks later? At least it wasn't a common poison. If we find even a trace, we've got our killer."

"It's a long shot, Jim. We'll need paternity tests." He turned the file around for Hardy and poked his cigar at names as he spoke. "Let's get the bartender, the construction guys, the cook, that drunken waiter, hell, and the other ones, too. If one of them knocked her up, we might have a motive. But Jim, you've got to kick these people's asses, 'cause most likely a confession or a rat is all we're gonna get."

"I had Matheson run down some names, though I haven't read her report. She says a waitress from New Orleans has a record."

Slaten frowned. He took the unlit cigar from his mouth, examined it with distaste. "I read her report, a fine bit of police work. So Jim, let's talk about Matheson. How come you haven't assigned her a partner?"

"I wanted to partner her with old Peck and spoke to him about it. He's got no issues working with a woman. He's the only one."

"He's on the sick list?"

"Shingles."

"Jim, what if you gave this case to Matheson? It's a nothing case, a nobody. The murder happened months ago, got no press. No scions of the eleven families involved?"

Hardy shook his head.

"It might be a good start for her, no outside pressure. If she solves it, good; if she doesn't, well, that's a story, too. At least we can say we gave her some real work to do. The way you've got things now leaves the department vulnerable. Besides, most of these people are her age, maybe she'll have some insight, be able to talk the talk, and she already knows the players."

Slaten could see the objections on his lieutenant's face and spoke before they could be voiced. "You can't keep her hanging around the bullpen like some kind of jumped-up secretary. She's a good cop; put her to work.

Act as her partner on this until Peck gets back. In the background as an advisor."

****

When two police officers strolled into The Open Door, Jazmin could tell they had business on their minds. If they were in for lunch, they would have chatted up Gail at the podium until she seated them, but instead, one of them prowled the bar, while the other peered into the kitchen and the dish room, checked out the hall. Like most people who engage in illegal activities, Jazmin made herself scarce in the presence of the law, but curiosity kept her close enough to see them escort Paul, in handcuffs, into the back of a patrol car.

She wanted this to be none of her business but had connected with both Yvonne, one of the few women on staff who treated her well, and Paul. He never leered, never made comments. Since she started working nights, he favored her with treats from the kitchen and the choicest cuts for her tables. She suspected he moved her orders up the line on busy nights. The waiters no longer messed with her. She attributed Paul and Hilton's behavior to Yvonne.

It felt like crossing a line to walk into the unattended office, pluck the phone list from the bulletin board, and dial the office phone. Yvonne didn't answer, and neither did Djuna, who must be at Johnny's. "Fuck 'em both," she said before she dialed. Johnny picked up. "Johnny, this is Jazmin. I need to talk to Djuna."

"Why?" he asked, his neutral voice revealing Djuna was there.

"Johnny, it's not about you," she began, but he hung up. She called again to no answer. She waited a moment and called a third time.

Djuna answered after four rings, "What?"

"The police took Paul. I tried to call Yvonne, but she didn't answer."

Djuna's voice softened. "Is that you, Jazmin? Thanks for letting me know."

"Don't make a mistake, Djuna. I didn't call 'cause of you."

****

Assistant D.A. Owen Fredricks made it clear he liked me yet managed to be both a gentleman and a complete professional. A handsome man, taller than me, with curly brown hair and an athletic build, he always gave me a smile and an encouraging word. In any room, he sought me out. People noticed, and this gave me some legitimacy. I appreciated him as an ally. One day he peeked into the detective's bullpen, caught my eye, and motioned with his head to follow. We walked down a short hallway to a darkened observation room. Inside, the D.A. made an impatient motion for me to close the door.

Owen said, "Hailey's first case. Her research led to the arrest."

Hardy sat, back to window, interrogating my beautiful guitar player from the park and the Japanese garden. He'd made arrests in Hennessey without telling me. The son of a bitch had gone around me, shut me out.

"Have a seat, Detective," said the D.A. "Yvonne L'Croix. Lieutenant Hardy has been badgering her for some time, but she hasn't said a word." When I'd dug up the dirt on her, I hadn't known Yvonne L'Croix was my guitar player from the park. In those days, pictures were not easily duplicated and traveled by mail.

Yvonne possessed a rare stillness, a poise. She simply sat, unreadable.

Owen spoke. "Hardy is usually pretty good at this, but this one is cold blooded as a snake. Look at those eyes, like she could cut your throat and not even blink."

The D.A. hesitated before he spoke. He had served ten years on the job because he proceeded slowly, listened, double-checked his facts, and challenged his own assumptions. "That's not what I see in her eyes," he told the younger man. "She isn't here. She's some other place, some other time. When Hardy gets her to speak, you might get a read on her. Remember, the longer they wait, the harder they crack." I didn't think she would crack because I saw a calm, beautiful, indomitable strength.

Hardy slowly turned the pages in a folder. When he looked up, his pale eyes took a long time to meet hers. Hardy appeared whittled down with sharp features, a pointed nose, cropped brown hair grayed at the temples. He projected boredom, so sure of the outcome that the process was tedium.

Yvonne closed her eyes. I imagined her thinking about Paul, her knight. She must have known we would question him. Did she wonder if he would talk, if he would betray her?

Hardy cleared his throat, spoke, a lingering pause between each sentence. "You're looking at premeditated first-degree murder. The death penalty. I've spoken to the D.A." He turned more pages, scanning each one. After a long while, he stopped and wrote a short note on a yellow legal pad. A long pause, a nod, a satisfied grin. "We've got a great case. If you confess, save the county some money, we'll let you keep your life."

Yvonne sat mute.

He continued turning pages and writing on the pad. "We know how you did it, why. We have witnesses to your threats." A conclusive gesture, hands raised, open wide. "You put poison in the coffee cup under the bar where she kept her wine." He stared her down. When he spoke again, his pace quickened. "You did it because she wanted your man. We know where you got the poison. We've picked up Fanny Mae Fontaine. We have teams searching her place, searching every inch of your apartment. When we find the poison, even a trace, you'll go to prison. Maybe Paul, too, unless he plays it smart." He returned to turning pages.

She closed her eyes again. Her face softened, thinking of him, I imagined.

"We've rounded up everyone from The Open Door: your friends, your enemies, her friends. They're talking to us right now, trying to help. Paul is here, helping us."

The corners of her beautiful lips turned up just a little. Beside me, Owen didn't notice, though he spoke without taking his eyes from her. "Her expression never changes. He's not going to crack her."

Hardy rose, looming over her. "He's horrified about Raina's murder. Everyone is helping us now. We have your file from New Orleans. This case will be very different, murder one. In your last trial, Officer Hiss revealed something we will use in court. How the man you killed bled to death slowly, how a long time passed before you called the police. The jury is going to hear all about your past."

She continued to sit, motionless, eyes far away.

"Look at me, Yvonne." Her hard, dark eyes turned to him. "This is your last chance to save your life. Once I leave this room, it's in the hands of the D.A. Talk to me. Maybe the murder wasn't your idea. Maybe Paul pressured you. Maybe he did it and set you up. Give me something so I can help you."

He waited. She tilted her head, weighting options, and sighed, about to speak. Something had gotten to her. I guessed Paul.

"You're very good at what you do," she said. Even though I knew better, her soft voice and gentle accent surprised me.

The D.A. jabbed Owen with an elbow. "Here we go."

"I'm terrified, and I didn't even do it. Given your skill, you can't possibly think Paul Tomaso killed anyone in cold blood. And I'd better have an attorney."

The D.A. pounded the table, rose. "He got nothing." He turned to Owen. "Tell Hardy to keep her for a couple of days, soften her up. Detective Matheson, you're well briefed on this case?"

"Yes, sir."

"Get to work on the cook. Play the good cop, tough but fair. Ready?" My first break as a detective, and I was oh so ready.

****

Paul sat in a gray room under a buzzing fluorescent light. He imagined such a room would be scarred by violent drama, but it struck him as merely too bright and government sterile: a gray metal table in front of him, gray metal chairs bolted to the floor, and a dark window through which he could not see. The silence numbed him, no rhythmic beating of knives on the board, no pans clanking, no buzz of conversation. Raina would crack in a room like this with no one to talk to, no way to get high. Did they think he killed her?

He had seen enough television to anticipate two detectives would occupy the chairs and grill him. They would be big men, one young, one old. They would be bored, having done this a thousand times. They would know tricks to counter each of his reactions and play the good cop/bad cop game, while men behind the glass would read his body language, evaluate him, function as a team, three or four against one.

Time passed. The gray walls seemed to suck the meaning out of life. They were making him wait to make him nervous, but mostly he was tired. After months of frantic motion, to sit alone in the quiet with nothing to do made him yawn. He looked at his hands. They were scabbed and scarred, marked with ghosts of injuries past. Yvonne provided all the softness in his life. She filled him to overflowing, introduced him to love, to the world, to himself. He wondered if they had picked her up, too. He lay his head on his arm, closed his eyes, and pictured her as clearly as if she stood before him. He would have slept, imagining her, but the door opened.

Her brass nameplate read: *Matheson*. She wore a white blouse with a black ribbon tie, a brown tweed suit. Except for her freckles and an intense, hawkish gaze, she might have been cast from the same mold as Raina, with redder hair and wider set blue eyes. She stood tall, lean, and muscled where Raina had been soft curves. She sat and precisely arranged a few manila file folders, a yellow pad, a black mechanical pencil, and a cassette recorder in parallel lines on the table. "Hello,

Paul. Sorry to keep you waiting." The good cop.

"Am I under arrest?"

"Did they give you that idea? We're all rushing around today, a misunderstanding." She hit the record button. "In fact, if you like, you're free to go, but we do need your help. We just want a little information, a little background," she said with a smile as drab as the walls.

Paul rose to his feet, indignant. "Slow down. You dragged me out of work in handcuffs. You've kept me in this room for hours, and now you tell me I'm free to go?"

"Well, yes, I'm sorry. Someone made a mistake. It's been a crazy day." She sighed, looking tired. Paul guessed it wasn't easy being a woman detective at what, twenty-five, twenty-six years old. She managed a sympathetic smile. "If you'll help us, I promise to call your employer and set the record straight."

"Help with what?" he said.

"Your friend Raina was poisoned, a very unusual poison out of Haiti and the Caribbean."

"Who did it?"

"That's what we're trying to find out. Will you help us?"

"Of course," he said, feeling manipulated. She gestured toward the chair and opened a file. A list of questions in red pen filled her pad, one every other line, written in a strong, angular hand. The file bore his name. He sat.

"How long have you worked at The Open Door?"

Her first questions were background about him, The Door, Raina, her drinking and drug use, the coffee cup under the bar, Hell House. He told her everything. When she asked about Djuna, he considered his answers more carefully, but Djuna wouldn't kill anyone. So he told the good cop about her and Johnny and their cheating game. He omitted the cocaine, and the night of three, when it occurred to him, Yvonne might be in another room, answering the same questions, Djuna, too, and Johnny. Questions about Djuna kept coming. She must be a suspect. The police already knew more than he did. Matheson asked about Djuna in places called the Polish Princess, the Brasserie, Cassidy's, and the Carriage Room. New in town, he didn't know any of these places. She asked about a man named Evan Piner.

"Don't know him, either."

"We were told anyone who knew both Raina Hennessey and June Novak would have to know Piner."

"I don't. Why don't you find him?"

Matheson studied him. "We tried. He's dead."

"Another murder?"

"Complications from a car wreck."

He tried to make eye contact with her, establish some kind of a connection, but her eyes were cold. She took her time, gave him weak smiles, thanked him repeatedly, apologized for the number of questions, and reminded him they were tracking down Raina's killer. She offered coffee, soda, a sandwich, but always her hawkish eyes looked into his, weighing, analyzing, evaluating.

She began asking about the night of Raina's death, the drunks, the fights, the crowd, the band. The questions covered minute details. What time did the band begin? How did the singer know his name? Her relentless questions wore him down. He wanted to object and leave when the good cop switched gears and asked about the speed incident in the banquet room. At the mention of Yvonne's name, he imagined her fingers on his lips, her lips puckered in a gentle shush.

He answered briefly, deflected the focus away from Yvonne and the threat she made. The good cop shifted back to the night of the murder. She asked about Bags in some detail. Then her demeanor changed. She put down her pencil, leaned forward. Her eyes narrowed. "How many people would you say had access to the coffee cup where Raina kept her wine?"

"Well, the cocktail waitresses, a bunch of the customers, the waiters."

"Did you have access?"

"Yes."

"Did Johnny?"

"Only if she put the cup on the bar. Sometimes, he poured it directly in her cup. So yeah."

"How about Randy Bogges?"

"Yes. As a waiter he would."

"Did Djuna?"

"Probably."

"Did Yvonne?"

He hesitated. Detective Matheson's hands, strong with long fingers, had what looked like grease in her cuticles and under short, unpainted fingernails. One knuckle wore a dark scab, the finger black and blue. "Yes."

"Yvonne felt jealous of Raina?" Again, he hesitated. She said, "Remember, we're here to solve the murder of your friend. Did Yvonne feel jealous of Raina?"

"No."

"Is she a jealous person?"

"A little."

"Tell me about the incident at the house party. What happened?"

He lied badly. She frowned and shook her head. "So she got jealous of a girl who gave you a light but didn't feel jealous of a woman who said, 'And when he's tired of the dark meat, maybe I'll get Paul'?"

"She wasn't jealous; she felt sorry for her. Everybody could see Raina falling apart. We all thought she drank herself to death." The good cop wrote, hand gripping the pencil. She flipped a page, flipped back.

"Who is Fanny Mae Fontaine?" He understood they also suspected Yvonne. He needed time to think.

"You've been asking me all these questions. Let me ask you one."

"You're here to answer questions."

"You said I could leave," he reminded her, rising.

"Sit. When we're finished, you can leave." The command in her voice surprised him, reminding him of his father.

"What happens if I leave now?"

"It's not up to me." Her eyes wandered to the darkened glass. "Sit. I'll answer one question if I can."

He sat, studied her. "Are you here because you look like her?"

"Who?" she asked, blushing.

"Raina. Like to drink?"

"Rarely. My father drank." Her face flushed a deeper red. She looked down at her yellow legal pad. A muscle in her jaw worked like her teeth were clenched. He remembered the men behind the mirror and wondered if he'd pissed off the good cop.

"I'm sorry. Mine, too."

She opened the file bearing his name. "Your father served in the Marines?"

"One tough old man, a sergeant. I'll tell you something about Raina. When I needed a place to live, she took me in. She teased me and taught me the ropes, and yeah, she drank too much and played around, but we were friends. She took care of me. She understood being a kid on your own. If I had any idea who killed her, I'd tell you."

She flipped pages, looking for something. "This report says you beat up three guys in a bar fight."

"They were after Jazmin and Yvonne."

"A man named Hilton says he was right behind you, but the fight was over in less than a minute. Did your dad teach you that?"

"Do we have to talk about my dad?"

Kindness in cold blue eyes seemed out of context. They made more sense predatory and judgmental but filled with sympathy, they were distracting. Then suddenly, they narrowed hawkish again.

"Paul, you've been less than honest. So now, you're going to tell me about Fanny Mae Fontaine, and then give us real answers to the other questions. We already know who did it. We have a full confession. Hiding the truth doesn't serve anyone, least of all, you if you want to walk out of here when this interview is done. Obstructing an investigation is a crime."

He frowned, shook his head, wouldn't meet her eyes.

She said, "You look like you're upset with me."

"I thought for a minute, 'cause of how you look, that you weren't just another cop."

An awkward silence lingered. The good cop stared at her pad, then raised her eyes. "But I am. I'm trying to solve the murder of your friend, and I'm asking you to help me. We're looking for information so we can see justice is done. Everyone says you're a stand-up guy and on the right side of the law on this, so tell me about Fanny Mae, and we'll figure out what happened."

"She's a friend of Yvonne's, and she sells fruit."

A man burst through the door, slamming it behind him. The bad cop, gray eyes and red face filled with anger. "We've arrested your girlfriend for murder. She's made a full confession. She put poison from Fanny Mae in the coffee cup under the bar. You were standing right there. You lived with the woman. She's going to jail. If you don't want to go with her, you're going to tell us everything, now. You two had a fight after she threatened Raina. She hit you. I want to know what she said, every word. I want to know about her jealous rage at the party. I want to know about Fanny Mae Fontaine. If I am not satisfied, you'll be booked as an accessory to murder."

Paul hesitated.

Hardy shouted, "I'm not fucking around. Book him!"

"Just a minute," said Matheson, her blue eyes, soft now, met his. "He's going to talk. He's thinking. He pauses before every question, even the easy ones." She kept her eyes on his and sensed his reluctance. "Look Paul, defending her is loyal and very sweet, but she may not be the person you think. Did she tell you she had been a prostitute?"

When wondering about the past she wouldn't tell, he rejected the idea, but it made sense: wild sex, the way she always said yes, her red vest and the queen of hearts, her sympathy for Jazmin.

The good cop said, "I see she didn't. Did she tell you she's killed before?"

Hardy said, "She cut a man's throat and watched him bleed to death."

Hard Yvonne, don't fuck with me Yvonne, capable of anything. "You shouldn't go out with girls like me," she had said. A tear rolled down his face. Another. He started to cry, tried to stop but couldn't. They let him.

After a while, the good cop said, "Okay, now don't fall apart. Start with something easy. Tell us what happened at the party."

She handed him a box of tissues. He wiped his eyes, blew his nose. "I already did." The door opened, and a thin, smallish man stepped in, about thirty-five, with very curly dark hair and small round glasses.

"I've been hired to represent Mr. Tomaso, and I'd like a moment with my client." Hardy cursed under his breath, stormed out. The good cop threw a look at Paul he read as, *I had you, twice*, then followed Hardy out. The man sat in Matheson's chair. "Hello, Paul. I'm Damien Novak, Connie Novak's nephew, Djuna's cousin. The family wanted you to have representation."

"If the Novaks called you, you know I can't pay."

"That has been taken care of."

"I don't want debt to fall to the family on my account."

Novak spoke quietly, brightly, reminding Paul of Djuna. "Let me explain. I never would have made it through college, much less law school, if not for Connie and her husband. They paid for most of it and sacrificed dearly. Had I known the extent of those sacrifices, I'd have made other arrangements. I've been practicing law for ten years, and never once has she allowed me to repay her. Today, Aunt Connie called and said she needed a favor. I'd like to clear my books, at least in part. If she wants this, I want to do it for her. Have they arrested you?"

"No."

"Did they tell you that you were free to leave?"

"Yes."

"Ever heard of Beheler?"

"What?"

"A case in California. Basically, if they say you're free to go, they don't have to read your rights, but anything you say can still be used against you, and they can still arrest you at any time."

"What should I do?"

"We're going to try to leave. If they let you, we'll walk to my office. When we get there, I'm going to ask some questions. On the way, you're going to decide if you're going to tell me the truth. My father was, to put it delicately, a worldly man. He once told me, *Damien, there are two people you never lie to—your doctor and your attorney.* I can't help you if I don't know the truth."

On the way to Novak's building, he began to get angry. They'd handcuffed him at work and tried to intimidate him, tried to come between him and Yvonne. Besides, if Yvonne had confessed, why had the bad cop been so angry? They'd lied to him. Novak sat at his desk and began to question Paul. "Did you kill Raina Hennessy?"

"No."

"Do you know who did?"

"No clue."

"Do you know anything about this crime?"

"Nothing. I told the police everything right after she died."

Novak settled in his chair, assessing Paul. "They've arrested your girlfriend."

"Are you representing her?"

Paul didn't like Novak's shifty eyes. "No. The family didn't ask me to. The public defender most likely."

Paul asked, "Did she confess? They told me she did."

"I don't know. You have to understand, Paul, the police can lie to you. It's legal, and they do it all the time. If one lie doesn't work, they'll try another."

Paul sprang from his chair, adamant. "We have to go back. She didn't do it. She had no reason. I have to make them understand."

Novak shook his head. "Not a good idea."

Paul waved an arm. "I don't care. She's innocent. I hope you're coming, but I'll go alone if I have to."

"I said I'd help. But please, if I tell you to shut up, do it. Connie told me sometimes you talk too much."

They put him and Damien Novak in the same room and made them wait. When Hardy and Matheson entered, Paul said, "Detective Hardy, you told me you wanted the truth. That's what you're going to get."

"It's about time," said Hardy. Paul let that pass. The man Yvonne inspired him to be stood beside him. "Go ahead," said Hardy. "Tell me the truth."

"Yvonne L'Croix didn't kill Raina. She had no reason. I love her with all of my heart, and she knows this. I would spend the rest of my life with her, and she knows this, too. I'm not interested in anyone else, certainly not Raina. Yvonne doesn't want me to love her this way, this much. But I do."

He couldn't say the rest. He took a deep breath, then another. He remembered Yvonne battering away with her tray in the bar, slashing with razor-sharp glass. You fight with whatever is at hand. His feelings for her were the only resource at his command.

"She's always thought our relationship was temporary. In fact, I think she's going to leave me, maybe when school starts." His throat tightened; he fought back tears, lost. "She thinks she's too old for me, and in ten years, I'll be looking at younger women, but she's wrong.

"When we're together, I'm a better man. I'm with her now. I can feel her, right here." He tapped his chest with a fist. "That's why I can talk to you when I'm scared shitless. That's why she had no reason to kill Raina, no reason to feel jealous."

Paul stared Hardy down. Matheson met his eyes briefly, gave him a faint smile, and then straightened her pad on the table.

"There's the first part. The second is this. If she's tried for murder, that's what I'm going to say on the stand. She didn't feel jealous of Raina. We never fought about her, except for the time she gave me speed, and that was about the drug, not the woman." He stared at Hardy until Hardy's eyes met his own. He spoke slowly. "She didn't do it. You've got the wrong person."

The good cop said, "We've still got a few questions."

"You can arrest me, do whatever you want. I just

gave you the only answer you're going to get from me. Ever." Hardy got up and walked out.

Matheson said, "You can go. We'll call if we need you." The way she looked at him seemed odd to Paul, but he couldn't read her.

When they left the station, Damien Novak shook his hand. "Wow, Paul, you rocked old Hardy. You ought to consider a career in law."

"Mr. Novak, I have to get her out. What do I do?"

"My guess is there will be a hearing on Monday where they'll set bail."

"How much will I need?"

"Maybe as much as twenty thousand."

He went begging. Constance Novak offered five hundred dollars. Djuna donated five hundred. Mitchell kicked in five hundred but only after Paul begged. Jazmin drove over, gave him a thousand dollars cash, and told him he wouldn't get the money back. The bail bondsman would keep it all.

On Sunday evening, he ventured to Yvonne's. The police had trashed the place, as they'd done to his apartment, drawers open, things taken out and replaced in a jumble or thrown on the floor. She kept her private papers in a cardboard box. He opened the closet and found it on a high shelf. He needed money to get her out of jail, so he opened it and found her checkbook: balance, two hundred and seventy-two dollars, and two one-hundred-dollar bills in a savings passbook with a balance of over twelve thousand. He flipped back through the book. In April, when they met, the balance was over fifteen. He examined the entries. Since then, instead of adding a little each month, the ledger was marked by withdrawals. Dim Sum, concert tickets, meals out, movies, clothes for him, organic food, fancy ingredients like truffles, nights in the clubs—mostly, she paid. He assumed that though she spent more, she made more, and since they would both be broke at the end of the month, they were in a way even. She'd never mentioned it. He felt incompetent, not man enough for his woman.

A cigar box lay on a high shelf. He tried to resist the temptation to open it. Inside he found a hawk's feather, a spool of red thread, and a picture of him on the riverbank by the restaurant, laughing, wearing jeans and a white tank top T-shirt, a blue L.A. Dodgers hat, his hair down. He found an ornate folding knife, very sharp, and a cameo locket, the ancient picture inside bearing a striking resemblance to Yvonne. At the very bottom lay a plain man's wedding band, platinum. She'd never told him about a marriage. She hadn't told him many things. He found a snapshot of Yvonne at twelve or thirteen, standing in front of an unpainted shack of a house, impossibly skinny, her face unscarred. She wore her familiar scowl, her angry, don't-fuck-with- me eyes. Next, he pulled out letters on cream-colored stationary clipped together. He scanned the first page for a signature—Dahlia. He assumed the police had read them, but they were arranged so neatly he couldn't be sure. He didn't. He put everything back and began to clean.

****

When my Marine father married my beatnik mother, the union produced a redheaded daughter with a temper who can cuss with anyone. After both Hardy and Novak interrupted my interview with Paul, I stomped up and down the parking lot hurling profanities. I wanted to kick something, but everything was metal or concrete, and I'm not stupid. People walked past and stared, but I didn't give a damn. I'd owned that cook. I'd spun a web and waited, and he was about to fall into it. I would have gotten everything but for Hardy.

Someone must have told Frank about my antics. He found me still pacing and cussing. "Calm down," he said, "and tell me about it." The man is unflappable because he knows precisely where he stands.

I explained how I'd sprung my trap, how Hardy had barged in and changed the game. "He wants me to fail and sabotaged me on purpose. He's done nothing but fuck me over. Slaten gave me this case."

"Where'd you hear that?"

"The women around here," I said, "are on my side. Think about that, buddy." This wasn't entirely true. Secretaries, clerical staff, and janitors were. The lady cops I beat out for the job were a mixed bag. Some wanted me to succeed to prove women could do this work but still resented me. Others stuck with pure resentment.

"And I'll tell you another thing. I'm going to be like a spider. I'm going to watch and wait, and he's going to make a mistake, and I swear I'm going to get him for this. I'm gonna rub his face in it, the belly-crawling, scum-sucking bastard."

"Hailey, that's no way to talk."

I fired off invective until Frank blushed, and then I said, "Is that the way you want me to talk, Frank?"

"Hailey, tell me again from the beginning. Go slowly and a little quieter."

Of course, I eventually calmed and said, "I'm tired

of him pushing me around."

"Slow down. You get so determined you forget to relax. Let's go have a drink."

"I don't drink."

"There's your problem right there," My glare announced this as a line that failed. "Well, what do you do to unwind? Do you have a man?"

There must have been fire in my voice when I said, "Kickboxing," because Frank took a step back.

"You go do that. I'll make your excuses, though I don't think anyone will miss you."

I said, "You're a wet fart of a condescending bastard," but my only friend in the department was undoubtedly correct.

Chapter 10
Killer in Your Eyes

We had no solid evidence against Yvonne except her threats. We found no poison traces at her apartment, Fannie Mae's house in North Portland, Djuna's, Johnny's, or Paul's. When Owen told me of her impending release, I told Hardy I wanted to be there when they let her out. Thinking I wanted to taunt or threaten, he said, "Let her know we'll be back. Make her fear you. Worry will sap her resistance and make things easier next time." Of course, he didn't understand me at all.

When they opened her cell door, she looked plain, strength spent and beauty with it, her face expressionless, dull. She registered surprise at seeing me but said nothing. We walked down the hall in silence, got into the elevator. When the door closed, she asked, "Do you remember me?"

"Of course. You never came back to the park. I looked for you all summer. I saw you and Paul once in the Japanese Garden. He was practicing martial arts with a gardener."

"You should've come over," she said, voice dull.

"You were in love, and I didn't want to intrude." She said nothing, so I continued. "He stood by you. We threatened him, bullied him. One reason you're getting out is because of him."

"I don't deserve him," she said.

I didn't answer until I thought of a soothing truth. "You must have done something to inspire such devotion." She looked at me with gratitude. "If I had a partner like that, I'd hang on tight."

She gripped my arm. "Nothing about my fucked-up life is that simple."

We walked to the phones. "I did the background research on you, the stuff from New Orleans. I didn't know who you were. The file came by teletype, no picture."

She made a bitter sound between a sob and a laugh.

"You should tell him," I said. She looked doubtful. "He knows now, anyway. Hardy told him. After what he did, he should hear it from you."

She might have nodded her head. She stopped when we arrived at the phones. I fumbled through my pocket for a dime.

After her call, she returned to my side, more composed. "Why did you come get me? You didn't have to."

"No, I didn't. I want him to know I admired his courage and his devotion. Will you tell him?"

She looked at me appraisingly, searching my eyes and seemed to see me in a new light. She said, "You should tell him yourself. You two are the same, in some ways. He's a good man. A little wild. I didn't help there." I wondered why she nudged me toward him.

"Tell him your story," I urged. "He needs to hear it. And you need to hear how he'll take it."

She considered. "This isn't over, is it?" she asked.

I thought of Hardy when I said, "No." We didn't say much after that, standing next to each other on the steps of the Justice Center as if we were friends. The statue of *Rebecca at the Well*, where I met her, was a couple of blocks up, a couple of blocks over. Paul stopped at the curb in an old battered, gray car.

She said, "You're kind. I would have hated waiting here alone. Thank you. I've never known a police officer to be kind."

"The times they are a-changin'," I said. "Know that song?"

She almost smiled. "Maybe I'll play it for you someday."

****

The Sunday after Yvonne got out of jail, Djuna called. "Hey, you guys up for Chinese?" They met at a converted Sambo's in Goose Hollow. Paul and Yvonne intended to see the Curtis Salgado Blues Band afterward. An hour later, Paul picked at morsels; everyone else sat listless, watching him. It had been a strained dinner. Johnny and Djuna quibbled; Yvonne said very little.

Johnny poured the last of his beer. "I've been wondering who killed Raina? Since they let Yvonne go, they haven't arrested anyone. Who better to solve the crime than us? We know the doings at The Door, all the players. We were there when the murder happened. We could figure it out. After all, somebody did it." His eyes darted to catch reactions.

Djuna said, "None of us are killers."

"Hear me out," said Johnny. "I know it wasn't me. That leaves you three. If we can eliminate you guys, we can work together and solve the crime."

"I'd like to know who did it," said Paul.

"Well, it must have been someone who knew

Fanny Mae," said Johnny.

Djuna replied, "We all did."

"But how many of us would she have sold poison to?" said Johnny. "That's why the police suspected you," he said to Yvonne.

"Which eliminates Paul," said Djuna. "She would never have sold him poison to protect Yvonne."

Johnny crowed, "The Gumbas are in the clear."

Djuna answered sharply, "Not in my book, buddy."

"Like I said, I know I didn't do it," Johnny replied.

"Paul, I'm ready to go," said Yvonne. "Signal for the check."

"Not interested in solving the case, Yvonne?" Johnny gloated, wearing a huge smile, his eyes bright.

Yvonne dug into her purse, threw two twenties on the table, and nudged Paul, "Come on, let's go." He stood and she slid out of the booth.

Johnny said, "Paolo, it might be pretty easy to find the killer."

Yvonne's face changed. No longer defeated or soft Yvonne, she glared at Johnny, fierce, ready for attack. "I'm sick of the shitty way you treat my friend. How'd your paternity test come out? Paul found out Friday." Johnny's face flushed; he studied his beer. "So are you a suspect or a sleaze? Or both? Come on, Johnny, tell us again how you didn't do it."

Djuna looked at the tabletop. "Why do you keep doing this to me?"

Yvonne answered, "Because you let him. Come with us. Say, *I'm done with you.* Walk away." Djuna shook her head. Yvonne scowled, "You're better than this, Djuna, I swear." Djuna turned away. Yvonne said, "Your life."

Yvonne frightened him, the way she marched him through town. Instead of taking his arm, she propelled him by it. "What's wrong?" he asked.

"We need to talk."

What could he have done wrong? Should he have defended her or stood up for Djuna? He speculated that she might leave him or might confess. They ran across Burnside, and she power-walked him to his apartment. Once there, she sat him on the sofa and planted his only chair in front of him. Her determination scared him, the coldness of her eyes.

"You need to know about me, about my past. I should have told you long ago, but I was selfish. I loved the way you loved me. I didn't want to lose you. So from just before my sixteenth birthday until I got arrested, I was a whore."

She growled the word, intending to wound. This would be the storm Ernie had predicted, and he would help her weather it. He said, "They told me at the police station, but I'd guessed before. I tried to figure out what you didn't want to tell."

She took his hands, looked into his eyes. "Paul, I was good at it, and everything we've done, I've done a dozen times with men who disgusted me, so it doesn't mean anything."

"You're lying, Yvonne. You meant all of it. Everything before was just practice for me." She tried not to smile. He knew in his bones her love for him.

"There's another thing. I killed a man."

He tried to keep his face neutral. "They told me."

"My pimp. When he found me, I was starving, eating out of trashcans. He took me in, and at first, he was kind. He made me his whore, and I learned to hate him. I decided to leave, to keep some of my money, a little at a time. One night, he found out and beat me. I fought back. He slashed me." She pointed to the scar. "Then he turned his back. He thought he'd ruined my face, broken me, and I'd crawl off and cry. I cut his throat."

He started to rise, to go to her.

She shook her head. Her eyes held his, and she spoke each word separately. "I…was…a…whore. I've done things I'll never tell you, things I'm ashamed of. I wanted to get ahead. I had rivals. I fought to stay alive, to keep my place, to rise, somehow from the shit. Even those people, those tough, vicious people were afraid of me. Sometimes, I think the things I've done show on my face, and everybody sees and hates me for them. You're the only one who doesn't, who doesn't see I'm no good for you, Paul. You should have someone young who is whole and clean and innocent and fucking naïve as you are."

"You're wrong, Yvonne, that's who you were. I know who you are. You are more than those years. I'm proud you fought back. I'm proud you survived. You're hard as nails on the outside, soft as flowers on the inside. That's the woman I love, the kind of woman I want beside me, the kind I will always want. When the police were grilling me, I kept thinking, *I've got to be tough as Yvonne.* All my life, whenever I'm in trouble, I'll tell myself, *Get on your feet and start fighting like Yvonne, with whatever you can find.*"

"No, Paul. You don't want a woman like me. You want someone moral and kind, someone innocent."

"What would I do with someone innocent? Drink whiskey till dawn? Take her in an alley against a wall after the erotic film festival? Who do you think I am? I work a man's job for shitty pay and get screwed because I'm twenty and Donny is incompetent, and Mitchell is too softhearted to fire anyone. If I were twenty-one, I'd be a manager, making more than you. I'm almost there. If this were 1969 instead of 1979, I'd be in Vietnam, and I damn well wouldn't be a private. I'd be running something, probably be a sergeant like my dad. I support myself. I'm smart and strong and tough. And because of you, I think I'm a good man. Stop treating me like a kid. I know what I want, and I want you."

She tried not to smile, shook her head. He put his hand under her chin, lifted her eyes to his. "Don't leave me, Yvonne, and don't stay in the past. Look to the future; go there with me." He rose and opened his arms. She threw herself into them, buried her face in his chest. "We can do it, Yvonne. We can make a good life together. Believe in me like I believe in you."

"Oh, Paul, I want to. I wish I could."

****

Yvonne sat quietly at the show, no whooping and hollering. Since coming home from jail, she'd stopped drinking and stuck to soda water and lime. Paul drank whiskey since the bar insisted on a two-drink minimum. They didn't talk much, but crying notes of blues guitar spoke the emotions they suppressed.

Yvonne's past haunted her. The ghost of it, after long absence, had reappeared. He wanted it to be a tangible monster he could fight and vanquish. He envisioned an image from a Dia de Los Muertos poster, a skeleton armed with bloody knife and bandoliers—a skeleton of exploitation, murder, jail, and scars which would never heal. If her ghosts kept her from him, they would haunt him, too. He wondered if Yvonne could transcend her history or if, for all her strength, it would defeat her.

After the show, back in her apartment, Yvonne changed into her white nightgown and curled up in bed, back to him. He held her, tangled his legs with hers. She said, "Paul, tell me the truth. Do you think I'm…tainted?"

"Of course not. Yvonne, it's the past. Let it go. Be here with me, now."

"I got through, *chérie*, but it still has a hold on me." She stifled a sob, whispered, "I'm too strong to cry."

Another of Ernie's storms. He would be sand, ballast, a stabilizing weight, steady and immobile. He stood, gathered her in his arms, lifted her off the bed, and cradled her close.

"You can cry with me."

"I'm too strong to cry," she said again.

"Nobody's that strong. You can cry with me."

"No." She sobbed, then sobbed again, then she wailed. At first, Paul carried her about the apartment, and she clung to him, her crying violent and hysterical. She would calm and then some memory would strike her, and she would grip him hard and wail again until she gasped for breath. She wouldn't stop crying. He tried to give her whiskey to calm her, but she wouldn't drink. He held her head upon his lap, stroked her brow. After a long while, she sobbed herself to sleep.

But sleep would not come to him. Wind buffeted the window, and through leaves, bone-white beams of streetlight danced about the room, triumphant skeletons, celebrating victory: Raina, a dead pimp, rivals, vicious things done long ago, the scar, Johnny, Djuna. He could not fight them all. He wondered if the four of them would remain friends or if tonight's dinner would end it.

Dinner bothered him. He could picture the table: teacups, beer bottles, smears of sauce on empty platters of orange chicken and kung pao shrimp. An ashtray full of butts. He recalled tea leaves on the bottom of his cup as if they held an answer. He tried to do a Holmes and think through each piece of dialogue but answers resisted him. He got out of bed and poured two fingers of whiskey into a glass, drank and paced, drank and sat in the big chair, drank and sat in bed, his leg against the warmth of Yvonne's back.

She stirred. "Is it morning?"

"No, *chérie*, go back to sleep." Then he realized his mistake. He had been looking for an answer, but the end of the thread turned out to be a question. "Who told the police about Fanny Mae?" Since he or Yvonne wouldn't have, there could be only two. Unable to unravel the knot, one of two it remained until finally, he sank into sleep.

On Tuesday night, Paul looked up from his prep to see someone new working behind the bar. He asked Mitchell who said, "Johnny found a job downtown, days. He said if I could find someone, he'd rather not come in. A few minutes later, Bob appeared at the podium, looking for work. Keep an eye on him, will you?"

Chapter 11
A Young Man's Blues

Two days after they released Yvonne from jail,
they transferred me to the narcotics unit. Mexican black
tar heroin had been flooding the streets, so Slaten
assembled a task force. Hennessey dropped off the
charts. For a while, no one had the case, but I couldn't
let it go. I fantasized about pursuing it after hours or at
lunch or on weekends, but they assigned me lots of
stakeouts or I took overtime or ended my shift
exhausted. The heroin case was interesting work,
wiretaps, snitches, undercover buys. Of course, as the
rookie, "The Golden Girl" as one of them called me,
they worked me hard and gave me shit jobs and most of
the paperwork. But they made use of me, kept me
involved and informed. I was back to being a cop.

One day after shift, they even asked me out for a
beer. When I told them I didn't drink, they never asked
again, but the pick-up lines and politics began to ebb.
More women were on patrol and in the lab. I had
proved myself in action and my novelty faded.

Then, things began to happen with Hennessey.
First, the FBI put a tag on it. They wanted updates and
to be informed of mysterious deaths or suspected
poisonings. They promised to fast-track toxicology.
Hardy put me back on the case because he had to have
someone's name on it but didn't relieve me of my

A. Molise

current duties.

An agent from D.C. called and, surprised to find himself talking to a woman, flirted some, and said more than he might have. Except for both an accident and new, computerized equipment, the poison that killed Raina Hennessey would have escaped detection. They wondered if it would surface again.

Next, Randy Bogges, known as Bags at The Open Door, got arrested for rape. Once in jail, he demanded to see Frank Clonch, claiming to have information about a murder. Hardy sprung me from Narcotics to interview him. My mother had been raped as a young woman, my roommate in college, too. Rape was a thing I grew up fearing and hating. It is a crime that often goes unpunished. It's sometimes hard to prove, but Bogges had been caught red-handed. Two bystanders ran to the rescue in time to see her kick him in the face. He appeared to be destined for prison, lined up to carry weight for all the promising young men who had made "an error in judgment" and gotten their wrists slapped.

If you're white and live in Oregon and work nights and drink until the wee hours and you've been in the tank for two weeks, you can become extremely pale. Bags did not look pretty. The victim must have connected dead-on. His eye and the side of his face were still discolored. His eyelid may have suffered permanent damage and hung at half-mast.

A public defender sat by his side. He opened with, "I want a deal."

"I'm not authorized to give you a deal," I said, "but I can run it past the D.A. I'll tell you this—the murder of Raina Hennessey has a higher profile now. If you can get us a conviction, I'm sure he'll be grateful."

154

"Not good enough," said Bags. "I want guarantees."

I rose and gathered my things.

"That's it?" he said. "No way." He turned to his attorney, "I want someone from the D.A.'s office."

"I tried," said the P.D., a strong, attractive brunette with blue eyes that made we want to look into them. "We got her. Maybe if you told her the nature of your information."

Bags bit his lower lip and nodded; I sat, knowing what he would say. I'd read the entire case file many times—the initial interviews by Clonch and French, as well as the murder investigation interviews. Hardy based Yvonne's arrest on statements by a few members of the staff, Bags most insistent among them.

"I know who committed the murder," he said triumphantly. "I know who did it."

"How do you know?"

"Raina and I talked all the time. She was my best friend. People think because we drink, we're stupid or something. *They think we're big water-heads,* she used to say. *A couple of lushes.* But we weren't stupid. Yvonne is a psycho. Half the people at The Door will tell you that. The other half she completely fooled."

I must have looked doubtful.

"You know she did it. You even arrested her. She hated Raina 'cause of Paul. Everybody knows. They fought. She threatened Raina. I thought Yvonne would kill her right there." He had nothing I could use. I put down my pencil, opened my briefcase. His mouth stood agape, incredulous, offended. "I mean, come on, you bust me on this chicken shit charge, and you won't even go after a killer?"

He looked at his attorney, who shook her head, "No."

Bags said, "I want a suspended sentence. I'll say anything you want. I'll say I saw her do it—the poison."

I stay in pretty good shape, weights, kickboxing, a little running. I could have made it over the table before the old sot could've lifted an arm. I rose, set my face like my father's, and then ran the kind of mind game he liked to play. "I'll take this upstairs," I said, looking Bags in his one good eye, "but I don't think it's going to save your ass from those prison boys. They like a rape as well as anyone."

****

School brought changes. Paul attended classes Monday through Thursday, so he dropped his Tuesday shift at The Door and tried to cut expenses. At work, he ate two meals. When not working, he skipped lunch or ate simply—brown rice and vegetables, fruit, bread. Since Yvonne insisted on paying for their entertainment, he tried to be a cheap date. The homework began to pile up after the third week, and he no longer stayed with her on Sundays.

One night, he sat at home studying Spanish, preparing for tomorrow's test. He wanted to achieve fluency, feeling as though Spanish would be a gateway to a whole other hemisphere. He yawned and looked out the window at the silent late-night street, the small circle of light from his desk lamp feeble against the darkness. Someone knocked. He opened the door to hard, scowling Yvonne. "Aren't you going to invite me in?" she asked.

He remembered their arrangement about endings

and his promise. "I'm afraid I know why you're here." He opened the door, and she stepped into his arms and kissed him long and thoroughly.

She tasted of whiskey, whispered, "Thank you, *mon ami*, for all you've done for me, but I'm sorry, it's over."

The ritual comforted him. He asked why.

She looked away. "I've met a man, not as fine a man as you, but one I think I could live with. There has been no behind the back. I've kept the bargain. We've talked at work; sat once over coffee. He might be the one for me, and I want to try."

"And if he isn't?"

"Then I'll go my way, and you'll go yours. No off and on again. You're getting an education, building a life, and I want to build a life, too." They stood in silence, bodies in proximity about to spin apart. "You don't know how much you've changed me. How could you know who I was before we met? The person at the restaurant they all hated was me. The night I abused you, that was me. The end of that night, soft Yvonne, you created her, someone only you could see. It feels so much better to be me. You did that; you loved me." Her smile broadcasted warmth and gratitude. He could not muster anger. He wanted to say many things their arrangement wouldn't allow. He stifled a sob. She put two fingers against his lips. "No, *mon ami*."

"It hurts."

"Two hundred good days for five, ten, thirty bad ones? You got what you wanted—a relationship next to perfect. Can't that be enough?"

"Can't we just continue?" She leaned over his Spanish book, turned some of pages.

"This is going to take you places, *cheri*, maybe all over the world. You want the cage of Yvonne because she's a great fuck and loves you till her heart breaks. But you know me, I'm not going anywhere. I want things simple and quiet."

"You'll only say *I love you* as you're walking out the door?"

Her smile fled. "Paul, I hate scenes. We agreed it would end like this. Those words hold a promise it would be wrong for me to keep. But I promise I will always care about you, always treasure what we had."

"But we might have made it."

"No, we're too different in where we come from and what we need next. I'm trying to move forward, be a real adult, whatever that means. I'm almost thirty and don't even know."

"I want to meet him."

"If you and I become friends. If you were not losing your woman, you would be proud to know him. He's a civil rights lawyer who donates time for people who have been oppressed. He is not dashing like my fiery grillman, but he's steady and calm."

"So this is goodbye forever?" He despised the plaintive note in his voice.

Her stern voice projected impatience. "Don't be dramatic. I'm hoping we'll be friends."

"I'd rather be your lover."

She softened. She examined the books on the table, opened his notebook at random, read a little then closed it abruptly. "We were more than lovers. We were best friends. Can we still be? You said you had no family, and you wanted to make lasting relationships. Well, you're my family, all I've got. When you graduate, I want to be there. And when you get married, I want to be there, too. You can call me your old Aunt Yvonne."

"Fucking hell, Yvonne," he said. A dull, dark ache in his chest grew into anger. He wanted to hurt her back. "I can't see you. I couldn't stand to know you were with another man." His words stung, and he regretted them. She would see him as petulant and childish.

She stepped toward the door but stopped, reluctant to leave things as they were. "What about this? In a month, when you don't hurt so much, I'll write you. If you want, you can write me back. If you don't and you ignore me, I'll write again and keep writing as long as I have your address. What I am now, you created. I was stuck when I met you. I probably would have ended up like my mother or Raina or Djuna or something worse. And if you decide you don't want to hear from me, just write return to sender on the envelope, and I'll get the message. But please don't do that, Paul." Then she turned, closing the door gently behind her.

****

He carried a great darkness he remembered from before Yvonne, from nights when he secretly lived in an attic storeroom in the Los Angeles restaurant, nights as a trainer in a cheap motel outside Scottsdale, nights wondering what Raina was doing and if she would come home, from the night after telling Johnny he would not pursue Djuna. As days grew shorter and the rains began, the darkness grew outside as well. Not used to such overcast and cold, he threw himself into schoolwork, completing every assignment and all the recommended reading. When school resisted him, he worked with weights, practiced martial arts, listened to

NPR. He wrote many pages, yet they were all the same: he had found his true love and lost her.

He tried to end each day too exhausted to think. Walking to school or riding the bus, he would drift into memories of Yvonne or fabricate situations where she would return. During busy times at work, he could, for a while, forget about her, but in slack moments, Yvonne haunted The Open Door, her face under red heat lamps, her body leaning against the bar, her long dark hair swinging as she turned from a table.

A memory of one late night stuck in his head. He had been cleaning and took a break to look for her, finding her at the well. She took an orange slice from the garnish tray, bit into it, closed her eyes for a moment, and threw the rind in the trash. She looked tired. She caught him watching, took another slice, bit it, and turned, flashing him an orange smile and wiggling her eyes.

He picked up shifts to make October's rent. He considered moving but couldn't stand another loss. A donut and coffee at the student union before class would last him until work, where he gorged on soup, salad, and bread. He kept the heat in his apartment low and wore layers of clothes. He tried to disconnect the phone, but they offered a reduced rate for those who could not pay, so he kept it.

One evening, he found himself in line at Thriftway behind Constance Novak. She quizzed him about school, they chatted while his groceries were bagged, and as they walked out together, Paul noticed her limping. She was a nurse. He imagined working all day with pained feet.

"Let me carry your bags," he said.

"Don't you live right here?"

"Yes, but I'd like the company. And I want to thank you for Mr. Novak's help." He walked her home and helped make dinner, talking all the while. In a torrent of words, he told her about Yvonne. Halfway through dinner, he realized he had dominated the conversation and apologized. "I've been going on and on. What a bore. How's June?"

"We've checked her into drug rehabilitation."

This seemed both bad and good. "That's terrible, but at least she's getting help. Can I see her?"

"Even April and I aren't encouraged to go. You could write."

At the door, as he was leaving, Constance Novak took his arm in a firm grip. "Paul, you were a friend to June, and what you said to Johnny, well, you should've punched him, too. So let me say, I've never had much use for Yvonne. She's too hard, too decadent."

Paul considered objecting but remembered Yvonne shushing him with a finger on his lips.

"I understand how an exotic woman could fascinate a young man, but when you're older, you'll understand women like that are nothing but trouble. Someday your perfect woman will come along, your own age, in the same stage of life."

"You don't get it, but even she didn't. I would never have wanted anyone else."

Yet walking home, he knew his inner darkness would lift one day. Yvonne had been many things to him: lover, best friend, teacher, coworker, other mother. He would have to replace her in many ways.

Chapter 12
Paul's Wild Ride

Hardy called me to his office. When I arrived, he said, "Shut the door." He looked intent, wired up, his squinting gray eyes checking me out tits to toes, not once but twice. His thumb and forefinger twitched to tap the eraser of a new yellow pencil on his desk. "We got another prodding from the FBI. Our poison showed up in Central America, a political assassination. I want everything on Hennessey."

"We found no poison anywhere. We found traces of cocaine with L'Croix, Novak, and Urbino, and also with Fanny Mae Fontaine, where we also turned up a quarter pound of marijuana, divided for sale. I'm stalled."

"Stir the pot. See what comes up."

Hardy offering what I wanted raised suspicions. "How much time do you want me to put into this?" I asked.

"Whatever it takes to nail the bitch," said Hardy. "I'll authorize overtime."

It took me a second to process who he meant. "What makes you certain it's her?"

Hardy shook his head, frustrated, pencil beating a compulsive rhythm on his desk. "Let's go through it. Novak is a nice kid from a good family, gone a little wild since her dad died. Did the technical boys turn up anything at her place?"

I didn't need notes. "Cocaine, a diary, a new one, maybe fifteen entries, which started after the murder, seemed kind of wild, out of control, the handwriting bigger with each entry. The last few were rants about the bartender, Urbino. He did something, betrayed her."

Hardy waved a dismissive hand. "He's a piece of work. Did he admit knocking up Hennessey?"

"Pretty hard to deny after the paternity test. But he claims he didn't know, and his attorney won't let him say more. If he didn't know, he doesn't have a motive, but he's still a suspect in my book. Right behind Novak. So back to the diary. We found one, but the first entries seemed like she'd always kept a diary. We didn't find any, and she denied having them."

Hardy fidgeted in his chair, again tapping his pencil on the desk. "So?"

"This diary starts about a week after the murder and never mentions Hennessey or her death. It doesn't mention our last interview even though it falls within the dates." The pencil kept beating its frenetic rhythm. "Look at it. I'll send it over."

The pencil stopped, eraser suspended in mid-air. "And the whore?"

Contrary in the face of repressive authority, I exaggerated. "I've got nothing on her, no motive, no evidence but gossip."

He looked at me like I was too stupid to understand how dumb I was. He may have read my discouragement for he sighed, changed his tone. "Hailey, sometimes in this business you've got to go with your gut. She's a killer. These others are fucked up people, true enough. But killers? I don't think so. It's a line few will cross.

But she did at least once and probably more."

"But there's no evidence. The stuff in New Orleans is rumor except for the trial which ended a verdict of in self-defense."

"Dig a little deeper there. Besides, it will play for a jury. I've got a waiter who will testify he saw her slip something into her coffee cup." Bags had gone around me. "And others who considered her unstable, dangerous. I've got witnesses to verbal threats on multiple occasions."

"Bogges? He's worthless on the stand. He makes my skin crawl. I talked to Owen Fredricks, who says they've got an airtight rape case on him. Besides, I dug up something else: attempted rape, three years ago, charges dropped by the victim. How's that gonna play for a jury?"

Hardy sat thinking, staring down at his legal pad. "With L'Croix, I've got threat, motive, opportunity, history. Let's stir the pot. I'll take a crack at the cook. Since he won't testify against her, the information we get doesn't have to be courtroom clean."

"What are you thinking?"

"Old fashioned police work." He smiled then turned his gaze back to the file on his desk and his pencil back to its reflexive tapping. I walked away. My father believed nerves were a sign of weakness. He would have steamrolled Hardy.

****

One slow night, Mitchell let Paul off at eight-thirty, and Hilton finished alone. Paul needed money desperately and considered quitting school and taking a second job. He sat in The Corner, head down, waiting for his bus. Jazmin sat beside him, "Can I buy you a drink?"

He wanted to say yes. "No, my bus is coming. Did you make any money?"

She shrugged. "Not much, but even this is better than lunch." She studied him. "You seem kind of down."

"I've got papers due, midterms. The other day, a waiter said, *Life is hard, then you die.* He was joking, but it felt true. With Yvonne, things were different."

Jazmin considered this. "Come home with me. The kid is at a sleepover."

Paul struggled for words. "Jazmin, I can't even afford to buy you a drink."

"Oh, don't worry about paying, not tonight," she said lightly.

The dirty, tattered carpet in the hall of her ramshackle building led him to expect squalor, but her apartment was brightly painted and clean. Her furniture matched. Knickknacks decorated her shelves, and the walls held art and pictures of her son in frames. She dropped her purse on the floor, keys on the counter, took off her coat, and flipped through the mail.

He had never noticed the extent of her beauty. Jazmin's eyes were green, wide apart, something about them gentle and sad. She stood almost as tall as he, skin a couple of shades darker, her curves more generous than Yvonne's slim frame.

"Jazmin, I don't understand why I'm here." She had never flirted or shown more than passing interest in him.

"Because you ran to save me. Because you stood up to Carl that night he harassed me. Because you and Hilton move my orders up the line. Because of those beautiful cuts of fish you give my tables."

"I didn't think you knew."

"That's another reason. Everybody knows. They gossip and are pissed but never once have you tried to…make something of it." She stepped toward him, kissed his cheek. He tried to kiss her lips but she leaned away. "Paul, this is just for tonight, okay?" She must have sensed his confusion and added, "Maybe we can become friends."

She took his hand and led him to a bedroom lit only by a pale night light in the hall. Her fingers brushed his cheek so lightly it made him tremble.

"I'm not sure what this is, what I should do," he said.

In the darkness, she brushed the hair from his forehead, and replied, "Just let me." Her voice and her touch were softer than Yvonne's, as though she were soothing a high-strung beast ready to bolt at the slightest provocation. Stroking his face, running her fingers through his long brown hair, she whispered in his ear. "You are a beautiful man, inside and out. Your body, your face. Your heart is beautiful, your spirit. Never forget that." Her fingers traced his lips giving him chills but there were no kisses. He didn't understand her tenderness, her soft way with him, her distance. As if she cared and she didn't. He wanted to ask, but she was giving him what he craved during his long nights alone.

Slowly, as she praised and caressed him, she took off his clothes then lay him down on the bed. He wanted to feel her body instead of her Open Door uniform. He wanted her lips to find his, to hold her close but instead she put her head on his stomach. "Just let me," she said again before her lips found his sex with gentle kisses and touches of her tongue. He surrendered to slow delight. A beautiful eternity passed before she took him in her mouth, another before she led him to a climax. He called out in ecstasy as she stripped him of disappointment and lifted hopelessness from the deepest places inside him. She purged him of exhaustion and fear, all of which flew from him in moans and writhing shudders. He released confusion and desperation. She emptied him completely, and he fell into sleep, and then awoke to boiling blood, her head still on his stomach. Again, she carried him though doors and chambers of pleasure and release.

When her mouth left him, he called her softly, "Jazmin?"

"Yes?"

"Why?"

She slid next to him on the pillow, kissed his forehead. "You know why. Yvonne. You even said her name. She asked me to keep an eye on you. If you looked stuck, like you needed to let go, she wanted me to…"

His mouth twisted into a frown.

"No, Paul. Not bitter. You know what she told me? It was love at first sight. The first time she met you, when she saw your hands, how they were burned and scarred, they looked how she imagined her heart would look. Your eyes were as sad as she felt. She loved you completely."

"She never told me. She would never say the words except when she left!" He wept in great heaving sobs,

"She wouldn't let herself say them, but she told you every day. She lived her life telling you."

He howled, "Then why did she leave?"

****

He cried hard and long. She said nothing but held him as gently as she wanted to be held. When he calmed, she whispered, "All her life, Yvonne wanted a home, a place she could feel safe and settle."

"But I would have settled with her."

"Paul, you have no furniture, no pictures, not even a table big enough to have her over for dinner." He moaned. "It's not your fault. You haven't found your place. Go out in the world, be a Marine or a scholar, wander, explore, accomplish something. That's what she wants. She's afraid one day you'd regret staying with her in some little apartment in this sleepy town."

Again, he cried. Jazmin envied his tears and wondered how long she would cry if she ever let herself start. Better to keep emotion tight inside, a solid bottom to push from when you were drowning.

****

One night after work, a white car with heavily tinted windows and too many antennas waited by the loading dock door. Rain pounded the pavement, drops shattering in great splashes. It was a long way to the uncovered bus stop. The car window slid down, and Detective Hardy said, "Get in, I'll give you a ride."

"My bus is coming."

Hardy said, "I want to have a friendly conversation, but doesn't have to be that way." Paul walked a few paces in silence. "Your time to choose is just about over." Paul walked on.

The car stopped abruptly. Hardy sprang out, twisted Paul's arm behind his back, shoved him against the car. Paul imagined how he would have used

Hardy's momentum and where he would have thrown him but let himself be cuffed. Hardy smashed Paul's head against the car as he stuffed him in the back seat.

Behind the wheel, Hardy hit the gas, fishtailing the turn onto Macadam, which slammed unseatbelted Paul against the opposite door. Hardy gunned it on the long straight, dodging traffic, running a red light, screeching around the corner onto Taylor's Ferry Road, which tossed Paul again, then accelerated into the hills.

Hardy spoke in a peculiar way, stopping for a long pause after every sentence. "We solved ninety-two percent of the murders last year." He switched lanes, passed a car on the shoulder, losing traction for an instant in the mud, then spoke again. "Those are just the convictions." The wipers worked furiously, yet the windshield remained a blur of water and lights in the heavy rain. He slammed on the breaks for a red light, driving Paul against the metal screen separating them, then squealed tires onto Terwilliger, knocking Paul back. He crossed the yellow line to pass, weaving in and out of traffic, hurling Paul with each turn. "We have a great team, years of experience. No such thing as the perfect crime, unless it's done by professionals. People always make mistakes."

Hardy drove fast as possible, with reckless disregard for both law and safety, tailgating, seizing every opening to fly down dark two-lane country roads. "So we're going to solve this case, convict the murderer, and damn it, Paul, if you know anything about this, you're going to jail, accessory to murder. Count on it. Once we get a break, things happen fast."

Hardy ran a red light, then a stop sign, just missing a speeding pickup, hurtling through the dark down a narrow road past mailboxes, driveways, a brightly lit country store. He hit a puddle at seventy, sending great arcs of water flying. The speedometer climbed to eight-five; Paul twisted to grip the armrest. "It's stupid to carry weight for someone else's crime. Most people cut a deal, immunity for testimony."

Paul remained silent like Yvonne, following Damien Novak's advice.

Hardy raced along through the rural darkness, crossing the line to pass or using the shoulder, tailgating, maneuvering with great jolts that flung Paul about. "The last time we talked to your girlfriend, she brought the most expensive attorney in town. Has she offered you his services?"

Hardy found an empty road, and the car leaped forward, careening around corners. "You'll need an attorney 'cause once things break, events happen fast." The speedometer rose to one-ten, inched toward one-twenty. Paul braced himself, feet pressed against the floor. "She has Wallace, Novak has her cousin, Urbino has some mob guy from the east coast. Everyone has an attorney. They're expensive, but a hotshot cook like you can probably afford the best." Hardy braked, tires squealed, the car fishtailed wildly and slid sideways, coming to rest on the shoulder in a spray of mud. The abrupt stop smashed Paul's face into the door on the opposite side.

"That's how fast things can turn around for you. What's it going to be? You want to come clean, come downtown for a little conversation?"

Paul struggled to get upright onto the seat, his nose bloodied.

"You're not helping me, Paul. Why did she do it?"

"I don't know." Paul hated the frantic, frightened note in his own voice.

Hardy stomped on the accelerator, wheels spinning to gain traction in the muddy shoulder. "You're lying."

Paul got mad. "Fuck you, Hardy. I'm not a liar, and I'm not talking. As far as I know, she didn't do it."

Hardy slowed. They were silent all the way back to town. To Paul's surprise, Hardy got off the freeway in Northwest Portland and dropped him at his building, saying as he uncuffed him, "Next time will be at the station."

****

For two days since coming home, Djuna occupied the sofa under a faded pink and white quilt an aunt had given her as a little girl. She spoke little, picked at her food, slept, or stared at the television. Nothing Constance did or said affected her much until she mentioned Paul. "I had a nice chat with Paul last week. He's been feeling down since Yvonne left."

"Why did she leave? She was crazy about him."

"He dropped off some things for you." Constance handed Djuna a large manila envelope paper clipped with a typed note card which read, "Help Wanted: Psychiatric Assistant, good pay, flexible hours. Must have excellent people and writing skills, positive outlook. Primary duties involve interviewing children in custody cases."

It pleased her to see her daughter's face come alive.

On the bottom of the envelope, he had scrawled. "I stole this from the job board so no one else would get it." The envelope held four papers, all "A's."

Constance presented another envelope, which held

an application for the Ph.D. program in Psychology. "He'll be home today. Why don't you go see him?"

Djuna showered and dressed. She got into his building without ringing the buzzer by following a guy with groceries and catching the door.

Paul's face lit up at the sight of her. "Djuna," he said softly. She fell into his arms. They stood in the doorway, holding each other. When he let her go, she squeezed him tighter until finally, he broke away. "Let me look at you."

Her arms were little more than bones. Her face and every gesture broadcast tentativeness, fragility. In her gray eyes he imagined a crystal vase hanging over the edge of a high shelf, poised to fall and shatter.

"Hold me, Paul. It's the first thing that's felt good in a long time." He did, gently. "Take me to bed," she whispered.

"Sit and talk to me. Tell me what you've gone through."

"I don't want to talk about my rehab, not ever. Take me to bed."

Savagely horny, Paul had been dreaming about sex. One day he embarrassed himself eyeing a woman getting onto the bus who glared at him and said, "Keep your eyes to yourself, fuckhead."

If Djuna had spoken with life in her voice or smiled, if her eyes hadn't held the fragile, teetering vase, he wouldn't have hesitated. "Is that what you want?" he asked.

She nodded.

"What about what I want?"

"What do you want?" she asked.

"The secret waits for the insight of eyes unclouded

172

by longing; those who are bound by desire see only the outward container." She looked puzzled. "The Tao. Teach me. Those notes you made, they're not enough."

"Paul, I don't know anything right now."

"That's the deal. Teach me, and I'll take you to bed."

"You sound like Yvonne with her fucking arrangements." He smiled. The Murphy bed was down, unmade behind him. She nudged him toward it. "This first," she said.

"No. After you teach me, we can get a couple of bags of groceries and stay in bed 'til they're gone."

"I need to sit down." He walked her to his one chair. When she sat, he grabbed her book from the shelf, set it before her.

"Why not desire? What about love?"

"Paul, I can't do this. My head is a desert, incapable of supporting thought."

"Djuna, you've got to help me. I'm desperate."

She gave him a dull counterfeit of her old smile. "I'm not Djuna. It's hard enough just to be June. This is about Yvonne?"

He nodded. "I love her, hate her and think about her at night so I can't sleep. It's making me crazy. Please, June, people have a summer romance and get over it."

"I got you into this," she said, opening the book. "Desire clouds your perception and makes you see the surface but not the depth. Look, this isn't working."

"Please don't stop."

She took a breath, started in. "You project all this stuff on her. You imagine her, tell stories about her. You create a fiction of Yvonne that obsesses you. She has become a product of your imagination."

"Perfect," he said. He knelt beside her, peppering her with questions through verse nine when she wilted visibly. "To take all you want is never as good as to stop when you should."

"Paul, I need to lie down." She fell onto his bed. He wrapped her in a blanket and lay next to her until she slept.

They met twice to discuss the book. By then, June looked better. Her color had returned, and though the vase in her eyes still perched on a narrow shelf, it no longer hung over the edge. Paul said, "You've done your part." He looked over at the bed.

"I may be all fucked up, but I'm not stupid. Not once have you shown the slightest interest in me, and frankly, I'm not interested in you. It's time for me to grow up. Thanks for helping me, though."

"You helped me, too, but I can't get over her. Have you spoken to her?"

"Yesterday."

Paul summoned the courage to ask, "Is she happy?"

Djuna's voice softened. "I think so. She just got a new sports car, and they're going to New York. She's excited." June winced, regretting her words. She laid a hand on his shoulder. "Let me tell you something not in the book. The darkness isn't real. Only the light is real; you're supposed to come back to the light. The sooner you let Yvonne go, the sooner she'll come back."

He considered this. "Sounds like bullshit. She's not coming back."

"Then let her go."

****

On a cold, gray day, on his way to work, Paul watched raindrops bead on the window of the bus, trying to remember lyrics to songs where rain stood for tears. The night before, he stayed up late working on a paper and studying. Classes all day, work until ten. He got off the bus anticipating another slow, rainy night, off early, few hours on the time card. At least he could go home and sleep.

He usually entered by the loading dock, preferring to walk first into the action of the kitchen. He loved the noise and whirl of motion, the laughter, the stew of Spanish and English seasoned with French cooking terms, the rhythmic beat of knife on board, clashing pans, rich scents of stock and caramelizing onion, a place of warmth and light.

Chains sealed the loading dock door. Mitchell had finally realized the amount of stuff disappearing out the back. Rumors circulated about a waiter who had compiled a complete four top in his dining room: table, chairs, linen, and settings.

Paul walked around to the front and noticed only two cars in the lot. One had been there for days. The polished brass handles of the front door were also wrapped in chains; The Door was closed. He traveled home in a daze and looked at his checkbook. "I'm completely screwed," he said.

He typed a résumé, grateful to Djuna for the time they worked through hers. He would do double shifts of job hunting—some restaurants before lunch, some after. With luck, he would only miss a couple of days of work, but fortune deserted him. It was winter when business slowed. A week of trying got him nowhere. One day after class, he stopped by the Student Union for coffee. A scalloped-edged paper placemat scrawled in blue felt pen said they needed a cook. The job paid a dollar over minimum wage, five hours a day, five days a week: burgers, fries, and cheese sandwiches. The smoking griddle man.

Chapter 13
This Ain't Torquemada

Hardy said to stir the pot on Hennessey, so I visited the Portland State Student Union to question Paul. He worked alone, cooking, serving customers. Wasted talent except he was paying his way through college; he had loved with a young man's great passion a woman who loved him back; people respected him. Those things mattered to me. He turned from the sizzling griddle and saw me, "What?" he complained, arms extended.

"I know you're about to get off, and I want to buy you a meal," I said, pointing toward the menu above his head, white plastic letters pressed into a ridged board.

"I'm not going anywhere with you, and if you try to take me out of here, I'm fighting. You people are fuckin' psycho." He turned back to work.

"Paul, "I said, using his name like we were friends, "what are you talking about?"

"As if you don't know."

"I don't. What happened?" When he told me, I couldn't speak for the anger boiling inside. I believe, in an ideal world, honest people should have great regard for police. My older brother served in the Los Angeles Police Department whose motto is "Protect and Serve" and that's the way people should think about police.

I said, "That's so fucked up." His eyes met mine

when I said, "All I want is to sit and talk."

He returned to his work, put up a hamburger and fries. "I'm not talking about Yvonne."

"I'm not after Yvonne."

He rolled his eyes to say, *yeah, right.* "Who are you after?"

"I'm after clarification, background, your opinion. When you said she didn't do it, I believed you. You loved her, didn't want to leave. Why would she commit murder? So sit with me, let me buy you a meal." I gestured toward a quiet corner.

"Here?" he asked. "Can we do better?"

"Well, I'm just a cop, but where do you want to go?"

"Rose's." The best deli in town: dark paneling, Formica and brown vinyl, a display case stuffed with tremendously portioned desserts. It was also near his apartment on a day soaked by wind-driven rain. We took a booth. He looked thinner, cheeks sunken, clothes hanging loose, with ragged sideburns, Levi's faded almost to white, the cuffs of his gray sweatshirt frayed. His light brown hair was tied back in its usual short ponytail.

I looked for an opener. "I like the jazz tag."

"I'm gonna shave it," he said, dismissive as young men can be. I wondered what she saw in him. He was handsome and fit, but so were many men. I wondered what the fuss was about except his eyes: light brown, soft and warm, sad, with a fire, perhaps of intellectual curiosity, certainly of passion, eyes you liked looking into. He didn't seem to mind. He ordered a bowl of matzo ball soup, a French dip with fries, a glass of milk, chocolate cake. The soup arrived first.

"You've been involved with quite a few women during your short stay in Portland." We engaged in a slow conversation with him eating and me wondering if a woman had committed murder for the love of this sweet-eyed, scruffy, young man.

"You think?" he said, he spooning soup greedily, polishing off half a glass of milk at a swallow.

"You've been here seven months. Raina, June, Yvonne. All older women. What's that about?"

"What does this have to do with the case?" The spoon clattered in his empty bowl. A young man eating with unconscious abandon filled me with warm nostalgia. My brother and his pack of boys were always raiding our refrigerator.

"Well, one is dead; the others are suspects. I'm just trying to get a handle on motives here, relationships. You like older women."

He turned to check the kitchen window for his sandwich. "I guess. Yvonne says I got issues and make shitty choices, but I didn't do it on purpose. Raina, I just rented a room, but stuff happened. Djuna, we were together a couple of times outside of work and talk about issues."

"What happened between you two?"

"She liked Johnny better." I had pegged him in the interview, could read his tells. I judged this a half-truth. When his sandwich arrived, he dove into it.

"And Yvonne? How did that end?"

He spoke with his mouth full. "You know we broke up?"

"She broke up with you. Paul, you're in the middle of a murder investigation. It's my business to know."

"I don't want to talk about it." He was aching to.

"I can imagine. You really loved her."

"What we had—I didn't give a fuck about her age. Maybe if one thing had gone right in her life, she would have stayed, would've mustered a little faith."

"Edward Wallace is a wealthy man. That turned out right."

"You cops are nuts. She didn't care about that. We were everything to each other. You know what attracted me to Yvonne?" I shook my head. "Right away, I trusted her."

This seemed a grave error in judgment. "She lied about her past."

He shook his head. "She didn't lie. She said it was bad, and she didn't want to talk about it. I don't think she lied to me but once. She told me she had no siblings, but 'cause she'd never lied to me, I knew. Her eyes wouldn't meet mine. She admitted she has a sister in jail."

I wanted to say apples don't fall far from the tree. I did check out the sister, five to ten, Louisiana Correctional Institute for Women for beating a college kid with a bat over a drug debt. Her record stretched over several pages. I called her to explore a deal. She said, "You wanna fuck with Sissy, that's your business—you police. I got four years served, good behavior, and a job when I get out. I'll pass."

Paul added, "What about you? Ever have someone you trusted completely?"

My mom, but it didn't seem detective-like to mention one's mother. "No."

"Single?"

I shook my head. "Not relevant." He winked a gotcha, and I understood what he meant and smiled involuntarily. Shorthand, intuitive conversation doesn't come easily to me. I'm not good when people get close.

My turn to lie. "My job right now is all-consuming."

"Excuse me," he said to the waitress as she passed, "can I order another sandwich? And a milk." He turned to me. "Yvonne met you once in the Park Blocks. She thought you were hot."

My face flushed. How the hell can you be a detective when you blush?

Paul nodded with a knowing smile. "She was right about you."

"About what?"

"You're strong, and you're a sweetheart."

"What's your point here?"

"Yvonne and I have a lot of integrity; you can trust us with anything."

I wondered if this was a threat or a promise. Even rumors about my orientation would make me vulnerable. "I'm sure I can," I said. Which I actually believed. I sensed depth of character.

"And I'm telling you she's innocent. She swore she didn't do it." He studied me just like she did in the park. "And I can trust you. You were pissed when I told you about Hardy, then disappointed, like he had violated some trust. Then you felt bad for me, and then," he broke into a proud grin, "you started plotting."

"You read me perfectly."

"Yvonne taught me how to assess people, their stance, their eyes, their faces. How to know who to trust. How to know when someone likes me." Was he talking about me?

"That sort of talent would give her tremendous

power," I said.

He considered this. He always considered what I said. "I'll bet you have that power, too."

When his second sandwich arrived, he ate more slowly. I liked him. I sized him up as genuine and thoughtful. He loved and was loyal to his woman. I'd be proud to introduce him as my friend.

When his cake arrived, he acted surprised and said to the waitress, "No way I can finish this by myself. How about a fork for my friend?"

"You could polish that off in about thirty seconds."

"Oh, yeah," he said with a big grin, but eased the plate to the middle of the table where it stood, glorious, between us. "You know, detective, you're kind of uptight. You've been watching me eat, and now, you're eyeing the cake. You know you want some. Those hawk eyes of yours tracked it across the room." He laughed. My fork arrived. My mother used to say, *To bait a trap for Hailey, use chocolate.*

"Are you afraid if we share cake, we'll be friends?" He verbalized my unconscious thought. "We could be. I could be the interesting one, and you could be the silent partner, the one with money." He laughed again, a completely happy laugh. "Come on, tell me about yourself. Tell me your last lover. You know about mine."

I said. "Can I get out of this by telling you who I think did it?"

"If you eat cake."

It was fantastic, rich, moist, bittersweet. I said, "If it wasn't Yvonne, it has to be June Novak."

Paul was quick to ask, "Why?"

"She had opportunity and motive. She knew Fanny

Mae better than Johnny. Maybe she found out Raina carried Johnny's baby."

He got defensive, raised his voice. "Why just us? What about the rest of the world? Raina had roommates, lovers, friends, a past. What about those construction guys? Maybe it was just bad drugs."

"Bad drugs would have shown up somewhere else. Besides, her speed was prescription from a quack. I checked the hospitals and tracked down the construction crew from a credit card. They're tough customers. We picked up one on an outstanding warrant, but poison doesn't seem like their style, and we couldn't connect them to Fanny Mae."

Paul demanded, "Who told you about Fanny Mae?"

"I have to pass, Paul. I take care of people who talk to me."

"Then think about this, whoever told you about Fannie Mae was trying to finger Yvonne. If she's innocent, they must be guilty."

I had considered that. "Or maybe they just wanted to help catch a murderer, a legitimate motive."

"Still, they have to be a suspect, and it must have been either June or Johnny because no one else knew her." He studied me, shook his head when I gave him nothing, took a bite of cake, drank milk, savored them together. "Why does it have to be Fanny Mae?"

" 'Cause we've got nothing else."

"Sounds like you have no evidence at all."

Not exactly right, but painfully close. With so much background, we needed one break, one domino to fall. I switched to offense. "Does June keep a diary?"

"I don't know."

I tacked. "What do you know about Evan Piner? Might help Yvonne."

"How?" he wanted to know.

"It might finger someone else."

"Who?"

"Can't say."

He accepted this. "Like I said, never heard of him. Who told you about him?"

"Raina's brother, the sober one."

He fingered his jazz tag. "Did he say anything else? That's not much to go on."

"He said you didn't do it. Are you going to help me?"

"I was always helping you. You made a mistake when you arrested Yvonne, and I was helping you overcome it." A smart-ass but one with a damned handsome, joyful, wicked grin.

I said, "You're so sure. I always doubt it when people are so sure."

"Me, too." He laughed. "I've said the exact same thing." He didn't want me to interrogate him and changed the subject. "You're in pretty good shape. You work out?"

I let him. Chocolate cake and sweet brown eyes had softened me. He didn't have an answer, but I figured he was motivated and smart enough to find out. "I run a little, work with weights, this new kickboxing thing. I used to ride dirt bikes but not here. I have a street bike I ride through the Columbia Gorge. I love speed, and cops don't really get tickets."

"And you do your own maintenance," he said, flashing his mischievous grin.

"How do you know?"

"When you interrogated me, you had grease under your nails."

"You should be a cop. Ever thought about it?"

"Not really. Why should I? Make your case." He listened, considered, asked questions, paid attention to me as no one at work did, engaging me with intelligence and courtesy, and so Hailey Matheson, the long-sealed can of worms, popped open.

When he asked, "Why did you become a cop?" I told him about my brother, a story I had never shared. On a routine traffic stop, he approached the wrong car, gangsters from South Central LA with drugs in the trunk. They shot him. I idolized my brother. I became a cop because if he couldn't be, I would for him. Every time I talk about Tommy, I feel this great darkness inside.

He sized me up, said, "You should let yourself cry."

I took a long moment to answer. His eyes were kind, sad for me. "I would fall apart completely. My father raised us to believe crying makes you weak and doesn't do any good. Did you cry when Yvonne left?"

"Not at first. But when I did, a friend held me, and I cried and cried. It helped."

The cop in me wanted to ask, "What friend?" Instead, I said, "I don't have a friend like that."

He picked black cake crumbs off the white plate with a fingertip, ate them. I could see responses come to mind and be rejected. Finally, he said, "If you care about people, they'll know and care about you."

One large crumb of cake stood alone on the plate, gooey with frosting. I anticipated his reach for it, and my finger arrived right before his so we touched. A spark of connection jumped between us. I had never felt that from a man or from anyone. His smile said he felt it, too. I had spent my adult life avoiding emotional entanglements, so this made me uncomfortable on many levels. I awkwardly changed the subject. "Do you remember the first time you and Yvonne touched?"

My question gave him pause. His mood shifted from joyful to somber. "I do. On our first training, Djuna took me to meet her in the break room. We shook hands. Her fingers were cool, and I remembered what my mother used to say, *Cold hands, warm heart.* I looked into her eyes and thought, she and I are the same. What we want most in the world is to be loved." His eyes met mine, and I recognized the same hope and longing I often saw in the mirror.

Feeling uncomfortable, I grasped an easy straw and fumbled again. "And the second time?"

He bit a lip, calculating my motives. "We were in her car, Djuna, Yvonne and me. I was kissing Djuna. Yvonne put her hand on my leg."

"Then what happened?"

"You want to hear this?"

I nodded.

"She kissed me." When I nodded for more, he said, "And then...we got on the freeway. You owe me stories, Detective, big time."

"But they'll have to come another time." I signaled for the check, then lied, "I have to get back to work." Meeting Paul had unsettled me: professionally in his revelation about Hardy; nostalgically about my brother; in the flush of my cheeks and a certain tingling from down low all the way up my spine and in the questions this raised about issues I believed decided.

When our waitress delivered the check, he said, "Thanks for the meal. I feel like I should pay something, but I'm flat broke right now." He hung his head. He'd gorged himself because he was hungry. "My life is such a mess. What a loser."

I'm not sure why I put my fingers on his. "You know why you're not a suspect? 'Cause Yvonne and Djuna and Mitchell and Hilton and Johnny all said you were a great kid, a heart of gold, and even Randy Bogges and that fool of a kitchen manager said there's no way you would have done it. Yvonne defended you adamantly."

As we were leaving, we had to wait for a large party to pass. I was standing behind Paul. On impulse, I took a twenty from my money clip and slipped it into a pocket of his leather jacket. It's what she would have wanted me to do, my guitar player at the feet of *Rebecca at the Well*, playing flamenco and giving money to hobos. I drove him home. Raindrops beat a frantic rhythm on the top of the car. In front of his building, I handed him my card and said, "Paul, would you help me if you got something on June Novak?"

He replied, "I don't know. The Novaks have been like family to me. Yvonne taught me you always take care of your own. My dad taught that, too. He was a Marine." I didn't tell him that my father was also a Marine. "So June Novak, I just don't know."

I said, "You know why I'm here?"

He shook his head.

"Because you could be a key to this case. People know you and trust you and might talk to you or let something slip. Don't you want to find Raina's killer?"

"I do."

187

"Fair enough." I extended my hand, "Pleasure to meet you, Paul." He got the wrong idea. His face lit up. His handshake felt like a caress, his eyes warm. His strong hand lingered on mine. He thought we were going to kiss.

I took back my hand. "Pleasure was mine," he said and added, "Warm hands, detective," flashing his devilish grin, slamming the door, and mounting the stairs to his building three at a time.

I sat for a few moments listening to rain pound the roof. I'd had a good day, confident my sort of policing was far superior to Hardy's. I was working on an intriguing case and had much to contemplate. I planned to sneak home early and savor it, but I stopped again at Rose's and bought a giant piece of that marvelous cake, to go.

When I got home, I changed into pajamas and slippers. I sat at my table, opened my box of cake. A heavy mist floated down on the tangle of gray and black bare branches arching over the Park Blocks. Eskimos supposedly have fifty words for snow; Portlanders should have at least that many for rain.

How many words does the English language have for attraction? I thought about Paul and couldn't find one to fit. As the light in my kitchen turned yellow against the dusk, I ate sugar and moist, dark chocolate. I had made a friend, kinda secret, kinda naughty, kicking the line of wrong. I once made a list of things I wanted to do in life and flirted with the idea of trying a man just to see. Had he not been tangled with my case, it might have been Paul. Our lips had been a foot apart, the feeling strong between us. He possessed the same magnetism that had attracted me to Yvonne. Did he too hesitate, a woman on each arm, before her lips touched his? Did she kiss him forcefully with strong desire or gently? Would that be the way to approach Paul, or was that what I wanted from her—dark lips sweet against mine?

****

Paul loved his Spanish class. He had grown up around the language, its rhythms and accents. He tried to think Spanish. He spoke some kitchen Spanish already, and while at The Door, enjoyed practicing with the Latino staff. They helped, laughing at his mistakes. He carried note cards with vocabulary in the pocket of his leather jacket. He was at his desk writing his next set of cards when someone knocked. He opened to Gary, the assistant apartment manager who lived across the hall. "You got a package. I signed for it. Hope you don't mind."

Paul examined a small package wrapped in brown paper, no return address but postmarked Aruba. Inside, he found a worn leather-bound journal with "Costa Rica" on the first page in a bold, flowing hand and bookmarked by a folded piece of stationery which matched the color of Yvonne's skin tone. It read:

Paul,

I'd erred in not meeting such an intriguing young man. Anyone who could awaken Yvonne's heart as you have must possess unique qualities, and when other sources tell a similar tale, I should have investigated. Insight and grace under pressure are very rare. I shall be interested to know what you make of yourself. Should you ever desire a more adventurous life, Yvonne knows how to contact me. I hope this token will allow me to someday make your acquaintance,

Dahlia

He glanced through the journal. The second page held Yvonne's old address. Scattered pages had been torn out. In 1975 and '76, Dahlia had traveled the width and breadth of the country, into Panama, Nicaragua, and El Salvador. Paul found sketched pictures of beach scenes, a waterfall in the forest, flowers, and shells resembling female genitalia. He found bars of melancholy music which he hummed. One page held a photograph of Yvonne, looking younger, defiant, with the caption, *Yvonne keeps her world small and will not let herself grow. Mine is the whole world.*

Other pages held detailed descriptions of mountain towns, coves by the sea, maps with crude topography. Two pages held calculations involving tens of millions of dollars. He read an account of being hunted in the jungle by helicopters and studied a sketch of Dahlia in someone else's hand. She sat half in, half out of a jeep on the driver's side, looking bold, confident, and rugged. Near the end, he found a sketch of a naked young woman and the story of her seduction and abandonment. Somehow this connected with Yvonne.

The journal upset Paul because he felt he would have to deal in some way with Dahlia, who intimidated him. He hid the book behind the sweaters in his closet.

Several days later, when he got home from work, he found a box outside his door, topped by Yvonne's gray fedora with a half-sized jack of hearts stuck in the hatband and a note, "In case you need a mojo." Under the hat lay an envelope, and under the envelope lay stuff he had left in her apartment, clothes, a beginning guitar book, The Rolling Stones' Songbook, an Italian cookbook. The envelope held a card—a buck on a ridge alone, silhouetted by the sunset. Inside he found a note in Yvonne's cramped, labored hand.

Dear Paul,

I heard about The Door. Probably Mitchell and I are the only people who know how hard you worked and how much the place meant to you.

I guess now you get to learn how to let things go. But two things at once like this must feel like a heavy burden. But I know you are strong enough to push through. If you weren't, I would not have loved (and continue to love) you so.

"Now?" he bellowed. "Why the fuck does she keep telling me now?" Frustration rose inside of him, and he ripped the card in half, snatched the envelope, stuffed the pieces inside, and scrawled the words, *Return to sender* when he realized it hadn't been mailed. His anger passed. He pieced the card together and read the rest.

I hope you've found a lover and are not alone. You're so damn handsome, you could find one whenever you're ready.

I am thinking of changing jobs, too. I have an interview tomorrow at Café Des Ami as a lunch waitress. Edward is embarrassed that I cocktail, so if I get the job, it will be a compromise. Wish me luck.

Last weekend we went to a party for Edward's work. I wore the wrong dress. The women all talked shit and pretty much ignored me. I guess this is where I learn to be an adult. Edward is good to me, so if you were worried, don't.

I hope this letter doesn't cause you pain. I think I did that enough already.

Love, your friend for life, Yvonne."

P.S. Please write back.

Paul put the letter away, not answering it. "I've barely looked at anyone because I'm still crazy in love with you" didn't seem like a winning line. Yet while reading her letter, some of the old connection vibrated in his chest. A few days later, he received a second letter, written on heavy cream-colored notepaper.

Dear Paul

Okay, I fucked up, really fucked up. I'm pregnant. It's a long story. Please write me back and tell me it's okay to talk to you or just call during the day. I'm freaked out, and Edward is working all the time. I can't be a mom. I'll be horrible. Please, please write (or call).

Yvonne

She left a new phone number and a new return address. She had moved in with Edward, crushing Paul's hope she would return. He sat down and dashed off a response beginning with, *I guess you fuck up a lot,* and ending with, *Have a nice life.* Addressed and stamped, he set it on his desk. He needed to review Trig and read *The Glass Bead Game*. He took these books from his backpack then reconsidered his letter. He wrote drafts until ten o'clock before finding his kindest truth.

Yvonne,

Remember when I used to call you my other mother? Well, you were a great mom to me. You explained your thinking and tried to teach what I needed to know. And when I deserved it, you kicked my ass. I only wish my real mom would have been as good. You will not make the mistakes of your mother. You will make other mistakes, sure, but who doesn't? I've never seen you do anything less than your best.

The man I want to be would tell you this until it sank in, but I can't. If I saw you, I would wish the baby were mine, and we were talking about names and where to put the crib. I would imagine kissing your belly and reading the baby poetry. This letter is the best I can do. I'm sorry it's so little.

You see, I'm not doing too well. I'm not used to all this rain. It's dark all the time. We don't even play basketball because it always rains on Sunday. I was broke even before the restaurant closed, and now I've got a shit job at the student union. I've got papers due and finals coming. This may be my last semester for a while. I wish I could help, Yvonne, but I'm having a hard time just taking care of myself.

I wish you and your baby and your man all the joy in the world. Maybe one day I can meet them and see the family you've created.

Paul

Money was indeed tight. He found a twenty-dollar bill in a pocket of his leather jacket and allowed himself to have an open-faced turkey sandwich with mashed potatoes and gravy at Quality Pie for Thanksgiving dinner. Hilton had invited him, but he'd shied away, feeling he would be poor company. Besides, with a chance to get straight A's, he wanted to do homework so at least something would turn out right. He intended to quit school. Paying bills had become his first priority. His final paper in sociology on income level and voting patterns in Oregon in the 1976 election was due on Monday. He faced a Monday deadline with a ream of statistics and a few scant pages of notes.

When he walked into his apartment Thanksgiving

night, he sensed something different. He wondered if he had been robbed. His clock radio flipped numbers on the window sill, his typewriter and his useless checkbook still sat on the table. He had nothing else to steal. He thought of Yvonne, and a wave of sadness flooded over him. He went into the kitchen for coffee so he could work through his last all-nighter and found her note on the refrigerator.

Paul,

I never should have sent that note. Just me fucking up yet again. I'm sorry, sorry for everything. I hope you will accept this as a little help from your other mother,

Yvonne

She had filled his fridge with food and stocked his pantry with boxes and cans. At first, he considered it miraculous someone had helped him, but then many people had: Mitchell, Hilton, Raina, Djuna, her mother, and of course, Yvonne. He thanked them, one by one, and got up to start his paper. Just before midnight, he got hungry for eggs. Underneath his cast iron pan, he found five hundred-dollar bills paper clipped to a note reading, *Shh.*

On December first, he crossed the hall to the assistant manager's to pay rent. His paycheck from the Student Union barely covered it. He would use Yvonne's money to rent a cheap room in a house. When Paul told Gary, the assistant manager, why he had come, Gary said, "Yvonne paid your rent through June with a check from Edward Wallace. It's not going to bounce, is it?"

Weeks later, Paul got a letter from Mitchell apologizing for the way The Door closed. He had also lost his job and now worked at a restaurant in Phoenix.

He offered Paul work and enclosed a two-page letter of recommendation detailing what Paul had done for The Open Door. On a separate sheet, Mitchell had written, *A week before Raina died, Yvonne threatened her in the break room, "If you touch Paul, I'll kill you." I told this to the police, but you ought to know.*

****

One sunny, frosty morning, Paul walked downtown, wandering no place special, imagining rainy winter with Yvonne. As he passed The Benson Hotel, Jazmin whistled and called, "Paul, hey, Paul." He turned; she took his arm as if he had offered it. She wore green heels and a long London Fog coat over a short green velvet dress. Behind her green eyes, an emptiness slowly filled as they spoke. He figured she had been working last night. As they walked, they made small talk until Paul said, "I know it's a strange thing to ask, but who do you think killed Raina? If I could figure out…" He shrugged.

"I don't know. All those weeks when we thought she drank herself to death made the murder seem unreal. Besides, I've got other things on my mind. I'm down to one job and have an eleven-year-old son who's starting to ask questions."

"Do you think Yvonne did it?"

"I don't want to think so. We talked about Raina once. Yvonne felt sorry for her. She was headed for trouble. But I know something I bet the police don't. Just before The Door went under, I heard two of the dishwashers talking in Spanish. One of them had been in Mexico when Raina died, but right before he left, he heard her and Johnny fighting about her pregnancy. Johnny wanted an abortion, but she wanted him to step up and be a dad."

"Who was the dishwasher?"

"Carlos." Jazmin walked for a while before she said, "I know something else about Johnny most people don't. He's mafia. At least his family is. He's got a huge trust fund coming."

"How do you know?"

She flashed him a pointed stare. Johnny had been a client, he guessed.

Paul walked her home. When they parted, she asked, "Are you doing okay?"

"A little better. You helped," he said. "I don't know if I ever thanked you. If I can repay the favor, give me a call."

****

After a week of clear skies and freezing cold, Paul, thinking about Costa Rica, got out Dahlia's journal and flipped pages, imagining waves on a white sand beach. An idea surfaced.

He crossed the hall, knocked on Gary's door. "Do you have a world map?"

"I have a globe."

Paul found Aruba, north of Venezuela, and recalled Detective Matheson's, *rare Caribbean poison*. It had come from Dahlia, not Fannie Mae, a slick sleight of hand, making the obvious wrong. He stood in the cold on the fire escape, staring at the city lights, and drinking whiskey from the remains of a pint he and Yvonne had shared at Cinema 21.

She had put poison from a hidden source in a coffee cup accessible to hundreds of people to commit a murder that wouldn't be detected for a month and had a stooge ready to swear she had no motive. "Fucking hell,

Yvonne," he said to the night, "you got me."

He rummaged through his drawer, finding Detective Matheson's card. He finished the whiskey and smoked until his throat was sore. He couldn't decide: rat or stooge?

****

One day after work, Paul walked home in a swirling mist. He planned to bathe and retire to bed with *Things Fall Apart*, a title which promised to speak to his experience.

In front of The Blue Moon, a black unmarked police car slid up beside him. Detective Matheson emerged from the passenger's side, an older gentleman from the other. He didn't like her expression, anger, disgust, frustration. "Paul Tomaso, you're under arrest for obstruction of justice." She cuffed him gently and whispered, "I am so sorry. Orders." She wouldn't look at him as she recited his rights.

Jailors took him to the drunk-tank, the door locking behind him with a heavy metallic click. The toilet gave off an overpowering stench. A man lay on the ground next to it, writhing and moaning. Two others sat next to each other talking. Paul sat on the ground in the corner farthest from the toilet. He wondered why they put him in the drunk-tank and hoped Damien Novak could get him out. Hardy must have found new evidence against Yvonne.

Hours later, a man shouted from down the hall, "You fuckin' mother fuckers. You fucked up fuckin' fuckers," or some variant, over and over. Three cops wrestled with a massive man, handcuffed and bleeding, blood running down his shaved head and down his face. He wore a green sweatshirt with the sleeves ripped out.

A swastika tattoo decorated his huge right arm. Paul recognized trouble, dubbed him Greeny. The police manhandled him into the cell. A billyclub descended, and Greeny fell to his knees. They took the cuffs off of him and slammed the door. After a moment, Greeny rose, grabbed the bars of the cell and began shouting again. "Fuckers, let me out of this fuckin' cell."

He turned to Paul. "What you staring at, you little fuck?" When Paul didn't answer, the man kicked him. "Answer, me fuck head." Paul rose, sliding up the wall. The man swung a huge roundhouse right.

Paul blocked, jabbed him hard in the solar plexus. The man bent slightly. Paul hit him under the chin with a straight punch that sat him on his ass.

He shook his head. "You little fucker. I'm gonna fuck you up." He rose, grabbed the bars, and again began yelling, rattling the cell door. Suddenly, he lunged at Paul.

Paul dodged, grabbed him by the shirt, and using the man's momentum, slammed his head into the wall. Paul positioned himself on the other side of the cell to watch his adversary.

"Better not sleep, fuck head," said Greeny, sitting on the ground, rubbing his head.

After a time, one of the other men rose to lean against the wall near Paul. He was short and thin, wearing a brown tweed jacket and corduroy pants, and smelled horrible. "You don't look drunk to me," he said.

"I'm not," answered Paul.

"Why are you here?"

"Obstruction of justice."

"A small badge of honor," said Tweedy.

"Why are you here?"

Tweedy closed his eyes and sighed. "Drinking problem. My wife stopped bailing me out." He turned bloodshot eyes to Paul. "They dumped a meth crazed guy like Baldy in here to soften you up, then they'll interrogate you in the morning when you're exhausted. But be careful of fighting. Did you see the guard with the billyclub? That's Big Felix. He's a sadist. He catches you fighting, he'll beat the shit out of you both."

Paul stayed awake, on his feet, leaning against the wall. Twice he fended off attacks by Greeny, escaping with only a knot in the middle of his forehead. Shortly after his adversary folded onto the ground in the personal hell of coming down, officers opened his cell and escorted Paul to a room without windows and handcuffed him to a chair. After a long while, Hardy walked in.

"I want my attorney," said Paul.

"There's no need. You can be out of here in an hour. You're not a suspect in this case. Answer my questions, and you can go, charges dropped."

"No attorney, no answers."

"You should cooperate. We're trying to bring a killer to justice. Is that wrong?"

Paul remained silent.

Hardy shook his head. "Last chance. Talk to me, Paul. Give me what I need, and I'll let you go."

"I want my attorney."

Hardy shook his head. "I wish I were more persuasive, but it's not my strong suit. Fortunately, I have colleagues who get better results."

As he left, Paul shouted, "I want to call Novak!"

Moments later, the door opened and Big Felix plodded in, grinning. He was shaped like a pear, huge girth and ass, smaller shoulders topped by a tiny head with greasy black hair standing on end; however, his arms were gigantic, fists twice the size of Paul's. His first blow hit Paul on the left side, just under the ribs, and Paul's world shrunk to black pain for a long moment before his senses returned. He opened his eyes to Big Felix's delighted smile.

Paul said, "I've been beat by a tougher man than you." He lost count at five blows. Felix never spoke, never lost his grin, and always waited until Paul had recovered before striking him again. Finally, when Paul returned from pain to awareness and opened his eyes, Big Felix had gone.

Hardy stood over him. "Give me what I need, and I'll let you go, your record clean."

"Attorney," he croaked.

"Another session then? Too bad. You'll talk eventually and to let yourself be abused this way; you could be damaged." A uniformed cop came in, spoke low to Hardy. "Fucking Novak," said Hardy. "Hustle him back to the tank."

Two officers dragged Paul to the drunk tank, each gripping him by an arm. Breathing hurt and being carried hurt worse, but his legs wouldn't function. They shoved him into his cell where he collapsed on the floor. A man was curled in the corner, snoring, and everyone else had gone. Time passed in dark pain until he heard voices and the knock of hard rubber heals on concrete. Hardy explained, "He gave one of the other inmates trouble, and Officer Felix had to restore order."

Novak helped Paul to his feet, said, "I'll get a

wheelchair."

Paul mumbled, "I can walk. Don't let the bastards grind you down."

Near the door, Matheson stood at a counter, writing in a file. She watched him pass; her eyes, brimming with emotion, met his trying to communicate something he could not catch. Paul rode home in Novak's car and wished the warm leather seats were his bed so he could spend hours not moving. "How'd you find me?"

"A woman called. Wouldn't leave her name. Said you were being roughed up."

"Did they take Yvonne, too?"

Novak said, "I don't believe they did."

Chapter 14
You Shook Me

At shift's end the day of Paul's beating, I paced in front of Frank Clonch's decrepit brown Rambler. After days of rain, the concrete parking structure dripped at the seams.

You have to like Frank; he simply said, "Get in."

He shut the car door gently as if the whole thing could fall apart with a jolt and asked, "Okay, Hailey, what did you do?"

I told him about Paul's beating and my call to his attorney.

"You're fucked," said Frank, "if Hardy ever finds out. Completely fucked."

"I'm going to give him time to calm down, then I'm going tell him."

"Not smart, Hailey."

"I'm fucked anyway—cold cases, paperwork, and late-night stakeouts. I'm not afraid of him. He's a bully, just like my father. If you show fear, it gets worse."

"Keep this to yourself."

"Look, if I'm going to do this First Woman Detective shit, I have to work in a way I can live with. Besides, if I don't tell him and he finds out, he's going to go nuts."

Staring ahead as if he were driving, hands on the wheel of his car going nowhere, Frank looked sad.

"You have to do it your way, as much as you can, as much as the world will let you." He rolled down the window, spat, and said, "I think I'm proud of you. If the kid doesn't sue, you found a hell of a solution. You didn't cause a stink, didn't get anyone in trouble. But if you tell Hardy, he'll kick your ass."

"Frank, I'm flying blind. If I were one of the boys, if this wasn't a gender thing, would I have to struggle to prove myself, do some infighting? 'Cause this son of bitch has been pushing me around, and now he does this on my case, and if I don't do something about it, he's going to push me right out the door."

"And if you tell him, he'll edge you out even faster. He's a good cop," said Clonch. "At least he was before the divorce. He's well liked by the bosses, and what he did, well, it used to be a regular thing. If you're planning on swinging that, it won't carry much weight."

"I figured."

"I'm telling you, lie low," he urged.

"It's my case—it's like he shit on my doorstep. It's like he shit on the job. And that poor kid."

Frank bit his lower lip, closed his eyes, opened them, and asked, "You sweet on the kid?"

"Me?" I said as if it were impossible.

"He's a handsome young man. But don't make this an issue 'cause you got a thing for him. You already put your career on the line to save his ass. If anybody finds out you turned on your own for some punk, you're fucked by everybody, not just Hardy. It's an us versus them thing."

My voice must have been a little too soft when I said, "He's not a punk; he's a student."

Frank didn't know whether to be angry or to smile.

"You're sweet on him."

"I am not."

"I'm telling you, Hailey, don't do it." He gave a great, tired, months before retirement sigh. "I guess the young have to learn for themselves."

****

A few days later, while sitting at my desk submerged in paperwork for narcotics, I got a call.

"This is Paul Tomaso. Were you the one who called Novak?"

I bluffed. "What are you're talking about?"

I hadn't intended to give myself away, but when our eyes met, I understood some part of me wanted him to know. A long silence followed as I wondered why. I said, "The police should abide by the law." Neither admission nor denial. Frank was right. If anyone found out, they'd find a way to take me down. About half of them were waiting for the slightest mistake to drive me from the building.

"Well, I owe you one. A dishwasher at The Door, Carlos Castro, heard Johnny and Raina fight about her pregnancy. Castro left for Mexico right after. He's back in town."

"You talk to him?" I asked.

"No."

"Who did?"

"It doesn't matter," said Paul, protecting someone, a woman I guessed. "You'll want to talk to him anyway. So thanks."

"Don't hang up," I pleaded.

"Okay," he said cautiously.

"Most of us respect the law. The police exist to help, to find the bad guys. I'm sorry."

"Of all people," he said, "you don't have to be sorry. I'll always remember what you did for me. I'll tell my kids about it. I hope this doesn't hurt you at work because it's pretty cool you're the first female detective and all."

"How did you know?"

"Research. So thanks, Hailey Matheson. Thanks a lot. You're exactly the sort of person who should be a cop."

****

Paul lay on his floor, trying to do sit-ups but was still sore and couldn't manage. When the phone rang, he answered to a woman. "My name is Sally, and I'm a manager at The Lovejoy Tavern. You put in an application a couple of weeks ago. If you're still looking for work, I have three shifts, Friday and Saturday nights and Sunday days."

"I'm a student and those work perfectly."

He found The Lovejoy Tavern five blocks from his apartment down 21st Avenue. Despite tavern in the name, café fit better, a bright place with white tablecloths, a black and white checked floor, and a display kitchen next to the bar. The servers wore long white aprons. A woman of about Yvonne's age with intriguing hazel eyes, a warm smile, and short curly brown hair introduced herself as Sally and sat with him at a round six top in the corner. He liked her instantly. She looked over his résumé and read Mitchell's letter. Handing his papers back, she said, "I understand you're a friend of Connie Novak. I used to sit her kids. Can you start tomorrow?"

The Lovejoy revived Paul. Cooking for an audience made him nervous at first, but he learned to love being watched, especially by children, when he lit his cooking sherry in pyrotechnic displays. The job required a lot of sautéing, and he sent silent gratitude to Hilton for what he learned.

One Sunday brunch, Yvonne and Edward walked into The Lovejoy. She saw Paul immediately, made eye contact and mouthed, "We'll go." He shook his head. She questioned him with her hands. He pointed to himself then Edward. She shrugged. The hostess led them to a table in front of the kitchen. Paul stole glances as he worked.

In his early forties, Wallace was a big man, going to fat, blond, balding on top, with a short, unkempt blond beard. Paul approved of the way he spoke to Yvonne, looking only at her, considering what she said. Yvonne dressed like the other rich ladies who patronized The Lovejoy every Sunday, a pale gold jacket and matching slacks, a cream silk blouse, heels. She had massed her hair on top of her head and held it in place by a clasp and pins of gold. She wore makeup like a mask, hiding her scar. He blew through his orders and hurried to their table.

He said to Edward, "Good morning, sir. I'm Paul Tomaso. I'm glad to meet you." Edward rose, offered his hand. He stood half a head taller than Paul. The two shook, but as Edward started to sit, Paul gripped his hand. "I have to thank you. I intended to quit school, and your generosity allowed me to continue. I wish I could explain how grateful I am."

Edward also spoke with a Southern accent. "You're welcome. Yvonne feels you two have a special connection."

Paul turned toward her and said, "I have something

for you. I was going to mail it." He reached into his back pocket for an envelope and gave it to her, said, "Have the salmon. It was caught this morning." He pointed to the kitchen. "Gotta go. Nice to meet you, sir."

Yvonne opened the envelope, said, "His report card, all A's."

As he worked, he couldn't keep his eyes off of her. She seemed sad, subdued, uncomfortable before him with her new man; throughout the meal, her left hand rested on the envelope. Her gold suit made him sad. He recalled her in her blues hat, slugging down whiskey, shouting at solos, shaking her ass at him on the dance floor. He supposed it childish to wish her unchanged. They both ordered salmon, and he grilled it perfectly.

After brunch, Yvonne approached the kitchen, and looking into her dark eyes across the counter in the noisy, hustling restaurant as he had done so many times felt like coming home. "Paul, I'm really proud of you."

"Thanks for helping me. Not just for the money but because you cared." His voice broke. "And congratulations. You'll be a great mom." He read negation, doubt, and fear in her expression. "Really, you will. I'm glad everything worked out." He turned to the stove because he didn't want to cry. When he next put-up orders, she was gone.

Chapter 15
The Yin Yang of Playing Rough

Dark bars remind me of my father when I was little, of waiting in the car until it got too hot and then fighting fear to come from bright morning to cool darkness and find him changed from the man I knew as daddy. He was an angry drunk.

Hardy sat alone at the bar, poking a cocktail with a swizzle stick. I sat next to him. "Sargent Croft told me you'd be here. I didn't know you were a drinking man."

"I don't drink much, can't even finish this one." He stared straight ahead, not looking at me, as subdued as I'd seen him.

"I hear you're taking a vacation."

"Yeah, personnel sent me a letter, said if I didn't use my time, I'd lose it. I haven't seen my kids in a while, so it's Christmas in Florida."

I ordered cranberry juice and asked, "What are you doing here?"

"Trying to figure how Novak found out about the Tomaso kid. Rumors are someone in the department dropped a dime."

"It was me."

"You?" he wondered, too astonished for anger.

"Hennessey has my name on it, and nobody gets beaten on my case—that's not the kind of police work I signed up to do; it's not what I believe in." When my juice arrived, I put a ten on the bar and drank deep. My mouth was dry.

Hardy began to warm from silence to pissed. "If lives were at stake, if you had a hardened criminal and needed information to save people, you wouldn't use force?"

"I don't think I would. But Paul Tomaso isn't a criminal; he's a kid, a student who's not even a suspect. Why does he get worked over?"

He argued stridently but couldn't quite get mad. "Lives are at stake. The whore is a killer. She killed Hennessey, killed the pimp. She's probably killed more we don't know. How many murders does she get before someone really goes after her? Where will your conscience be if she kills again? Hell, she even might decide the kid has to go."

"I don't know, Lieutenant. I've seen the evidence you have and more, and I can't come to those conclusions. The pimp was self-defense, the rest rumors. Urbino, Novak, even Frank's idea of Bogges messing up a date rape, these cases are just as strong."

He shook his head. "I've been doing this work a long time. I know in my bones it's her."

"Seems like you're obsessed."

"Look, if you believed the whore is a two-time killer, wouldn't you bend the rules?"

My father used to say, "Watch and wait, and you'll get an opening." I spoke before I could wonder if I should. "Whore. You keep using that word. I don't listen to gossip much, but I heard something about you. Did your wife leave 'cause she caught you in her bed with a prostitute?"

He didn't deny, rattled the ice in his glass with his

red swizzle stick.

I rose, downed my juice. "I'm asking you to take me off of Hennessey." I pointed toward the ten. "Buy yourself another. Maybe it'll help you figure things out."

The next day when I got to work, Hardy had taken his name off Hennessey and gone to Florida. The case was all mine. If I had told him, my father would have been proud.

****

A week before Christmas, Djuna and her sister, April, knocked on Paul's door.

He and Djuna met occasionally for "a decent breakfast" at the monastery coffee shop on 21st or dinner at his place or an occasional movie at Cinema 21. She no longer drank or saw Johnny. She looked better, though still too skinny. Every time they met, he urged a walk and when cooking for her added extra oil or cheese and served dessert. She had gotten the psychiatric assistant job, would hear about her PhD application after the first of the year. They were friends, no fire between them.

Djuna said, "I think you've met April."

April extended her hand. "I've heard so much about you. All good. Even from Ma. Oh, and big hands. June, can I hit on him or is he still yours, somehow?"

Djuna touched his arm. "Be careful, Paul. She has even less self-control than I do."

"I have plenty of self-control, most of the time," April said.

Paul compared sisters. Their faces bore a striking resemblance. They had the same pale gray eyes, but April stood taller with a thinner face, freckles, hair straight instead of curls. She attended the University of Oregon and was a math whiz but lazy, and a worry to her mother, although he didn't know why.

"Anyway," said Djuna, "Ma says you're coming to dinner Christmas Eve, and will you come early and help cook?"

"She thinks we're worthless in the kitchen," said April, "and June is, but I'm not. I just pretend to be incompetent so I won't have to cook."

"I'll be there. I was thinking about dinner. Want to join me?"

"I will," said April.

"We can't," said Djuna, "relatives coming."

****

When Paul arrived on Christmas Eve, Constance sighed with relief. "Thank heavens you're here. We have four more coming." While he was peeling potatoes, April appeared at the kitchen door.

"Tell me what to do," she announced, looking straight at Paul, "I'm yours to command."

Constance shot her a sour look; Paul put her to work on a salad. She worked carefully and without stopping, the same way he worked, the same way Yvonne did. He could never be with someone who didn't know how to work, which led him to know he wanted to be with her. As they navigated the kitchen, she kept finding ways to touch him: a hand on his shoulder as she passed behind him, fingers brushing his arm when she spoke.

When Constance hustled a tray of appetizers out to the dining room, she stole a kiss and whispered, "Hold that thought."

April switched name tags at the table so they could

sit together at dinner. They held hands under the table, nodding to conversation they barely heard. After dinner and the dishes, when April grabbed him by the arm and said to Constance, "We're going outside," her mother did not seem pleased.

They stood on the porch, their breath steaming in the yellow light. He kissed her, an exploratory kiss then a playful one which grew passionate and begged to become more than kissing.

She leaned back, said, "Wow! You're still single, right?"

"Yep. And you?"

"Freshly dumped, thank you," she replied.

"Know the feeling. Want to talk about it?"

April broke away and looked out at the night. "It's the same damn thing every time. I like a guy, fuck him, fall head over heels, then cling so hard he runs away. But I'm coming to understand, none of these men have character, and I'm always secretly glad when they leave."

"Is that what you're going to do with me?" asked Paul.

Her eyes held his. "I keep thinking when I find the right guy, I'll get to the fall in love part and stop. How about you? I know Mom's opinion, June's, and even a little of Yvonne's. What's your side of the story?"

"What did Yvonne say?"

She shook her head, her lips expressing distaste. "Ask her yourself. I don't want to get on the wrong side of Yvonne. She creeps me out. What do *you* say?"

"I would have stayed with her forever, but she didn't believe it."

April laughed, incredulous. He didn't want to think

of Yvonne, and said, "How about another kiss?"

It began at enthusiastic and quickly warmed until, again, she broke away. "How about after the party, I come over, and we give each other Christmas presents?"

"I don't know. What if I wanted to play for keeps?"

"What do you mean?"

"You say you fuck them and end up glad they've gone. I don't want to do that. If you can't look at me and say, *I want to be with this guy because he has a real possibility of working out,* then I would rather just be your friend."

"Sounds like you want a guarantee."

"Not a guarantee, just a bet to win, not to show. I want to get to the love part and stop."

"What if we go for a hike tomorrow and talk things out?" she asked.

Their next kiss began as a wondering which tested locked doors and said, *I'm scared but would like to hope.* Back in the house, they sat on the sofa, hand in hand in front of the family, a little proud, a little embarrassed, very unsure. The scowls her mother fired at April didn't affect her at all. They made Paul uneasy as he suspected Constance worried more about him than her daughter.

The family exchanged presents. Thanks to the money from Yvonne, Paul bought Constance slippers and Djuna a beautifully illustrated copy of *The Way of Life.* He sent Yvonne a woolen baby blanket.

Djuna said, "We bought a present for you. Yvonne, too." She returned from the bedroom with a guitar wrapped with a red ribbon. Running his fingers over the strings, it felt like a missing piece. He had a job he liked, a great apartment in a neighborhood he loved. He had done well in college and now, maybe, he had April. He thanked them and added, "This will fill the empty hours."

April whispered, "Save some hours for me."

On a cold, clear Christmas afternoon, Paul rang the bell, and April skidded to the door, socks on the hardwood floor. She guided him to Forest Park. He enjoyed watching her walk the trail ahead of him, her lean ass moving in tight jeans. They sat on a downed pine in a clearing, gazing at the city, the stump of a branch between them. She picked up stones. "I tried to come see you last night. Ma stopped me." She threw a stone down the slope into a tangle of young fir. "I was coming for a fuck." She threw another stone. "I really like you and feel we might have something, but you should know since I was thirteen, I've always had a boyfriend. I've never been alone for more than a week or two. So after I go back to school, I could try to wait for you, but if I can't, it's not because I don't like you. It's because I can't be alone."

"Let's see what we have before school starts."

"I can't sleep with you. I promised Ma. I told her I liked you, and she said if I don't want to mess up as usual, I should go slow."

"How long is slow?"

"Valentine's Day."

"At least I won't be another fuck and forget." He picked up a bit of branch, breaking it into small pieces. "April, it doesn't add up. You can't go fast. You're leaving, but you can't wait, so you can't go slow."

April threw all her pebbles down the hill, wiped her hands on her jeans. "There's something else. The night before June and I saw you, Wade dumped me. I got home at six, cried until past midnight. I cried again in the morning. Then that afternoon, I see you, and there's April up to her tricks. June gave me hell on the way home. We didn't have relatives coming; she just wanted to get me out of there. Maybe now isn't the time. Maybe we get to know each other like Ma said, and then, spring break or summer, we'll be making out on the porch with no doubts, no questions."

Paul remembered the Tao. *It is wealth to be content and willful to force one's way on others.*

"Can you give me a hug?" he asked.

"I could, but I'd rather have one of those kisses, the sweet ones first."

On the way home, Paul put his arm around her as they walked through the neighborhood in the deepening twilight. He loved the feel of her against him, the way her shoulder fit under his arm, the softness of her hair against his cheek. He loved the shabby Victorians yearning to be restored; the red brick apartments blackened by the soot of time; the old trees which made shadows to kiss in under the street lamps. He loved the rundown shops that might not make it through another winter: Paolo's Market, The Arcane Book Store, Quality Pie; someone's dream, their days, the lifeblood of their family slipping into the past. He turned her to face him, tried to give her a kiss that communicated the urgency of the transitory. Her arms circled his shoulders, held him tight. He loved the cold air, the warmth of her through her brown sweater, and the soft way of her tongue in his mouth.

Twice they sat together in the Novak kitchen before New Year's Eve when Sally, The Lovejoy manager and April's old babysitter, invited them to a party. They spent most of the evening making out on the couch. About ten-thirty, Sally tapped him on the shoulder. "Time to breathe. Paul, go get yourself a drink." April eluded Sally and found him in the kitchen standing next to the keg. He told her, "I have to go. I can't take this anymore. I haven't gotten laid since months ago."

At one in the morning, the buzzer to his apartment sounded. He stumbled out of bed, pushed the intercom button. "It's April. If you don't want me, I'll go."

His heart fell. A fuck and forget. "I want you. But you have to say it," he said.

She waited a beat or two. "I'm here for a fuck." She paused, left the speaker on. "I hate you for that." She sounded ashamed. He felt the same on both counts: hated himself and felt ashamed. As she walked into the darkened room, he took her in his arms, kissed her hard and angry. She fell back against the wall. He pinned her to it. When he paused to breathe, she whispered, "You can do anything you want to me."

A hand on her back, he hustled her toward the bed and pushed her down, the anger, hurt, and frustration of the break up with Yvonne and his months alone surging through him. At one point, he tried to stop himself, but the way she called out in pleasure at what should have been pain inflamed him further. When he finished with her, they were on the floor. As his mind reengaged, he tried to understand how, despite his aggression, she had been in control. She crawled to the wall and leaned against it. He imagined she would have bruises in the morning.

In the red light of the Thriftway sign, she looked

him in the eye. "Feel better?"

"I feel like a jerk." If not for his experiences with Yvonne, he wouldn't have been able to do what he had done. She had broken barriers, taught him about deep places in his psyche.

She smiled. "I guess you do."

"*You can do anything you want.* You say that to all the guys?"

She ignored his question. "Got a cigarette?" He rose, found a pack of Yvonne's, lit one, and handed it to her. It unnerved him how she watched him, how she flicked her ashes on his windowsill, how she sat against the wall, naked, silent, knees up, feet apart, moving only to smoke. The clock radio flipped its numbers. She asked, "You and Yvonne ever do that kind of thing?"

"Yes, but never mean."

"You were thinking about her, weren't you?"

"How did you know?"

"I didn't think you were angry at me. It's funny. She's June's best friend, and she's always been nice to me, but I've always been afraid of her. I'm sure you've seen the look. Once, she brought some guy to June's birthday. I'm a flirt, and I admit, I flirted with him. I was seventeen; we had relatives over; he didn't know anybody. Well, she gave me the look, like she'd just as soon kill me as spit in my eye. She gives me the creeps."

She stretched and yawned. "You interested in doing that again sometime?"

"Not really."

"Too bad." She dropped the lit butt out the open window and rose to gather her clothes. "You know, Paul, you ought to be finished with one woman before you go making promises to another."

"I'm sorry."

She shrugged. "It's not a surprise. As for the other, I liked it. A lot. Now you know." She held up her shirt. "You ripped the buttons off."

He found her a sweatshirt. "Can I walk you home?"

Again, she gave him a troubling smile. "Are you afraid someone is going to assault me?"

"April, I'm sorry."

"You'll get over it." She sat on the bed to put on jeans and tennis shoes. When she finished, she stood, eased another smoke from the pack, lit it, and smiled. "You know, I still feel the same way about you. You could visit." When he couldn't meet her eyes, she added. "Look, maybe I can help with the Yvonne thing. You know why I think she dumped you?"

"Why?"

" 'Cause she killed Raina."

"Go on."

"She kills Raina and doesn't think the police will figure out it's murder, but they do. They know she did it, so they arrest her but with no proof have to let her go. If they find some evidence, she's back in jail. She's stuck with this constant jeopardy hanging over her. Then luck intervenes. She meets a defense attorney."

"He's not a defense attorney. He's a civil rights lawyer."

"And a criminal defense attorney who charges even more than my cousin. Anyway, he likes her and wants to get married. He's insurance and that's why she dumped you: he has money and if she gets arrested again, she won't have to use the public defender. To seal the deal, she gets pregnant."

"She made it sound like an accident."

"An accident? Yvonne? That's like if you burned down your kitchen. Did you know they've set a date?" He shook his head. "August, after the baby is born. We could go together." She smiled.

Paul stepped into jeans. "But why would she kill Raina?"

"Jealousy. Did you ever wonder why she paid your rent?"

"A little."

"Because you're insurance, too, her stooge. You'll stand up in court and swear she had no motive and you would have loved her forever. With weak evidence, no motive, and a high-powered attorney, they'll never get her. So she throws you a bone every now and then. Gives you money, sends you a card saying, *Oh, how I miss my sweet boy.*"

"But why does she need me? They dropped the charges."

"She didn't tell you? The police are still working. You had your adventures with Hardy, and Detective Matheson's been to see June twice since she got back from rehab."

"But still: why would she want to kill Raina?"

April hesitated. "She was a very expensive hooker. One night when she and June first met, she got drunk and told June stories. When she was sixteen, with her thin body and colt legs, the old guys could pretend they were sleeping with a girl and paid big bucks. She played games with them."

The images this invoked made Paul weak. April studied his reaction, flashed a thin smile, continued.

"She did things to get her tricks, fucked people up, bad, real bad."

Paul must have glowered, for she seemed to shrink back.

"All I'm saying is—for you or me to kill someone, we'd need a drastic reason. But maybe Yvonne didn't need much of a reason, like those gang guys you told me about who'd kill you for wearing the wrong color shirt."

"How do you know this?"

"June keeps a diary. Always has. I've read every word."

Paul pulled on a shirt, reached for the pack, and lit a cigarette.

"I have to go," she said and started to the door. He didn't answer. "Hey, are you okay?"

"Not really. I guess there's lots of ways to play rough."

"I guess there are. Does it hurt?" He nodded; she smiled again. Then she didn't. "I guess I messed things up between us," she said.

"We both did."

"Remember when you said, *If you screw up in the beginning, it's hopeless?* Well, I hope you're wrong." Then she walked out, leaving the door open behind her.

****

One Saturday morning, Paul treated himself to breakfast at The Steppingstone Café. He walked home down Irving Street in a rain which floated lightly to earth. Suddenly, a black unmarked car raced down the street, followed by several patrol cars.

Paul said, "No way, not again."

Detective Matheson popped out of the black car

and motioned him to cover. He ducked behind the brick railing of stairs leading to a large apartment building and peered over the top. She wordlessly began directing officers toward a house across the street. When the officers were deployed, Matheson gave a signal, and a huge man with a battering ram bashed the door open. Matheson, gun drawn, charged in first, yelling. They took three men in handcuffs from the house. After the black and whites rolled away, Matheson crossed the street toward him. "What are you doing here?" Her eyes burned with predatory intensity.

"Coming home from breakfast. Watching you. I love to watch people work. It reveals character."

"What did you learn?" He loved how her blue eyes were bright and hard.

"You're tough. I didn't realize. Was your dad in the military?"

She relaxed a little, smiled. "How'd you know?"

"The way you hold your shoulders, the way you went balls out, as my dad used to say."

"My dad was a Marine, too, a colonel."

"Guess you outrank me on dads. Mine was a sergeant." She smiled again. "So Hailey, there's a mystery this weekend at Cinema 21…"

"You think hitting on your arresting officer is a viable plan?"

"When you put it that way, no."

"Smart man. I have to go back to work." She turned away, striding across the street on long legs with an athlete's grace.

He called after her. "You should come and see me work sometime. Lovejoy Tavern."

She turned in the middle of the street. "I know

where you work, what shifts, where you bank, and your phone number. If I wanted, I could find out a hell of a lot more."

Two days later, she and another woman, obviously related, showed up at The Lovejoy for brunch. At Matheson's suggestion, Sally seated them at a counter facing the kitchen. She gave Paul a thumbs up. They were not exotic beauties with carved faces like Yvonne. They were fit and neat with blue eyes and reddish hair. Hailey wore jeans that caressed her long legs and a red, button-down shirt, rolled at the sleeves. "Paul, this is my sister, Cat."

Cat offered her hand. Paul wiped his on the kitchen rag hanging at his waist. Her fingers were long, her touch warm. Something jaded in her look put him off. Where Hailey's eyes were clear, sharp, and bright, Cat's held what he saw as anger and a sense of impending defeat. Yvonne had taught him to read character in faces. Even when looking at other women, he couldn't stop thinking of Yvonne.

He prepared them an off-menu appetizer. Chef had ordered fresh scallops for a dinner special, still in the shell. He shucked a few, sliced them thin, firmed them for a moment under the salamander, and topped them with a sauce of sherry, lemon, shallot, and butter.

Throughout lunch, the two women discussed the wedding of a friend, and Paul had little chance to talk, but when her sister left for the restroom, Matheson asked, "What did you think I would get from watching you work?"

"That I'm a hardworking guy with a lot of integrity who likes to do things right."

"I got more than that. My sister is a lot like you, a

222

little toughie who ran away from home. She likes fast men, but she's a good kid, just finished her first semester at Portland State, grades not as good as yours. If you come out of this clean, call me."

A break in the work allowed him to face her. "How's the case going?"

"I got the dirt on your ex from New Orleans. You interested?"

"No. It's not who she is now."

Detective Matheson considered. "You may be right, but let me ask you, is she still accountable for her past?"

Paul mumbled something about transcendence and redemption, but orders were stacking up, and he couldn't really think.

She said, "A conversation for another time. You should come clean with either me or Hardy. He's usually by the book, but with this, there's no telling. Your ex got under his skin."

"I thought you had my back."

"Things don't work that way."

"But you tipped Novak."

She spoke firmly. "Don't take it personally. The police should obey the law." But if it wasn't personal, why had she come?

When Cat returned from the bathroom, she smiled, and again offered her hand. "Very nice to meet you, Paul."

After they left, Paul suspected Detective Matheson had played good cop again with an assist from kid sister. He trusted her but wasn't sure. He simply didn't understand Hailey Matheson.

Chapter 16
Eraser, Call Girl, Aruba, and Child Care

The Monday morning meeting of the violent crimes unit lasted almost two hours. They'd had a rough weekend. "Anything else?" asked Major Slaten.

I glanced at Hardy, took a deep breath, and spoke. "I learned a couple of things on Hennessy, the poisoned waitress. Urbino, the bartender, knew the victim carried his child. He and Hennessey fought about her pregnancy one night after the restaurant closed. A dishwasher heard them. Yelling, bullying, tears. He wanted abortion; she wanted the kid. I've got a witness, a family man, and a deacon of his church. I dropped in on Urbino at work, tried to get him to say something; he picked up the phone the second he saw me. His attorney arrived ten minutes later."

Owen Fredrick, the Assistant D.A., spoke up. "I got something on your suspect, L'Croix. Guess who she dumped the cook for. Ed Wallace."

"*The* Ed Wallace?" asked Slaten.

"Indeed. Now, when she won't talk, she'll have one of Wallace's boys sitting next to her to help."

The eraser of Hardy's pencil began drumming on the table, and he asked, "Does he know about her past?"

"Rumor has it," said Owen.

"What's he thinking?" asked Slaten.

Owen grinned. "Well, she's a pro, and he is by no

stretch a lady's man. Remember when he got left at the altar?"

I said, "Now we've got Novak and Wallace both on this case. Novak has his client sewn up. Won't let her say a word. He believed we were about to charge her last go-around, so he's gun shy."

Owen said, "I was talking to Damien about another matter, and he mentioned Hennessey. He can't understand why we're still putting hours into a case this cold.

"We're not," said Slaten. "Hailey's been moonlighting. So they're all lawyered up. What else have we got? Does the cook know anything?"

"No," I said at the same time Hardy said, "Yes."

Hardy's pencil stopped its ceaseless tapping. He glared at me, said, "I'll have another crack at him."

"Shit," I said under my breath.

"Got something to say, Matheson?" asked Slaten.

I could have said things about beatings and car rides and obsession with the word "whore". I remembered how Yvonne had studied me and what she had taught Paul, and looked long at Hardy. His eyes were not right. Two weeks in Florida hadn't helped. He still had his sights set on Yvonne and Paul, too. But most of all, I figured, he wanted to take another shot at me. I had something on him. One of his subordinates had rebelled and gotten away with it. I guessed he wanted to pressure me into a mistake.

I calculated the odds, took my best chance. "Let me press him. I've been working with Tomaso."

"What did that get you?" countered Hardy, his pencil tapping a rhythm on the table.

"He gave me the bit about Urbino."

Hardy dismissed my comment. "That just muddied the waters. I've been working with him, too." He stared me down this time, daring me to tell. Which meant he owned Big Felix. I looked around the room. It would be a stupid play. When I said nothing, Hardy added, "Detective Matheson and I will work something out."

"Good," said Slaten. "This meeting has gone on long enough."

Hardy stood up and left, the first man out the door. I sat staring at my legal pad until Slaten and I were alone.

"What's on your mind?" said Slaten.

I tapped my pencil on my pad three times.

Slaten nodded, mouthed his cigar, said, "Lieutenant Hardy off his game on this?"

I said nothing, rose, and gathered my stuff.

He tapped his pencil twice himself, maybe just to see how it felt. "You'll report important developments to me."

****

One cold, foggy Saturday at the end of March, sick of his apartment and tired of studying, Paul gave away his shift and walked downtown. Old doors seemed closed to him. June worked full-time for one psychologist and dated another. She had been accepted into her Ph.D. program and had begun reading. He wouldn't allow himself to see Yvonne. He would have taken her back without hesitation, child and all. He loved her still and didn't want to think of her as Raina's killer, the moral position he would choose.

He was not alone. He played ball on Sunday with Hilton and became part of the work gang at The Lovejoy. He also developed a friendship outside of work with his manager, Sally. He had lied about his age on his application and could drink with the others at the round table in a corner of the bar. No longer The Grillman, he was Paul, one of the cooks, good at his job, and people liked him well enough. Always, he had school. But at night, he would mourn Yvonne, not desperate or broken-hearted but simply feeling something extraordinary had been lost.

While waiting for the light to cross 16th, it struck him that even though the poison hadn't come through Fanny Mae, she might know something. He decided to find out. He walked through China Town to the Burnside Bridge and the nearly empty market and stood where she could see him, pretending to look at pottery. When she noticed him, she shook her head, held two fingers against her watch, a signal Yvonne used to use, and turned to a customer, "Samples, oranges sweet as honey."

He killed two hours in Powell's. When he returned, Fanny Mae's had packed her ancient gray van and sat behind the wheel, smoking. She gestured toward where trucks were exiting the market onto First Street. She drove up, stopped for an instant so he could climb in, then sped off. Orange peels, crumpled cigarette packs, candy wrappers, and paper coffee cups littered her van. "What you want?"

"The love potion you gave us. Does it last forever, or does it wear off?"

She laughed her cackling laugh, long and loud. "You still in love with my witch-baby? I thought you were here about some murder."

"You didn't have anything to do with it."

She looked at him sternly. "Keep silent what you

think you know."

"You think she did it?"

The van darted to the curb and stopped with a lurch. "You with the police?"

"No."

"You wearin' a wire? Open your coat. Pull up your shirt. All the way."

He did as she asked and blurted, "I love her, Fanny Mae. I would never turn her in." He wondered if this was true.

"I'm gonna trust you. She does. Witch-baby's so nuts about you she coulda done anything. One day she's gonna leave you; next time bought you a ring, gonna get down on her knees and propose." Had the ring in the closet been for him?

"Why do you call her witch-girl, witch-baby?"

"She bewitched 'em all. Even me. I used to be young and pretty as you please. She has powers, and if you don't know, I can't tell you. You should have seen those men, pledging their love, their money. She knew how to do each one, to give 'em exactly what they needed to fall in love. And how many of those men did she care for? None. Only man she ever been in love with is you."

"Does she love him?"

Fannie Mae snorted. "He's good to her, treat her like a china doll. That's a good thing when you having a baby. He's a decent man, and there's many kinds of love."

"Is she happy?"

"Who the fuck is happy? Are you happy? Am I happy? Stupid damn question." She drove for a while, said in a softer voice, "No. Does that make you feel better?"

"And the love potion?"

She laughed again, her gaze meeting his. "Baking powder, spice for smell. Gives people hope."

Back in his apartment, he sat at his desk trying to see through heavy fog, wondering if Yvonne had tricked him into loving her, and if Fanny Mae told him what he wanted to hear to protect her witch-baby, her oldest friend, and former lover.

****

Paul enjoyed his English class, World Lit, but fell in love with *One Hundred Years of Solitude*, certain Marquez would understand his love for Yvonne, because he had seen magic, too. Paul learned magic from how beams of light slanted through Yvonne's window differently every time. From the way hard Yvonne changed to soft, and the way he sometimes saw her as she had been years ago. He knew it in the way she completed him, and the way, when with her, he could envision the man he wanted to be. He imagined Marquez would have sage insight about love and murder and tried to write him. He started several letters but couldn't craft one that satisfied.

One Friday after work, planning to go home and read the last eighty pages of *Solitude*, Sally stopped him, "Phone call, someone named Hasmean. Did I pronounce it right?" Paul's heart leapt. Yvonne confided in Jazmin.

"Paul, I'm sorry to call you at work, but I'm desperate. I have a date tonight, and Ricky's sitter is sick. I've called everyone. It's a lot of money for me. Could you stay with him? Till late?"

Paul wanted to finish *Solitude*. He planned to

bathe, eat, read, and try to decide what to do about Hardy and Yvonne, hoping Marquez would provide insight. He didn't want to give evidence against her, but arguments about transcendence seemed thin. "Do we have to stay at your place?"

"What do you have in mind?"

"Guy stuff. Either whiskey, cigars, and the dog track or a movie."

"A movie would be okay."

Ricky was eleven and pissed. Actually, he was nervous but past the age where he wanted to show it. He had not enjoyed the men his mother brought home, and the prospect of being out with one felt both bleak and a little frightening. He knew, in a vague eleven-year-old sort of way, what she did and why. But Paul was young and fit and called him Rick instead of Ricky. Burgers at The Lovejoy helped. Learning to roll the basketball off the tips of his fingers when he shot made everything just fine,—six in a row from the free-throw line.

After basketball, Rick guided them to a bench at Couch Park, something on his mind. "My mom says you protected her and know how to fight."

"I guess. Why?"

"This kid at school is a bully, beats everybody up. He's started picking on me, but he never picks on anybody who fights back." Ricky inherited his mother's black hair and big green eyes. Looking into them, Paul saw both fear and nascent strength.

Paul showed Rick how to block, how to take a hit to give a more dangerous one, about vulnerable places in the body: the solar plexus, the throat, the in-step, the temple, the knee.

"Jeez," grumbled a rough voice behind him. "You're gonna get the kid in trouble showing him that shit. You should teach him to box."

The voice came from a large, tremendously ugly man, with a huge red patch of skin on one side of his wrinkled face, a red, bulbous and mangled nose, and two cauliflower ears. His bottom lip drooped to one side.

"I don't know how to box," said Paul.

"I do," said the man.

A graying gentleman in wire rim glasses stepped up, wearing khaki, a green plaid shirt, and a tan windbreaker jacket. "He does. Fought for a shot at the middleweight title once, coached Gold Gloves around here for years."

Paul looked at Rick who shrugged. Introductions were made, hands shaken. The boxer was named Gabe. Paul's open palms served as punching bags. Gabe demonstrated, gave directions. Sometime later, Paul noticed Detective Hardy standing by a tree, watching.

Paul said, "I gotta talk to this guy. Be right back."

Hardy smiled at him. "Who's the kid?"

Paul shrugged and glared.

"Just trying to be friendly," said Hardy.

"You almost kill me in your car, then you turn some thug loose on me, and now you want to be my friend? You're schizophrenic. Stay the fuck away from me."

"I was passing by on another matter, but I saw you and wanted to apologize."

"Apologize? Tell you what: let me tie you to a chair, give you ten of my best shots in the gut, and we'll call it even."

A. Molise

"Paul, you don't understand the situation. Yvonne is a confirmed killer, suspected in multiple murders. It's my job to take those people off the street. I went overboard because I don't want her to kill again. I shouldn't have done it. My mistake. I'm sorry." They glared at each other for an awkward moment. "Who's the kid?"

"A friend's. You're wrong about Yvonne."

"Paul, I do this five, six, sometimes seven days a week. After a while, you get an instinct for things. I don't think I'm wrong. Come by the station. I'll show you what we got from New Orleans. It's against policy, but I owe you. Talk to me. Make your case. Give me more information, and I might change my mind. But it looks like you're doing a good thing here, so I'll let you go. Gabe over there, he's the best. His fighters dominated the Gold Gloves around here for years." Hardy started to walk away, then stopped. "But Paul, count on this: you and I aren't done. Better find yourself a criminal attorney. Being an accessory to murder can get you five to ten, and if you don't talk to me, you're going to end up on the wrong side of this thing."

"I got Novak."

"I don't think so. Constance Novak filed a complaint, something about bruises and ripped clothing on her daughter. April declined to press charges, or you'd be in jail right now, begging for a deal. And deals, Paul, aren't open forever. If you're going to play chicken with me, you have to know, it's a dangerous game."

After boxing, they agreed to meet Gabe for another lesson next Thursday after school, pending Jazmin's approval. The older man shook Rick's hand, said, "You know what my dad told me when a bully tormented me? Look 'em right between the eyes."

Rick and Paul went to Silver Dollar for pizza, took the bus downtown, and saw a movie, sharing a giant bag of popcorn and a huge orange soda. They theater-hopped to see another. Paul and Rick arrived home after eleven. Since bus service had ended, they walked, and along the way, Rick ran out of steam, so Paul carried him piggyback. At Jazmin's building, Paul balanced the sleeping kid on his back while he fumbled with the key. He walked into her dark apartment, and Jazmin said from the blackness, "Paul, where the fuck have you been? My God, what happened to him?"

"He's sleeping. I guess I wore him out."

"You wore out Ricky?"

"Where's his room? I'll put him to bed."

She pointed toward the hall. "To the left. Be careful; the floor is a disaster."

Back in the living room, he asked, "What's with the lights?"

"He hit me, Paul. Twice. I said something. I don't remember what. Then boom, forehand, backhand. I think that's what he wanted all along."

Paul found a light. Jazmin wore a bruise on one cheek, and her other eye was blackened. "Let's get some ice on that." He rummaged through the kitchen, put ice in a plastic bag.

"I need to lay down," she said. "Come, talk to me." She lay on her bed, ice pack over one eye. Paul sat on the floor against the wall. White light from the kitchen oozed into the darkness. Jazmin was older, experienced, and had been friends with Yvonne.

He said, "I need some advice. This detective, Hardy, thinks Yvonne killed Raina, thinks I have evidence against her and says he'll jail me as an accessory." He told her of his crazy ride, his beating, Hardy's promise to return. He left out his misadventures with April, saying only that Novak had dropped him.

"Do you have evidence?" Jazmin asked.

"I know where the poison came from. What am I supposed to do?"

Jazmin sighed. "If you turned her in, you'd have to get on the witness stand, look her in the eye, and testify against her. What if she delivered her baby in jail and spent the rest of her life in prison? How would you feel?"

"It's not about how I feel. It's about justice and doing what's right."

"Or about living with the consequences of your actions. I don't know anything about justice. Maybe I'm not smart about big ideas, or maybe I haven't seen it, but I do know a little about you, and you'd feel like hell. You should see her. Maybe you'd know what to do."

"See her? My heart breaks thinking about her."

"Maybe you need to get your heart broken one more time, so you'll know. It's been a long day, Paul. I'm going to sleep. If you stay here tonight, I'd feel a lot safer."

Paul sighed. "One more thing. Rick has a boxing lesson on Thursday."

"Boxing! I've had enough of violent men."

He told her about the bully, about boxing with Gabe and added, "Sometimes, if you know you can fight, you don't have to. The look in your eye changes and the way you carry yourself. It shows."

Jazmin took the ice from her eye, gave a half sigh, half cry that sounded like internal collapse. "Shit, he's growing up. I'm so fucked up about men. How can I help him?"

"Don't worry. He's a great kid and I'll help you with him."

Jazmin bit her thumbnail for a long moment. "I'm going to trust your judgment. If you think it's a good idea, I'll say yes. But I can never take him on Thursday."

"I'll take him. And one more thing—can we be friends?"

"We are friends."

"No, really friends. Like you tell me your birthday and Rick's. And if you have something on your mind, you'll call and we'll talk. That kind of friends."

She laughed. "You're just like Yvonne said. Yes, Paul, I'll be your friend. And if you fuck me over, you'll be just another shitty man, but if you screw over my kid, I'll come after you. No lie."

"Rick? Nah. We're bros. Throw me a pillow, I'll sleep on the sofa."

The aged sofa sagged due to some internal collapse. The holes in the crocheted comforter trapped his toes and let out heat. The railroad yard below wouldn't let him sleep, a booming workshop of men shaping, cutting, and binding metal. The light of their efforts rose in showers of golden sparks, then fell into darkness. It amazed him that on a torture rack of a sofa, in a room he had no business being, in a part of Portland he'd never been, sleeping with near strangers, he could feel connected, as though he had a place and maybe something like a home, which made no sense but made him happy.

****

After Paul left in the morning, Jazmin sat with coffee at the kitchen table, looking out the window at the sun for a long time before she called Yvonne. "This is Jazmin."

"Everything okay?"

"Some good, some bad. I had a date last night, and Paul stayed with Ricky. Yvonne, he offered to help with my son."

"I told you how he is. He'll be great. He wants to be a dad."

Conversation stalled. Jazmin said, "Well, that's the good stuff. My date hit me."

"Shit, Jazmin, I'm sorry."

"No big deal. Just bruises. Just my face. It didn't even hurt much this time. But that's not why I called. Paul's got some detective after him, Hardy. Yvonne, they put him in a room and beat the shit out of him, body shots that wouldn't leave any marks. He took those punches for you. Djuna's cousin Novak saved him and the cop, Hailey Matheson."

"Fucking Hardy. I'll make him pay. Why would he do it? Paul doesn't know anything."

"He knows where the poison came from."

"Fanny Mae?"

"Somewhere else. But Novak dropped him, and Hardy is coming back." Jazmin became angry. "I thought you loved him. If you can't help him, I'm going to tell him to talk, to get himself off the hook."

Yvonne said nothing for a long while. "I can help. I

know someone who is interested in him, who has resources." Silence filled the line, and then Yvonne asked, "Are you two involved? Because I don't think Paul needs…"

Jazmin had been taught it was rude to hang up on someone, and she had never done it, but after gently cradling the phone, she felt pretty good.

****

I began consulting with Major Slaten on Hennessey, brief meetings, or a few words in passing, awkwardly outside the chain of command. Things should never have gone that far. I learned that Slaten had designed the recruitment program and advocated for hiring me. He and Hardy had argued over his treatment of me. His daughter, in the Air Force, wanted to be an astronaut and may have been the foundation of my success.

When I suggested we interview Yvonne not as a suspect but as a witness, Slaten gave me a leery wince, "You'd better have good reason to tangle with Wallace. You're going to run into his crew eventually."

"I'm not going to mess with Wallace. I believe the cook. She had no motive and didn't do it. But she was there and knows the people involved. Because Hardy focused on her as a suspect, he didn't find out what she knew as a witness."

Slaten arranged it. Yvonne arrived with an entourage, Wallace and two other suits. At Slaten's suggestion, I met them, shook hands all around. Yvonne gave me a smile and said in her soft drawl, "We meet again, detective."

It was a cold, dry day, below freezing, and we shared a shock when we shook hands. She laughed and winked.

She wore rich bitch: a woven dress in a black-and-white pattern with a rounded collar and a bow in front, a dress which possessed an innocence which seemed nothing like her, black leather pumps, diamonds at the ears, a huge rock on an engagement ring on a gold chain around her neck, many rubies on a ring on her other hand. A slight curve of her belly revealed pregnancy. Her lips and nails were painted red. Two bows which echoed the one on her dress restrained her long dark hair in a ponytail, one at the nape, the other at the small of her back. Her fiery dark eyes were exquisitely made up. Detectives traveled out of their way to walk past and stare. Bad to the bone, except for her gentle handshake, which lingered in my hand like Paul's.

Yvonne and her man appeared ill-matched. In his early forties, blond, balding, larger than husky, Ed Wallace wore a suit bordering on frumpy, a ragged beard, and hair crying for a trim, but Wallace carried a certain gravity. Like Yvonne, he wielded a soft Southern accent, played the gentleman, genial, as if operating under the assumption that in service of justice reasonable men could reach understandings. However, he brought a ruthless reputation to court. Officers stayed awake nights worrying when they had to face him. Quietly confident, he was the most successful man in the room with a budding national reputation. Brilliant but…

I had done my homework. One day around noon, Frank laid eyes on his secretary, and I followed her a couple of blocks to lunch and stood in line behind her to order. She was a very attractive woman, maybe fifteen years older than me: blonde, trim, petite, and well-dressed in a light blue woolen skirt and jacket ensemble. It had been a pleasure to watch her walk down the street. Without trying to hit on them, a woman can flirt with another woman, make her feel good about herself. As a gender, we are easy to seduce into conversation. We like engagement, expressions of vulnerability, wit, shared confidences. A touch of flattery never hurts.

I asked her what to order. Loved her skirt, needed to upscale my clothes, and had just arrived in town. Got any suggestions? She appraised my aged navy skirt and jacket combo, nodded sadly, and took me under her wing. We shared a table. She directed me to shops, wrote them on a little pad with a note about each one. I like her kind of woman, quietly confident, thorough, and energetic. She had a warm smile, sympathetic eyes, a wedding ring.

Turned out we were both in legal with high-powered bosses who were very competent but had well, juicy quirks which I made up as I went along. She confided in me because we were strangers, because I could not know who she was talking about, because I seemed either innocent or naive. Edward Wallace played cards, a gambler who loved a wager and more often than not won sometimes startling amounts. He made regular trips to Vegas and occasional ones to Monte Carlo. He liked fast cars and luxury hotels. He had come from money but had made plenty on his own account.

Wallace, Slaten, a pissed and silent Hardy, and others would be watching from the observation room. Wallace would not be representing his fiancée. The nervous man present was the associate selected for this duty—little to be gained protecting the necessarily innocent betrothed of the boss but much to be lost. I wasn't nervous. I only wanted to ask one specific question about Yvonne. I stole a page from Hardy's book; I wouldn't go for evidence. If I surprised her, maybe I could read her and get an inkling if she had been the killer.

Yvonne, junior partner Michaels, and I sat in the largest interrogation room, my back to the observation window. She said, "I want to…" I anticipated an expression of gratitude and gave her a look. She got it, said, "Edward didn't think I should come but." Her eyes said she wanted me to protect Paul and hoped this voluntary interview would serve as payment. I loved the easy way we understood each other.

I asked my questions, and she answered in detail. Both she and Paul had left the bar after the fight to ice Paul's face and huddle in the peace of the office, where they calmed and comforted Jazmin. She confirmed that Djuna spent hours sitting by the well where Raina kept her wine, talking to Johnny and Yvonne as they worked, watching the show. After finishing his tables, Bags showed up and found a place a few seats down. At no time did Yvonne see either Djuna or Bags approach the well though the scene was wild, and all the servers had to fight their way through the crowd. All night, customers jammed the cocktail station to get drinks. Approaching the bar would have been difficult for either of them. Yes, Bags bought Raina numerous shots, Yvonne didn't know how many, but he probably didn't handle Raina's drinks, just paid for what Johnny served. Could Bags have seen Johnny tamper with a drink? Yes, the whole bar could have, but people were focused on the band. Could it have been Paul?

"Sure," she said, "he stayed close by the bar to protect me, but it could also have been any of the dozens of customers crowding the bar. I'd been elbowing them out of the way whenever I ordered drinks.

"Besides," she added, "You know Paul didn't do it." She ran a finger down her scar and asked, "Could the poison have come from somewhere besides the coffee cup?" Of course. Anywhere. Anytime. Which spelled out the pathetic state of our case.

A disturbance roiled the hall, voices raised, a loud slam against the wall, a bellowing, and another loud slam, this time against the door of our interrogation room. I popped up, opened the door, and a writhing mess fell in. A prisoner had slipped his handcuffs and was using them to throttle a uniformed officer. Two detectives were trying to get at him, but the downed cop was on top and in the way. I kicked the prisoner in the head, and he lay still. They lifted the uniform to a chair and dragged the prisoner away.

I closed the door, turned back into the room. Yvonne's eyes were laughing. She offered me a wide smile and said, "Just like my boy. You should have seen him take those guys, the way he moved. Damn." I remembered him at the Japanese Garden, his silken, powerful motions transposed to that scene in the bar, the flashing lights, the raucous music, the pressing crowd. Yvonne wore an odd expression. Both joyful and guilty.

She had looked at my pad and left it askew. The black mechanical pencil I had arranged precisely next to it was crooked. Yvonne offered an *I know I've done bad, but can you blame me?* smile. I could and did. I was furious, amped up with action. My question had been revealed, my trap sprung.

She looked into my eyes. "Anything more?" She knew what I would ask and had prepared a lie to counter it and another to explain why she'd checked my notes. Her eyes were alight as if her bet was on the table, and the roulette wheel was in spin. I hated her and fell in love again at the same moment, a worthy adversary, a worthy partner.

My question concerned a phone number in Aruba. When Hardy mentioned death in Central America by the same poison, I checked her phone records. Two weeks before the murder, she called the number written on my pad twice, once, for two minutes, and several days later, for fifteen seconds.

Perhaps I should have asked. I had questions to follow half a dozen possible answers. But to what purpose? The number led to an answering machine locked in a room in a bar in Savaneta, Aruba, owned by a dead man. I could get no further. The poison originated in the Caribbean, and Yvonne called Aruba two weeks before the murder. It proved nothing.

The suits sat behind me, staring through the glass: Wallace, Slaten, Hardy, even Frank. I'd given my word to Slaten; he'd given his. And deep inside Yvonne's black eyes, behind the fire, I caught a glimpse of cold wickedness. She wouldn't hesitate to make me look bad. She and Edward Wallace might not be a bad match.

If you wrapped my desires in a package, they would look like her: dangerous, wild, intimate, knowing, strong, a survivor. I had been stricken since that day in the park. With her sitting across from me, those damned eyes lusting after awkward, gawky me, I almost messed up. But Edward Wallace is not the only one who plays a fair hand of poker. I figured odds, examined my hunches, and folded. "Nope," I said, "not now."

I rose first. As we approached the door, she bade her attorney precede her and hung back, blocking the doorway. She turned and whispered, "Take care of my boy. And you know what else? You two would be perfect. He'd understand your this and that. See him." Again, she nudged me toward Paul, and I wondered why.

At shifts end, Mrs. Joanna Reedy, Slaten's secretary, rushed to join me in the elevator. I held the door. Petite and trim, she wore a light gray wool skirt and a pale blue blouse buttoned to the top, every gray hair in place. We would become friends after she retired, and I would learn she hid the richness of her being behind a demeanor of cool competence. I respected her, in part, because everyone else did. Her boss confided in her, honored her opinion, and often sought it. She'd been around the department for years and functioned as a keeper of history and a voice for continuity. She knew where all the bones were buried.

She said, "Did you notice her outfit?"

"The puffy dress?"

Mrs. Reedy laughed. "That puffy dress is, I think, a museum piece or a knock-off of one from the late fifties. I sketched it." She took paper from her purse, unfolded it to reveal a detailed picture of the dress, a cartoon sketch of Yvonne that portrayed her as doe-eyed, innocent, fragile, and beautiful. Ah, how we see what we want to see. "If you want me to confirm it, I could send this to my daughter, who is a fashion designer in New York."

When Joanna Reedy found Yvonne's dress to be part of a rare and tremendously expensive haute couture collection from 1958, I did a bad thing. A court order is a court order; we type them all the time; a signature is often a scrawl; a judge could have any name at all; a court seal goes on some documents but not others and really, outside of the legal cognoscenti, who knows which gets which? I spent an afternoon trolling branches of U.S. Bank, Edward Wallace's bank, evaluating managers until I found a woman who looked harried, overworked, and a little unhappy. There weren't many female bank managers then. Her left hand carried no ring. I told her I was a detective working on my first case, securities fraud, a big deal. I began to flirt and flatter, and it pleased me on many levels when her fingers touched my arm and lingered. I waved my document as if it were real. She said, looking into my eyes, "Everything seems just so. With our new computer system, I think we can find what you want."

Records revealed, among other things, that Ed Wallace and Yvonne stayed two weeks in New York, partaking of fine restaurants, clubs, shows, and other cosmopolitan delights. Yvonne must have visited every premium house of fashion and shop selling vintage clothing on the island of Manhattan. It would have taken me years to earn what she spent in those two weeks, but not Edward Wallace. He must have been successful gambling, for on their return, he made a cash deposit for an amount close to half of what she had spent.

Right before I left, the manager looked me in the eyes and said, "If you're looking for anything else, come back. I'll do my best to help you."

I said, "I wouldn't think of seeing anyone else." Months later, I returned to the bank and stood at the counter and watched her work for a minute or two, but she wasn't for me: too plain, too tame, too safe, not at all like my heart's desire.

Chapter 17
My Plan Was Loose

Major Slaten sat at his desk considering his cigar, a constant which accompanied him to every meeting, press conference, and crime scene, but he never lit up until the end of the day. His wife, Denise, wouldn't tolerate smoke in her house, so he smoked on the way home. In good weather, he might stop at a park. In winter, bundled however he must, he would smoke sitting on an old chair in the garage, looking out at endless drizzle. The cigar helped him leave behind the persona of Major Slaten and become Robert Slaten, husband and father, a ritual to which he clung. He organized his life around constants: his morning routine, his menu of lunches that Denise packed dutifully, a different one for every day, the meticulous way he ordered his work.

He counted on Jim Hardy to be one of these constants, steady, calm, hard-working, and careful, but these days, Hardy appeared to be slipping. He hadn't been the same since his divorce. Slaten hit the intercom button. "Send in Lieutenant Hardy."

Slaten studied Hardy as he entered and sat. He looked twitchy. Slaten shook his head and began. "Jim, I took an unusual phone call yesterday. A man named Ambrose Lambrecht from Brussels, which is in Belgium; I looked it up. I don't often like lawyers, but at first, I liked him. He spoke with a funny accent, made a few jokes. Then he wanted to talk about you, you and the cook on Hennessey."

Hardy flushed. Lambrecht had spoken some truth. Slaten studied his cigar. "He said you're a little nuts over the kid, had him worked over, took him for a high-speed ride." Hardy's mouth tightened. "Back when we first started, a quiet work out on a sleazeball in a big case—everybody looked the other way, but things are different now. This is not an important case, and it's not twenty years ago. Lambrecht told me his client wants Tomaso treated by the letter of the law. This seems a simple request."

"The kid isn't his client?"

"Nope. The client put down a sizable retainer. Lambrecht considered it a ridiculous amount. They're not planning to file charges or sue, which is the good news. On the other side of the coin, he made jokes about the mischief young attorneys could cause scrambling to reach their quota of billable hours. His firm has an arrangement with a law firm in Salem. Apparently, the boys down there have a contest to make your life miserable. The winners get to yank your chain and bill the hours, nothing illegal, but you might want to make sure the details of your life conform to the letter of the law."

Hardy frowned. "I don't understand."

"Well, Jim, off the top of my head, that gazebo you built last summer. You got permits for that, right?"

Hardy bit his lip. "Who's the client?"

"No clue. In any case, you're going to let go of Hennessey, completely, not on my time or your own. You're taking this personally. Nobody cares about

Hennessey. We've got a dozen cases pending, some of which got headlines. It's been almost a year. If we had something to go on…" He spread his palms in a gesture of surrender. "We solved ninety-two percent last year, Jim. We're a good team, and you're more valuable than any one case."

"Lieutenant, if I've got markers out with you, I'm calling them in. I know in my bones it's her. We can't let her walk this time. I'll play it clean."

Slaten considered the look on Hardy's face, then his cigar. He wanted to make a decision that wouldn't haunt him hours later when he'd finished smoking it. "We gave this case to Matheson, and she'll keep it with strict instructions: letter of the law, no trouble with Tomaso. You're done."

****

On a hot Sunday afternoon, defiantly kicking the line drawn by my new orders, I strolled down a 21st Avenue awash in green on my way to The Lovejoy Tavern to see Paul. In detective shows, the cops are masters of improvisation. They thrust themselves into danger on a hunch to confront the suspect, jive and banter, ask probing questions, badger, threaten and bully, strip the suspect bare of secrets, induce confessions, discover the missing clue. But I'm not that way. I need to plan and prepare, take notes when I ask questions and review the answers, calculate, and add things up. I also need to not be fucking interrupted every time I close in on an interview.

Yvonne had nudged me toward Paul twice. Could she read me, as Paul said, and tell I had feelings for him? Perhaps this was a calculated maneuver to line me up as an ally or a gambit by Paul to protect the woman he loved. I wanted to find out.

When I walked in, a woman with beautiful hazel eyes rose from a table covered in papers to greet me. "You're Detective Matheson, aren't you?"

"Yes."

She offered her hand. "Sally," she said. "Paul told me what you did. It was heroic, really, gallant, a tremendously ethical thing to do. I thought of writing a letter in support."

"Please don't. It's best as a private matter. And call me Hailey."

"So you're not here as a cop?"

Paul emerged from The Lovejoy bathroom in blue Bermuda shorts, a white T-shirt, and flip-flops. "It's complicated. Hello, Paul."

Both happy to see me and worried, it confused his face. He held out his hands, wrists together. "Go ahead. I'm getting used to it."

I blurted out, "I'd love to, but I left my handcuffs in my other shorts." Both Paul and Sally checked out my skinny legs, once San Diego tan but now a fluorescent Oregon pale. "Can I buy you a beer?"

He looked to Sally, who smiled, "She looks dangerous." Paul shrugged. To me, she said, "What can I get you?"

"Cranberry juice on the rocks."

Sally said, "Careful, Paul. She's trying to get you drunk, so you'll spill your secrets about the Kennedy assassination."

Paul ushered me toward a big round table in a corner of the bar. "I witnessed the whole thing from the grassy knoll."

My plan was loose: conversation fueled by alcohol,

punctuated by a few strategically inserted questions. But from the beginning, talking with Paul felt more like a date than an interrogation, filled with awkward fencing and testing. But once we got comfortable, we had a lot to say to each other.

We had both lived on base at Pendleton at the same time, but I was older, and our paths didn't cross. He had seen my brother's name on the athletic record board at school. We experienced some of the same teachers. He told stories set in places we shared, about his childhood as a Marine brat, about workers at The Lovejoy, about The Open Door, and about Raina. He made me laugh. So I bought him one beer, Red Hook, then another. He had been cooking, working hard, surrounded by fire on a hot day. Sally waited on us, eavesdropping shamelessly. I tried to buy him a third, but he balked. "I'd drink with you all day, but you're not really drinking."

Paul could have been an interrogator himself. When it's your turn to talk, he just sits, a picture of expectation and interest. "I don't drink much," I said. He waited, nodded. "I drank my first year in college, but when summer vacation rolled around and I saw my father again, well, I didn't want to end up like him."

"I could put a little vodka in your cranberry," Sally said over my shoulder.

They were both looking at me. I hadn't asked any of my questions. "Sure," I said. "Why not?

At a blatant signal from Sally, Paul rose, mumbled, "Restroom."

Her hospitality industry smile fled, leaving her dead serious. "I don't know what you're thinking here, but he's my friend. We talk a lot, go to dinner. He really likes you—what you did for him and something about breaking down a door. He was disappointed when you tried to set him up with your sister."

First Frank, then Yvonne, then this Sally, ushering me toward Paul. "With my sister, it was a compliment, really, not many guys like that on the market." I figured if I gave her an answer, I could get in a question too. "He's not still seeing Yvonne? It's an issue for me."

Sally smiled. "No, she came in to eat, a surprise to them both. It upset him for a week. He hasn't gone out with anyone except around Christmas."

"Who?" I asked, a little too sharply.

"Friend or foe?" she demanded. "Cop or friend?"

"Honestly," I said. "If you're a cop, you're always a cop, which is one reason why I'm here, but my questions are trivial, so I don't know."

"Go on."

"You know what it is about him? The way he stuck by her, defended her, the things he said. He would have gone to jail for the woman he loved. He suffered through all the shit we threw at him and didn't talk. Did he tell you he got in a fight to protect her?" Should have been "Her" with a capital "H."

"I don't see him as fighter."

"Martial arts, took out three guys in minutes. I majored in English for a while; I'm a sucker for the knightly virtues," which I suppose was true.

She laughed. "Fair enough. Philosophy for me. With Paul, it's the reading. He's well read, and he thinks about it. I've never had a friend like that. You know what he does? He'll call me in the morning on my day off and say, "I've made this huge breakfast." When I come over, he'll have coffee and the New York

Times, great food and something he wants to talk about, maybe a book or an idea. We'll read and eat and talk." When jealousy warmed my cheeks, I should have said thanks for the tip about Johnny Urbino and hot-footed it to Cinema 21.

"So you two ever?" I ventured. He seemed to like older gals, and with Paul, there would always be too many women. I wondered if it revealed a hole in his character.

"No, not the one for me. I'm too old to get hung up on someone not the one. Like she did." She with a capital *S*.

"Tell me about this last girl," I asked conspiratorially.

"I used to babysit her. I tried to tell him he and April were no good."

"April Novak?" You should have seen her go pale.

"I think I've said too much. I just wanted to tell you he has a crush. If you get him drunk, he's going to make a pass at you. So if you're here as a cop, go easy. Yvonne hurt him badly. A couple of girls around here have tested the waters, nothing. You seem to be doing pretty well. Here he comes; I'll get the drinks." Mine arrived rich with vodka, the cranberry diluted with vodka to the palest pink—a green light from Sally.

I chose honesty. "Sally wanted me to tell you, I'm working on Hennessey. After hours only."

"Is that why you're here?"

"Paul, I don't know why I'm here." Though I should have admitted I came because *she* sent me. "I had questions about the case. I wanted to talk to you. That day a Rose's, I thought we could be friends." My words felt almost true.

He frowned. "Go ahead, ask your questions." And be judged by them.

"What happened with April."

He looked ashamed, blushing, eyes avoiding mine.

"I fucked up."

"Did you attack her?"

"No. But everything I did that felt wrong she liked, and she didn't like anything that felt right. Which sounds like bullshit."

"She didn't file the complaint. She refused to sign it." He seemed relieved but knew they had something on him. "What's with those Novak girls?"

"I have no idea. They're brilliant. Kind of lost. You know their dad died, right? Kind of suddenly, but who am I to talk? I'm kind of lost, too. All obsessed with Yvonne." Being honest.

"Loyalty to your first love is admirable." Which pleased him, and the tension dropped. He drank beer, enjoyed it. "What do you think of Johnny Urbino?"

"He's a sleaze. He helped me when I first started at The Door, but he lies, he cheats, he would feed drinks to Raina and fuck her when she was too drunk to speak."

"Did he kill her?"

Paul speculated, "Maybe he didn't want to pay child support out of his big trust fund."

"You know about that?"

"I know lots of useless information. Maybe I should be a detective." I must have looked hurt. "Hey, isn't the witness in detective stories supposed to crack wise to the cop. Or the dame."

"I guess I'm both," was the best line I could muster.

"In spades," he said, big brown eyes sparkling. He imagined I liked him.

I let everything go. Eventually, I ordered another round, said, "Sally tells me she treasures your friendship." He told stories about the two of them; he loved to tell stories. He tried to make me jealous with a gleam in his eye. He told stories about other employees at The Door, then apologized for talking too much. "I'm kind of starved for conversation. Yvonne and I talked all the time."

After the day shift, Sally sat at our table with offerings of garlic bread, stuffed mushrooms and another round. A couple of brunch servers joined us. Then the magic happened. I had fun for the first time since coming to Portland. Paul and Sally didn't mention my being a cop. I was just Hailey Matheson, another twenty-something, a little drunk on Sunday evening, laughing around a table in a bar.

Paul conducted himself with great maturity. He didn't talk much but directed the conversation, a man beyond his years, asking questions, drawing this one out, or changing a sensitive subject. Raconteur and quipster, he made us laugh. They started talking about Ernest Holmes, and I knew of him because of my mother, and several times I led the conversation, and Paul helped, giving me an opening to speak. Twice, I made them laugh and pound the table.

I got through one potent drink and at least two more. I was thirsty on a hot day. I'm a lightweight and so became gloriously and unselfconsciously drunk. I flirted, touching his hand, his arm, his leg, as if he were mine. Energy flowed between us. I'd experienced that flow once before, but it had turned aggressive and selfish before things got worse.

Alcohol prevailed. In books and movies, no one ever drinks the detective under the table. Detectives make nearly fatal mistakes, get slipped mickeys, end up in bed with dangerous women, and wake up with deadly hangovers, but they don't pass out, useless. They don't vomit. I found myself sitting at the table, completely pissed, telling myself, *The detective doesn't vomit.*

Paul said, "I have to get her out of here. She looks kind of green. Stacy, will you call a cab?" I believe I walked out of The Lovejoy on my own power, but I'm told he all but carried me.

He took me outside and sat me at a bus stop. The air helped, and I got a foggy idea that he was drunk, too, and I could pump him for information. "I'm jealous of you and Yvonne. I've never had a relationship that good."

He looked me over, trying to decide if this connected to Hennessey or was a dating question about a partner's past. Either he trusted me or figured I wouldn't remember. He told about how she picked him up at the employee party and the strange light in her apartment, about meals they cooked, musicians they'd seen, the way she made him laugh, the red she wore for luck, her patience, and how she taught him consideration.

Suddenly, he stopped talking. I guess he realized, if he were wooing me, he had revealed a heart still entwined with hers. He chose honesty. "Sometimes I think she ruined me, and I'll never have a relationship as sweet. Other times I think she taught me how things were supposed to be, and when I find the right woman,

I'll know what I want and how to make it work."

He poured me into the cab. He leaned over me to open the window on my side, saying, "If you have to hurl, remember the window."

I grabbed him, kissing him a short hard kiss, and bursting out laughing. "The lady cop will never tell. Whatever happens after this. That should be a great comfort to you, who likes to keep secrets. I know you're keeping secrets."

He carried me up my building's front stairs. I wondered: how can arms be both gentle and strong? What would it be like to love him gentle and strong? In the elevator, he propped me in the corner and laughed at me kindly. I sat on the floor and laughed at myself. "I never do this. Ever. Why did you let me get this way?"

"It seemed like you needed to cut loose."

He helped me up, and I navigated to my door. Fumbling with the key, I pictured Yvonne, leading him down her own too bright hallway into her own small apartment with its strange light, the two of them filled with loneliness. I imagined a story about the gentle way love flowed between them. I slid next to him, put my arms around his neck, and kissed him deeply. I fell back against the wall.

I had never been kissed by a man, a few boys as a teen, a couple of women years ago. A long time had passed since anyone. Most kisses felt like a soft, wet, pleasurable friction, the way I kissed him. But that's not how he kissed me back. His kiss felt like a whispered conversation, like a poem where we traded couplets. He expressed tender affection. He wanted me. I wanted him back. He wanted to be gentle with me, soft. He wanted to be rough. I liked all the ways he wanted me. I wanted to know everything she taught him about making love. My emotions swirled dizzy, foggy, hot, and sloppy. I could feel him hard against me, very near my warm, longing spot. His hand touched the back of my thigh, just under my ass, a guiding touch, a suggestion: if I wrapped my leg around his, he would be where I needed him, a move he must have practiced with her. I followed his lead because I felt safe, clothes on, the drunken excuse, an easy retreat with my door open beside me. I held him close, devoured him with kisses. Our bodies found a rhythm. I broke off long enough to say, "You come inside."

He backed away. The disconnect staggered him for a moment. He leaned against the opposite wall, shook his head as if to clear it. "Something's not right. I like you but I don't want our first time to be drunk. Or maybe it's something I can't put my finger on. But like you said, you know my number and when I get off work. Call me or just stop by. We can talk. I had a great time with you tonight. I don't want to ruin it."

He kissed me once, a soft, sweet kiss, and said, "Good night, Hailey," then he turned away, weaved into the wall, turned, saw me watching, caught my smile, and gave one back. He stepped back toward me. "June has kept a diary all her life, but there's something I gotta know. Why was she in the hospital?"

I leaned forward so we were eye-to-eye, inches apart and put my hands on his shoulders. "I can't tell you," I whispered. We laughed.

He put his hands on my shoulders and whispered, "They said rehab."

I poked his nose. "They lied. Evan Piner, find out." We stared into each other's eyes, tempted by the idea of another kiss. My head cleared a bit, and I turned away, weaved through my door, closed it behind me, and leaned against it, relieved. It could have been a disaster.

I liked him, but *like* has nuances. I admired and respected his character and enjoyed his company. I appreciated his insights. He made me laugh. We shared a kindred spirit. I would be proud to have him beside me. I appreciated that he had been perceptive enough to prevent a mistake. But even though I liked him, it had been his stories about loving Yvonne had gotten me hot. Thoughts of her made me turn and kiss him and induced me to slip my tongue into his mouth and press hungrily against him.

Leaning against my door, in memory and imagination, his kisses changed to her dark lips and whispered in her voice. His strong arms and gentle embrace turned into her graceful arms and demanding hands. I struggled through a long night. A great dark mass hung heavily inside me. Books, a bath, herb tea, bed, all were futile. I couldn't sleep, couldn't relax, couldn't cry, couldn't stop thinking about the two of them. They ran hot and bright through my consciousness like a red thread braided into black hair. The only other thing I could do provided no real relief. But another thread ran through my insomnia: why would the Novaks lie to Paul Tomaso about Djuna coming unglued?

In the morning, hungover and feverish, I called in sick and called my mother, who brought wor wonton soup. As we ate, I told her about Yvonne and Paul, and what I suspected about June Novak. When I'd finished, she said, "Well, I don't know why you're upset. You made a friend and maybe solved your case." But as much as I wanted him to be, he was not my friend but a material witness, and my case was not based on hard evidence but on a hunch. And the hunch could be rooted in my desire for a woman I wanted more than I'd ever wanted anyone.

****

A few days after his encounter with Hailey Matheson, Paul found himself walking home past Café des Ami where Yvonne worked. He doubted she would be there because lunch had long been over, which gave him courage. Two well-dressed, middle-aged ladies chatting over white wine were the last remnants of the lunch crowd. A waitress with graying blond braids approached him, said, "Can I help you?"

"Is Yvonne here?"

"She's in back. Can I give her your name?"

"Paul."

She looked him over. "You're Paul? Finally." Yvonne swung open the kitchen door, roundly pregnant, her white tuxedo shirt unbuttoned, revealing a black leotard, her belly high and full like some ripe, dark fruit. She had wrapped her hair in a tight bun. Her lips were set in a scowl, anger replaced by sadness.

She saw him and shouted, "Oh my God, Paul," and ran across the dining room, flinging her arms around him in a tight hug. It felt like coming home, the energy flowing between them. "I kept hoping I would see you," she said. When she let him go, she added, "It took you long enough, you little shit."

He couldn't resist rubbing her belly. "You look beautiful. How is he ever able to keep his hands off of you?"

"Because I'm a vicious, grumpy bitch." She linked

her arm in his as she liked to do. "Walk me home." On the way, she told him about a day when the chef got sick, and she had helped cook. "You would've been proud of me. I kicked ass and thought of you the whole time."

"I was always proud of you."

They turned on Vista, headed up the hill. He believed they belonged together and imagined caressing her belly, whispering to the baby within. Yielding to an impulse to make wild declarations, he blurted, "I wish it were mine."

She put two fingers to his lips, "Shh." They walked in silence.

He took refuge in small talk. "Why are you still working?"

"I would go crazy. I've never spent so much time doing so little. And the sympathy tips. They're throwing money at me. I like serving food, and I'm good at it, and I love the restaurant. I'll never work at a corporate place again."

"Will you work after the baby?"

"Edward says no, but if I don't, I'll be three dirty diapers short of over the edge. He works a lot, sixty hours a week. A few lunch shifts will keep me sane. How's school?"

"Not hard, just a lot of work."

"Can we be friends now?" Her smiling eyes were warm for him. How could he say no?

"Will Edward be okay with that? I don't want to cause trouble."

He laughed to see her stern with him once more. "Paul, remember when we made our arrangement? Edward and I have arrangements. One of them is about you." Two fire trucks, sirens blaring, roared up past Vista into the hills. When they had passed, she said, "As long as there's no hanky-panky, I get to keep my boy. Are you going to talk to me now? If you don't, you don't get to babysit."

"I'll babysit."

"How about Monday through Saturday, eight to six?"

Again, they walked in silence. She stopped in front of a huge white house with a manicured yard, black shutters, and trim.

"You live here? Nice place."

She looked dismayed. "I'd rather have my one-room apartment and my lusty boy and…"

He touched her lips with his index finger, "Shh, I have to go."

He hugged her hard, and she hugged him harder back. In her arms, he wanted nothing. She whispered, "Will you be my friend? I really need a friend."

"Yvonne, are you scared?"

"What if I'm a shitty mom, and she turns out like I did?"

"Then you're in for one hell of a kid." He tried to let go, but she held on. "You won't be able to pass as a respectable upper-class lady if you keep this up."

"They already know I'm a fraud. They'll just add this to the growing list of my social fuck-ups," she said and stepped away. "Promise you'll call?"

He walked alone up King's Court to the middle of the Vista Bridge and leaned on the concrete rail. Below lay Goose Hollow with downtown beyond, then the river and suburban neighborhoods stretching toward the horizon. He could see Yvonne's old building, a spot of soot-blackened red brick. Good for you, Yvonne, from Goose Hollow to King's Hill, from a streetlight like bones to the city glistening at your feet, and farther back, from used, slashed, and bloody to this safety, this prosperity. She was living a life he couldn't provide for years, if ever.

He envisioned them growing apart. One day she would be a Christmas card, a lunch, a drunken phone call when the wife was out. But now, she lived in Edward's big house, surrounded by his things and filled with his baby, but Paul knew she was thinking of him. Portland rumbled below. In all the city, Yvonne cared about him more than anyone. If she had killed Raina, her intent had been to protect him from stagnation and decadence. She had risked her life for his. He would never turn her in, never leave her baby without a mother. He took Matheson's card from his wallet and dropped it over the railing, watching it spin and twist away.

She waited at the foot of the bridge, stern and beautiful. He wanted to both laugh and cry. He stopped two paces away. She said, "Paul, in that note where I said I fucked up, what I meant…"

"No, Yvonne. Don't say it. I'm at peace with things. I'm glad we met. Please, don't say anything."

She turned from him, wrestled with silence, said, "I want to see you."

"You promised to teach me guitar. So once a week?"

"I'd like that."

"You can't come to my apartment. I don't trust myself with you. We'll meet at a park if it's sunny, a café if it's raining. But we can't talk about us." He hesitated for a long moment before asking, unsure if he wanted an answer. "Who is Evan Piner?"

"Where did you hear that name?"

"Hailey Matheson."

"Hailey, is it?"

He wanted her to be jealous. "We got drunk one night at The Lovejoy. I'd like to talk to you about it, but first, this Piner guy."

"Forget it, Paul. It happened years ago."

He reached over, grasped her chin, and turned her head to face him. For an instant, she resisted. "Raina and Djuna fought over him. He was a little older than you, a carpenter who did some work at the Polish Princess. He couldn't decide, kept going back and forth. One night, drinking with Raina, he snuck into the other room to call Djuna. She made him come to her, made him drive. He got in an accident and ended up paralyzed from the neck down. Djuna used to visit him, Raina, too. Of course, they blamed each other. He died a couple of years ago."

He took his best guess. "And Djuna had a breakdown?"

"Paul, don't jump to conclusions."

"Why not?"

"Djuna may be a mess, but she's gentle and kind and wouldn't hurt anyone but herself. You and Officer Honey? That's what I've been talking about: someone moral and responsible with a place in the community—the first good choice you've made."

"I don't think it's gonna work out. She said she'd call but never did. I'll tell you the whole story next time. How about Couch Park, Wednesday?" She nodded. He looked for a long moment into her eyes and said, "Goodbye, Yvonne." The man she had taught him to be walked him home.

Chapter 18
The Dead, The Killer, The Crazy, and Everybody's Next Girlfriend

On a hot, windy evening after work, too restless to go home, I took refuge in the cavernous, oh-so-urban Metro café. Nothing there was very good: the food, the coffee, the pastries, but I had just started drinking café mochas, and The Metro catered to a fascinating though somewhat ragged selection of Portlanders. I had been thinking about Yvonne and about Raina Hennessey and wanted to make something happen, but instead I sat and brooded. Then two soft hands covered my eyes, giving me chills all the way down to my sensible navy-blue flats. "Guess who," she drawled.

Even before I covered her hands with mine, I knew. "Yvonne," I said, "what are you doing?" as if we were friends.

"Can't fool the detective," she said. She wore a punitively expensive dress—Joanna Reedy confirmed it to be more haute couture, this from 1975—a single length of gauzy black fabric which hung to her ankles with an opening for the neck, accented by slashes of red, yellow, and green. With the light behind her, you could see through it to the leotard and tights underneath. She had wrapped her hair in a red and black silk scarf. The huge rock on a ring still hung from a chain around her neck. She sat, heavily pregnant, and said, "You look beside yourself."

"Is it so obvious?"

She nodded. "Thank you for helping Paul."

"I didn't do anything."

"You're lying," she said, without anger. "Edward heard; Paul is certain; his attorney guessed—the way you shushed me with your eyes."

They were seeing each other again. "An officer could find trouble doing something like that," I said.

She nodded, serious, studying me with eyes I imagined could see right through me. "You like him, don't you?"

"Paul? Me? Not my type."

Yvonne laughed, changing her face, all severity and ferocity fleeing, leaving behind delight, tenderness, sympathy, an echo of my guitar player from the park. As we talked, the planes of her face refracted an array of emotions and personas at the slightest tilt of the head or set of the mouth; the scar appeared and disappeared as she turned to scan The Metro. You could see her any way you wanted: a lover, a killer, the personification of a hope, a confidante, a desire. But heavens, how her sculpted face stood out in the crowd.

"Well, he likes you." She leaned over and touched my hand. "Poor Hailey. You don't know who or what you are. Have you ever given yourself a chance to find out?"

"Once," I said in a voice barely audible, even to me.

Again, she studied me. "I know the question you didn't ask. Thank you for that, too." Her eyes held mine. "You know a lot about me, don't you? Well, maybe we're even. I know about you, too."

So I had no secrets, could say anything, tell my long-suppressed truth. She put her long beautiful fingers on mine, and a tender energy connected us. My whole body wanted to open to the flow, but I held back. "I don't get what you're trying to do here," I said.

"It's no great mystery. That day in the park, the way you looked at me. You've been good to Paul and me. We're grateful for what you did, but we admire you for what you are doing, your job, breaking through. Paul looked you up, the articles about you, the bullshit. So why are you here if not to question me? Why did you almost have Paul? You look at me with your wanting eyes. And don't even try to act as if you haven't had me tailed, as if you didn't know I always come here after my massage." I could feel my face burn. She read me perfectly. "It's been you following me in a trench coat and that hat! Oh, Hailey." She seemed delighted and a little embarrassed for me.

"I'm working Hennessey alone," I said to defend myself, "on my own time."

"So, again, why are you here?" My face flushed. "Is it possible you don't even know?"

"It's possible," I mumbled.

She laughed. "It probably is. Poor thing. Look, I have to go; I cook dinner most nights; Edward has come to expect it." She struggled to her feet. "It is surprising where we end up, isn't it? Do you ever let yourself be surprised? After the baby comes, I'll be home alone all day. Edward won't let me work. You should drop by. Call it an interrogation, ask about The Open Door."

I couldn't say yes, couldn't say no.

The smile disappeared. "You think I did it, killed

267

Raina. Well, I didn't. I would never have put Paul in that position. He's like my boy, my beautiful boy." Standing right next to me, with one finger, she traced a line on my face along the line of her own scar. "I already have too many regrets."

I didn't believe her. She looked smaller, diminished from her wildness of the park, from the grim determination of her first interrogation and the bravado of our interview with attorneys present.

She asked, "Do you ever talk about your scars?"

I wanted to express my affection and desire. "If I did, I'd want the person I told to be you." She waited for more, but the best I could do was say, "When you're a mom, you should try to stay out of trouble."

"What fun is that?" she laughed. "Paul and I will always be grateful." Her expression sobered. "You should see him again. He isn't a suspect; he's a man." I began to object. "You'd make a pretty couple. He's the perfect height. You two are like bookends that are different but matched." I remembered fitting comfortably under his arm. "He would be good for you. He likes to go real slow, talk a little, love a little. He's a sweet-talker, my boy." Her eyes filled with mischief. "I taught him everything about pleasing a woman. He would know how to be with you."

"I'm not attracted to men," I said.

I couldn't tell if her smile held tenderness for Paul and me or hid a scheme to protect herself. "I understand, beautiful, but you like Paul, so you should try, just to know. Anyway, come see the baby." She pointed toward my cup. "I make way better coffee than this, and I use good chocolate."

As I spoke, she bent to kiss me, then stopped to

hear my words. "Yvonne, who did you call in Aruba?"

She straightened, looked me in the eye. "Wrong number."

"Twice?"

"Just to make sure." She moved closer. I fell into her dark eyes, inhaled her warm, peppermint breath. My lips parted with wanting; my eyes closed with hoping. Considering her past, I feared her kiss would be rough and lustful. Her lips brushed mine and set me shivering. I sensed our kiss meant much to her and scared her, too. How I relished her tenderness and the hope of love. Her bold second kiss whispered of lust and sweet satisfaction. Her third kiss promised belonging, a freedom from limits, kinship. I'd never experienced such careful and deliberate kisses. Her fingers played against my neck as if she would hold me by my most vulnerable part. Everything melted away, the café, the city, my life. Nothing in the world existed but the two of us, wholly connected. The world with all its weight, its edges hard as stone, crashed down around me.

She broke off. "You'll come?" Her eyes captured mine. I longed to see if the feeling there mirrored my own—and it did! I wish I had paused before the world with all its weight, its edges hard as stone, crashed down around me. I wish I had paused before speaking, taken and released a single breath. "I can't, and you know why."

Her mouth, sweet against mine a moment before, broadcast pain, frustration, and what I took to be collapse. Before I could think or react, she gathered her bag, turned, and walked through the indifference of the crowded café, through glass doors into the night.

Sometimes, on a Thursday evening, I go to the Metro Café about five o'clock and drink shitty coffee with cheap chocolate and watch the shabby people. She never came back.

****

Yvonne and Paul met for three guitar sessions on Wednesday mornings in Couch Park before she gave birth, casual, breezy, chaste, old friends having fun, making music. They stopped meeting after baby Vivian's birth, but one hot afternoon, he ran into her at Fred Meyer. A stream of profanity in a familiar voice rose from the next aisle. She stood there, babe in arms, badgering a clerk. She looked like trouble, near to naked in frayed, short cutoff Levi's, a black stripe of a tube top, gold platforms, elaborate eye make-up, and hair piled on her head. When they were together, she'd worn simple clothes, jeans, more often than not. She stood unsteady, reeking of whiskey, wildness in her eyes. "Well, well, if it isn't Paulie, my beautiful boy." Surprised at her compliance, for she could be a stubborn drunk, he got her and her child into the car. As he drove her home, she started to talk, angry and profane.

She called Edward a tyrant who wouldn't let her work and "made stupid fucking rules" whenever anything went wrong. He worked "all the fucking time" and bored her to death when he came home tired from the long hours. Variations in strict routine upset him. He was terrible in bed. His weight smothered her. Music bored him, and the blues were too fucking loud. He had the damned gall to accuse her of cheating, then tried to buy her off with absurdly expensive clothes as an apology. Their fights were frequent and bitter. She hinted at violence, said, "I taught that fat ass not to fuck with me." She couldn't live like this, couldn't marry him, could barely stay. Paul sensed trouble when she made him carry Vivian inside and escalation when she snatched the baby from his arms and spirited her upstairs.

He could tell she wanted to get laid. Part of him wanted to leave, part to oblige. He fidgeted by the door at the foot of the stairs, fascinated by the opulence, knowing he ought to make a decision before she returned. He started toward the door. She hurried downstairs, fire in her eyes, and fell into his arms, her mouth hot and hungry. They hadn't kissed for most of a year. A liaison with her would plague his conscience. A part of him didn't care. He had never said no to her.

He said, "No."

She laughed and kissed him, a biting kiss which told him she wanted him to be wild for her, out of control with lust, willing to hurt to be satisfied. She wanted him to force her to do exactly what she craved. Remembering his time with April, he took her by the shoulders, gripping her roughly, and caught her gaze. "No."

When she reached for his belt, he grabbed her hand. Laughing, she said, "You know you will," and fell back against the stairs, pulling him on top of her. He could have held her upright and didn't have to fall. She wrapped her legs around him, grabbed his hair, bit his neck, and rocked against him. He bit her shoulder hard. The cry she made was primeval: pain and pleasure, lust and triumph. They attacked each other. She opened his pants, pushed aside the crotch of her cut-offs. They made savage love on the stairs, the

271

dining room table, then in front of the cold, stone fireplace. She sat in Edward's chair, made him kneel before her, and satisfy her there. His many fantasies about her were never like this, tenderness and joy subsumed by an aching need mirroring his own, their once exalted love debased by ferocious desire.

When finally satiated, she lay beside him on the floor and took him in her arms,—her first tenderness. She said, "I could spend days telling you I'm sorry." She held him, stroking his head, but soon their position shifted, and he found himself holding and comforting a despondent Yvonne. "See why I couldn't stay? I would've fucked it up, Paul. I always do."

Paul didn't say much as he gathered his clothes, unsure of his feelings. He had never imagined their reunion like this. Walking home alone, he felt used and at the same time like he had taken advantage of her sadness. He didn't feel at all guilty for what he'd done to Edward Wallace. Fuck Wallace, payback is a bitch. He liked feeling low and mean like the blues Yvonne used to play. Yvonne's amorality did not surprise him, but his own capacity for vengeance did. Yvonne always seemed to reveal hidden facets of his personality, and he would have to amend the belief that he was a person of refined character.

By the time he got home, he had decided to say yes to an overseas trip to Costa Rica and worked on his application and the student loan to pay for it. Someone had dropped out last minute, and his Spanish teacher recommended him. He couldn't see how he could continue an affair like this. He ran down to Thriftway that night for coffee, and at the register, he found she had slipped two hundred dollars into his wallet. At first incredulous, he got angry, then practical—she had given money he wouldn't have to borrow—then horny. Anticipation of Wednesday's guitar session put him on lusty edge.

He waited for her on a blanket under a tree in Couch Park, guitar on his lap. She ambled across the grass in the hot August sun, carrying V (as they called baby Vivian) but no guitar, the wind playing with dark hair let loose, hanging long. She wore a skirt of black lace, an off-black embroidered jacket, high heeled ankle boots. "Is this one of your outfits?"

"Vintage, 1962." She stood on the blanket, black boots on white fabric. "Play for me," she said.

He played an old cowboy song, sad and simple, and sang low, "I ride an old paint, I lead an old dan. I'm going to Montana to throw the hoolihan." As he played, he stared at the lace of her skirt, knots, holes, and tangles. *Just like us.*

When he finished, she said, "Let's go to your place."

He looked up at her, rubbed his thumb and fingertips together, palm up.

Her eyes were unreadable. "That's what you want?"

He nodded.

She opened her purse and let a hundred-dollar bill flutter to the blanket. She dropped another, then another. Paul nodded.

They ended, spent, side-by-side on the floor of his apartment, drenched in sweat. V fussed from her place on his couch. Paul sat up, took her in his arms, rubbed noses and cooed at her, laughing at her innocent gurgling. "I'm in love with your baby, Yvonne."

"I wish I could be," she said.

"She will love you even more than I did. You just have to bring her in, engage her." Paul cooed again, delighting in the smile he provoked. He touched Vivian's forehead with an index finger then touched his own and closed his eyes. "I predict she's going to be a witch baby who will break a hundred hearts before she finds a man who loves her completely, and then she's going to hang on and never let go."

"I hope she gets the last part," said Yvonne. "Seems to me, the heart you break most is your own."

He pitied her and hesitated before speaking his truth. "I'm going to Costa Rica. End of the summer. Turned in the papers yesterday."

"Take me," she said in a tone which threatened argument.

He turned to face her, rocking the baby. "Yvonne, you got issues. You always called me on my shit, and, honestly, you got issues."

Scowling, eyes like daggers, she rose and began to dress. Her anger passed, and she replied in a soft voice, "I know. Do I get to see you before you go?"

They arranged it; she would call mornings, say, "When can I come?" Relations between them calmed and lost their desperation. They made love, played guitar. He tried to teach her to love her baby. Her fights with Edward diminished, anger replaced by melancholy.

****

On a hot twilight, someone knocked at Paul's door. He guessed Gary from across the hall or old man Joe needed something to finish dinner. He opened to April, one hand against the frame. "Hi. Busy?"

"You Novaks have a gift for subverting front door security. How'd you get in?"

"Smile nicely," she said, demonstrating.

"I'll bet you get everything you want with that smile," he said.

"We're gonna find out soon, I think. I understand you're still single."

"True." She fell into his arms. Their lips met. He leaned away.

"Not working?" she asked. He shook his head. "Damn. I wanted to try again. You sure?"

"Bad taste from New Year's."

"We could talk it out," she proposed.

"Do you drink?" he asked, recalling the tactics of Hailey Matheson.

"Only when I'm thirsty."

"You thirsty?" he asked.

"Buy me a drink, and we'll find out."

They took a booth at King's Second, and Paul ordered a pitcher of beer. "Nice place, Paul. You know how to make a girl feel like a chronic alcoholic."

"It's a dive, but it's a working-class place: these are my people. The guy at the end of the bar with a mustache is a chef at the Benson. The guy next to him works at a factory bakery. I'm going to write about these people someday. Would you rather go somewhere else?"

"No, it's perfect. I feel kind of low down and sleazy."

In the middle of the pitcher, she shifted to his side of the table, and he put his arm around her just in time to see Johnny Urbino hold the door open for a tiny woman with short, spiked hair. They walked past Paul and April, weaving drunk, without seeing them.

"Look who's here," said April. "I hate that fucking sleazeball. Know the girl?"

"I do. Goes by Valentine."

Johnny stepped over to their table. "It's nice when sisters share. Hey, gumba. The dead, the killer, the crazy, and now everybody's next girlfriend? Surely you can do better."

Paul started to get up. April grabbed his arm. "Let it go. Don't go to jail 'cause of this asshole."

Paul said, "And you're with?"

"It's all for kicks, Paolo," he said, turning and signaling the bartender. "The killer," Paul whispered to himself. It must have been Johnny who told the police about Fanny Mae.

"We're smarter than he is. Let's get him," said April.

Paul gave her an appraising stare. "Can you act?"

"What do you want me to do?"

"Yell a lot and hold me back."

"Grab you and yell something like, "No, Paul, stop, he's not worth it?"

"Perfect. He knows I'd kick his ass." Paul remembered a movie where a guy in a white T-shirt bellowed the name, "Stella," then he yelled from deep in his gut, "Johnny!" Johnny whirled around, everyone in the bar turned. "It was you who ratted Yvonne to the cops."

April threw her arms around his neck and held him back while he struggled, yelling, "Forget it, Paul, he's not worth it." Paul fell back, landing on top of her.

"Let me go, April. He ratted out Yvonne!"

"Paul, stop! You're hurting me!"

"Let me go!" Paul struggled to rise with April gripping his shirt.

Johnny stood frozen, wide-eyed. "I never said a word. I'd never snitch, my family is…"

"Run, Johnny. I can't hold him!" shouted April.

Johnny ran, knocking into a man on his way out the door, spilling beer all over him. Paul and April untangled. Paul said softly, "Run, Johnny, run."

"You put the fear in that rat," she answered.

Paul rose and sat across from her. Valentine, flushed and tipsy, stumbled into the booth next to Paul and grabbed April's hand.

"Djuna, you straightened your hair. I love it. Have you heard from Dahlia? You must miss her."

"Dahlia?" asked April.

Valentine squinted across the table. "Sorry. You look like this woman I know."

"Djuna is my sister."

"My mistake," said Valentine, still holding April's hand. "Johnny was my ride. You two could take me home." Her wide blue eyes shifted back and forth between them, burning with a certain fire.

"We'd love to give you a ride," said Paul, "but we've got no car."

"Too bad," she said. "Did Johnny really rat out Yvonne?"

April said, "Yeah."

Paul said nothing.

"I'll tell everyone at the Brasserie. Guess I better see where the little snitch went so I can get home." Valentine stared into April's eyes. "You guys should come see me. You look like fun. Paul knows where to find me."

After she left, April asked, "Did what I think just happened happen? I've always wanted to have a threesome. I think it would be scary and exciting. Was it?"

"What do you mean?"

"The threesome with you, Yvonne, and June."

"I keep forgetting you know everything your sister knows. Who's Dahlia?"

"I'd forgotten her. Some woman June slept with a couple of times."

He began to sip his beer then put it down. "Look, I'm tired. I'll walk you home."

On a warm evening, crickets competed with the sounds of the city. She seemed unsteady and leaned on his arm. At the foot of the stairs to his building, she said. "We could try again. Kiss me."

He shook his head. "What's up?" she questioned.

"April, I want the truth."

"What are you talking about?"

"June, Raina."

Her face changed. "You can't possibly think…"

"You know everything June knows. You've read all her diaries."

"Paul, we've had a lot to drink."

"You and your mother knew all the time. The dinners she gave me, the knocks on Yvonne, the job, Christmas with the family."

She shook her head, "You're jumping to conclusions."

He grabbed her shoulders. "You Novaks wanted me to be insurance for June, and you tried to buy it with Damien Novak, with those nights in December, with New Year's Eve."

"How could you say that? Those moments we shared."

"You didn't feel anything. You can't feel anything. All those lovers, you never felt a thing, except when they pounded you, except when they left. I was just next in line. You wanted to hold every card, cover every angle. If they sent Yvonne to prison for killing Raina, you were fine as long as it wasn't June."

"What a horrible thing to say." She stepped back, frowning.

"June wasn't in rehab; she suffered a breakdown. You lied to me."

"Paul, you can't imagine we would feign affection for you. It's too farfetched. Go home, get some sleep. You'll wake up in the morning and see this is all a drunken fantasy. I'll call tomorrow, and maybe we can get together to say goodbye." She walked perhaps ten steps then turned, a skeletal emptiness in the grin she wore. "You know, Paul, I'll talk about New Year's anytime you want. In my desk at home, there's a complaint about sexual abuse, waiting to be signed. Lieutenant Hardy keeps calling, asking me for it."

****

Some days, Portland seduces you and makes you want to stay forever. The city put on its best show for Paul on his last day: an immaculate blue sky, the thermometer at seventy-five, a soft dry breeze from the east rustling the leaves of the poplars. He chose to walk down 22nd Avenue in the shade and quiet. Redevelopment on 23rd made that street busy and strange, shabby old places turning into expensive new ones. He couldn't remember what had gone. Soon, he too would be going.

June Novak now lived in a huge, yellow Victorian up Thurman Street with the psychiatrist she had been dating. Paul found her sweeping the front porch. She looked good in jeans and a button-down white shirt, her wild hair tamed under a powder blue scarf. No longer bony, she looked healthy and stronger. When she saw him, she put down her broom. "Paul, I was hoping you'd come say goodbye." She hugged him and then grabbed his arm reminding him of the time she took him to meet Yvonne. "I can't wait to show off my new house. Ben is out back. The old lady who lived here before let everything grow, and he's trying to get us some light." Their furniture looked meager and forlorn on vast oak floors. He would have left it empty, with lots of space.

"It suits you, June. You were born to live in a house like this."

Her smile couldn't manage its former radiance, dimmed by tentativeness at the corners. "I wouldn't be here if not for you. Everything I treasure came through you, my job, my graduate classes, even, in a way, Ben."

"I could say the same. My apartment, my job, college, Yvonne."

"It's sweet how you're still loyal to her after all she's done." Her comment helped him decide what to do, but he didn't know how to start, so said nothing. "We all appreciate your loyalty, Yvonne, April, and I. It's a very attractive quality." When he said nothing, she continued. "I have something I've been meaning to give to you, but my life has been such a whirl, but a good whirl, as if I'm finally growing up."

She vanished into a dark hall. A broad bolt of sun poured in the open front window exposing dust motes hanging suspended. Each would eventually fall to earth. She returned, something in her fist. "Open your hand and close your eyes." He did. She put a small piece of paper in his palm. "I'll bet you forgot about this," she said. He held the receipt with the phone number of a job in Costa Rica.

"Thank you," he said, looking into her eyes. The vase sat on the edge of a high shelf, precarious and fragile.

"You could use it in case you wanted to stay after your semester. I'm glad you get to live your dream. We all do, Yvonne and you and I, even that asshole, Johnny."

"Everyone but Raina." Her pale gray eyes opened wide.

"Poor Raina," she said.

"I got a letter a while back. From Dahlia."

In her eyes, the vase on the shelf jumped forward. "You know Dahlia? You can't know Dahlia." She covered her mouth with one hand.

"Met her through Yvonne. You stayed with her while she was in town and said nice things about me. That was sweet, June."

The hand that covered June's mouth began to tremble. "No," she whispered.

"When did you last hear from her? The day before Raina died?"

She bolted. A door slammed then glass shattered, and Djuna screamed. He walked through the dining room into the kitchen and out the back door. A thin, pale man with a thin, neat, brown beard worked with a pruning saw on a pole, surrounded by fallen branches. Paul stepped onto the porch. "Something I said upset

June. You should go to her."

"Who are you?"

"Paul, used to be a friend of the Novaks. You should go."

"I'm almost done."

"Now," barked Paul in his father's voice. The pale man started toward the door. June wailed from the depths of the house. Her man clambered through downed branches, shot Paul a dirty look and dashed inside. Paul walked out through the side yard and headed home. Yvonne would come soon, and then he would be done with Portland, all but the leaving.

****

Yvonne arrived three hours late, swooping into the Thriftway parking lot in her red Corvette. She couldn't get organized, dropped her keys, forgot the diaper bag, her usually graceful movements short and choppy as she gathered baby Vivian and her guitar. He wondered if she had been drinking or fighting with Edward or both. It was not soft Yvonne who showed up at his door, face stern, holding a fussing child. "Will you take her? She's been a pain all day."

Paul took the baby. "She needs to be changed."

"She always needs to be changed." Yvonne took the diaper bag from her shoulders. "Will you?"

"Sure." He set Vivian on the sofa, got to work. Yvonne rolled his typing chair from the other room and took out her guitar.

She dressed as she used to, in neither couture nor slut-wear, wearing high-heeled black leather boots, tight jeans, and a tight black leotard cut very low. She wore a black hat with a short crown and a wide brim, her hair tucked underneath. Her engagement ring adorned her finger.

"How's motherhood?"

"Glad you asked. I haven't complained in what, thirty seconds?"

"She's got a bit of diaper rash."

"There's cream." Yvonne began to play the blues, simple chords. "I want you to know, this is original material." Then she began to sing. She rarely sang. Her voice was soft, though rough like the blues.

"I get to see my baby, every single day,

Yeah, I get to see my baby, every single day,

But I'd like her so much better, if she'd just go away."

"Jeez, Yvonne, you can't sing shit like that, you'll traumatize her."

"That's the tame stuff for when people are around. You should hear what I sing when we're alone." She cooed at her child. "Auntie Djuna promised you a lifetime of free therapy, hasn't she, sweetie?" She closed her eyes and played her blues.

"My baby's always hungry, and she always wants a drink.

Oh, my baby's always hungry, and she always wants a drink.

And when she's done with that, her diapers start to stink."

Paul shook his head. Yvonne said, "I told everyone I'd be a shitty mom. Poor kid."

"She's sweet. She'll turn out just fine."

"We'll see. Edward wants her to be a lawyer, 'cause she's loud and obnoxious, but I'm determined to make her a blues singer, call her Leadbottom. I'm going to make a tape loop to play while she sleeps, *Lawyers bad, whiskey good,* over and over." She switched to a more intricate blues, fingerpicking, no words. Paul finished with the diaper, set the baby on his lap. As Yvonne played, her face softened.

Since she left him, they had never discussed the murder. He asked, "Do you ever think of Raina?"

"She comes up sometimes." Her eyes avoided his.

He looked out the window. He would miss his view of Mount Hood, the I-5 bridge, the St. John's. He turned back to Yvonne and said, "What an unfortunate life. One night when she didn't come home, I looked through her stuff. She was as smart as Djuna, her report cards all A's. I don't know what happened. Maybe a hard life broke her, maybe alcohol or drugs or too many poor choices."

"We all make bad decisions, Paul. I've certainly made my share." Her eyes lingered on his, apologizing, though he didn't know what for. "Do you think I killed her?" she asked, looking down at the chords she played.

"Not anymore."

"When did you change your mind?"

"Last night."

Yvonne played hard and angry. Then she stopped, looked up. "I'm late because I visited Djuna at the hospital. Connie called me. Djuna is pretty bad. She smashed a mirror; her hands are all cut up; she's not real coherent. Suicide watch. What did you do?"

"I told her I knew who killed Raina, where she got the poison."

"Why?" Yvonne asked.

"I was tired of those people fucking with you. Nobody messes with my family. You know Connie was fucking with you, right? April, too. Every time I talked to them, they knocked you a little, told me to let you go, hinted you did it. Djuna told the police about Fanny Mae."

"How do you know?

"Johnny denied it. I looked into his eyes like you taught me, and I believed him. He's Mafia, raised not to talk to the police. Did I blow it?"

She bowed her head and took a deep breath, then looked at him as she had the night he fought for her, with admiration and longing. "You handled it perfectly."

"Why did she do it?"

Yvonne hunched over her guitar, playing a blues for which he could only remember the chorus about rain and kitchens. "For Johnny, but also for you. Remember Evan Piner? He was a lot like you, young, wanted to be in love, devilishly handsome." She grinned, playing as she spoke. "Raina corrupted him, booze, speed, partying all night. The night of his accident, Djuna was trying to save him. She wasn't going to let Raina take you or Johnny." His eyes met those of hard Yvonne, and he saw no guilt, no remorse.

"How come you didn't tell me?"

"You're pretty straight, Paul. I didn't know if I could trust you to protect Djuna. Would you have taken a beating for her?"

"You left me hanging. Hardy's been after me since the beginning."

"I didn't know. You wouldn't talk to me; Djuna didn't tell me. Djuna and I both told Hardy it couldn't be you. I thought you were safe because you didn't know anything. Our arrangement was to make sure nothing happened to you. That's why Damien Novak helped you."

Yvonne stopped playing and shook her head, scowling. "I promised myself I wasn't going to lie to you. What I said before isn't the whole truth. Before she did it, she asked me if she should. I said, *Yes.* Raina had her sights on you. I didn't want her life to be your life. I couldn't let you end up with her."

Paul got angry. "You know I wouldn't have gone back with her, ever."

"I do, but not here," she put her hand on her chest, "I wasn't how you taught me to be. I was Yvonne from before. I had to make sure. I fucked up, Paul. I tried to tell you on the bridge. For a month, I made every wrong choice. I'm sorry. I don't know what you think of me now, but at least believe I am so sorry."

He turned from her to look out the window. A cloud shadow passed over Mount Hood. She said, "I was crazy in love with you. You know that, despite what I said or didn't say. I wanted to protect you. I wanted you to find somebody better than me, certainly better than her. I knew I should let you go, but I wanted to hold on forever. Please, look at me." He looked into soft Yvonne's pleading eyes. "Paul, I would have stayed, but the police thought I did it. I didn't want to go to jail. I couldn't betray Djuna. I found Edward. I didn't know what else to do."

She covered her face with her hands and started to cry, not the hysterical cries of the night she wrestled with her past, but soft sobbing. Months ago, he would have rushed to comfort her. Now, he didn't know what to do. She didn't do it, then she did, then she didn't, then she kind of did. They had loved each other, but now he was leaving, and she was marrying someone else. He watched her cry. When her tears stopped, she looked up at him, eyes red, pleading for something, forgiveness, tenderness, reassurance—he couldn't tell.

He gave her half a smile, shook his head. She put down her guitar, sat next to him on the sofa, and kissed him deep and long. The magic worked. The entire world vanished except for the woman in his arms: Costa Rica, Edward, the baby in his lap, school, work, and money. There was no Raina or Djuna, no police, no law, no right and wrong. Tenderness flowed between them. When she pulled away, she picked up her guitar and resumed the blues.

"Will you take off your hat and let down your hair?"

"My hair? Why?"

"Because that's how I want to remember you."

"Paul, when you're gone, forget about me. This is your time in the world. You're only young once. Don't pine away for the married old lady you left behind."

"Good advice." He petted the baby's cheek with a finger. "Let me give you some: don't marry him. What you have isn't love, it's one of your damned arrangements, and you can make magic." She turned away, fussed with the tuning. He leaned over, put two fingers under her chin, and raised her eyes to meet his. "Your hair." Her scowl contained defiance then fear. She lifted her hat, and her hair fell, cropped to the shoulders. "You cut your hair?"

"It seems fitting of my position." She closed her eyes, sighed, put her guitar away, and rose, leaning the case against the sofa. "This is for you."

"I can't take your guitar."

"Rumor is I'm getting one far too expensive for my

talents. Inside is Dahlia's number. If you need anything down there, call her; it's her turf. She did some things for you already, so you ought to thank her, but don't trust her. She's liable to do anything."

"Sure, Mom. Just like you."

"You know I hate scenes." She put the diaper bag over her shoulder, took Vivian from his lap. "The attorney is coming home early tonight. I told him you were leaving, so he's going to favor us with his presence." He followed her toward the door. "He's afraid we'll have wild will-I-ever-see-you-again sex, and I'll run off to foreign lands."

He found her in his arms. She kissed him a firm, short kiss, and turned, opening the door. She stopped and faced him: hard Yvonne, scowling, determined. "You're a good man, *cherie*. You deserve the truth so you can let me go and live your life in peace. Djuna is not the guilty one. I am. She just did what I told her; she's always been in love with me, and I've always been able to play her. How do you think I got you? The night of three was my idea to get you away from Raina. You and Djuna were never going to last."

Her eyes wouldn't meet his. He studied her face using all the tricks she taught him. He felt she was lying. Her dark eyes rose. "Now you're free from all of us. Go, live a good life."

She walked down the hall a few steps before she turned. "I love you," she said. "I will always love you."

Chapter 19
Play It Low and Lonesome

I kept notes on Paul and Yvonne which never left my apartment. Evenings alone, I typed my discoveries: history, new information, and tidbits from interviews. I put feelers out. A woman at the overseas office at Portland State gave me Paul's flight information. The lonely, old man down the hall from him talked too much and suggested no one would be at the airport to say goodbye. After pacing my apartment for an hour, at the last possible moment, I dashed to the motorcycle I keep in a garage near my place and raced through a wild rain to the airport.

I found him in the terminal, apart from the other students, hunched over Yvonne's old guitar, playing a simple blues. He looked older than they, grim and thin, unshaven, kind of hard, wearing an old, gray, fedora with a half-sized jack of hearts tucked in the black hatband, a brown leather jacket, and a serious scowl. He didn't look up until I stood before him and said, "Hey." He reminded me of something I'd read about a young man, "No job, no woman, no house, no city." Did his expression hold damage or pain or something I couldn't pin down?

He has a way of noticing me, like he is thrilled to see me, as if my arrival is the best thing that could have happened. "You're dripping wet," he said, breaking into his devilish grin. "But you don't look like you're going to arrest me."

"Should I?"

A question he declined to answer. "How'd you find me?"

"I'm a detective." Without looking up, he nodded and kept playing. I added, "June Novak is in the hospital."

We held a slow conversation, silent spaces between question and reply. He avoided my gaze, laboring over his blues. "She okay?"

"Not really. I guess she'll get help." When he didn't respond, I added, "They used your name in vain."

"I'm not surprised."

"So June Novak?" I proposed. He shrugged. "What do you know?" I asked.

He still wouldn't look at me. "Nothing you can use."

"You should let me decide."

He strummed a few chords, focused on his fingering, letting the pick linger after each string, playing nothing. His eyes met mine. "Let it go. Dostoyevsky said, *If he has a conscience, he will suffer for his mistake. That will be punishment.*"

"*As well as prison,*" I said, finishing the quote.

He gazed at me with happy wonder. "You know Dostoyevsky?"

"Chekhov better. Paul, you and Yvonne have to know, there's no statute of limitations on murder."

He said nothing and sang nothing but played part of a cowboy song I remembered from childhood. "I ride an old Paint. I lead an old Dan. I'm going to Montana to throw the hoolihan," a sad song. That thing I saw in his face—it was rot, corruption, a faint echo of the look in June Novak's eyes, a thing I had seen in my own. "I have to know," I whispered, "was it her?" I don't know why I whispered.

He gave me an odd smile. "You know she's madly in love with you right? She and Edward have an arrangement about her seeing women. And you want her. Is it because she's dangerous? I think you like danger."

I didn't want to think about riding hard through the rain, passing and weaving on the wet, dark, rush hour freeway, desperate to see this man. "Paul, please tell her I feel the same way. But I can't see her, can't let our relationship go that far. Even if she were innocent. My job." He nodded and returned to playing.

I didn't want the conversation to be over. "You know what draws me to her?" He shook his head. "The bad in me, the parts of myself I don't like, they don't matter to her. She'll take me for who I am."

"It's the opposite for me. The good parts of me are the most wonderful qualities in the world." I waited. He was holding something back. He said, "I'm afraid the murder was my fault—that it was done because of me. She goes after the weak ones, you know: homely Edward Wallace, Djuna, the lonely boy new in town, the cop who can't be who she is, Raina, the drunk. I'm afraid I'm just like her. Raina, Djuna, April. You. Hailey, I've made mistakes, bad mistakes."

He was handsome as she was beautiful, and like her, charismatic and seductive. Again, I found myself wanting to help him. "Paul, everyone makes mistakes; it means you're human." His expression said this wasn't enough. "Make yourself into the man you want to be. You're strong enough to do that."

He looked doubtful.

"Do you know why I'm here? Because every time I see you, you're trying to do the right thing, protecting someone—even me, my drunken night. Whatever you did to June, you're not letting her go to jail, and I think if you wanted, you could put her there. That's why I wanted to say goodbye."

"Thanks," he said. They called his flight. He put her guitar away, gathered some things, rose.

"And stay out of trouble down there. You'll be in a foreign country. I can't…"

"…help me," he finished. He guessed I'd helped with Connie and Damien Novak. He called me by name in a tone I longed to hear from her, a lover's tone of great intimacy. "Hailey, everyone I ever care about will know how you saved me and what you risked. It was generous and honorable, and I'll never forget it." His brown, sad eyes filled with strong emotion: gratitude, admiration, and affection like I'd never known. We connected. He put his hand on my shoulder, took my other hand, and kissed it. "I like you, Hailey Matheson."

I caressed his cheek. "I like you, too. When you come back to Portland, call me. But you have to know, I'm not into men."

He smiled like we shared a secret. "Yvonne told me about you. I like you just the same."

"I'm glad," I said. He stepped up and kissed me chastely on the lips. I liked the man-smell of him, the strength of his arms, his gentle way. Then he kissed me again. The airport vanished, the people, the planes, the case, obligation and responsibility, fundamental differences. Everything vanished except memories of her deep, dark eyes, the touch of her fingers on my face, the sweet messages of her lips on mine, and these would long linger. His hands slid from my back to grip my shoulders. He looked me in the eyes, his voice low and soft. "Goodbye, Hailey."

We drank in the sight of each other. I saw affection for me and sympathy. Maybe I saw hope. He was leaving her, leaving them all, trying to craft a better future. "Goodbye, Paul. See you at the end of the semester."

He picked up his things.

I had to know. "Was she involved?"

The next bit took a long time coming as he wrestled with himself. "What would you do if I said 'yes'?"

I couldn't decide. "I don't know. Try to forget her. Go after her. Yes, go after her, I think."

He gave the slightest nod, a bit of a smile I chose to read as approval. Maybe that's why I came—to have someone see the real me and approve. "She didn't do it," he said, eyes sliding past mine as he picked up her guitar and turned. He boarded the plane without looking back. He never wrote, didn't return at the end of the semester, and would be a changed man two years later when I saw him again.

A word about the author...

A. Molise is a writing collective with roots in Portland, Seattle, and Sonoma County.

www.2amolise.weebly.com

Thank you for purchasing
this publication of The Wild Rose Press, Inc.

For questions or more information
contact us at
info@thewildrosepress.com.

The Wild Rose Press, Inc.